KU-589-335

THE DANCE OF DEATH

Roger the Chapman is far from pleased when the Spymaster General to the King commands him to accompany the beautiful but manipulative Eloise Gray on a special journey to Paris, pretending to be her husband. Roger guesses that the French king is making overtures to the Duke of Burgundy on behalf of the Dauphin - a move which could wreck the relationship with England's staunch ally and most important customer for her wool exports...

*Kate Sedley titles available from
Severn House Large Print*

The Green Man
The Three Kings of Cologne
The Prodigal Son
The Burgundian's Tale
Nine Men Dancing

THE DANCE OF DEATH

Kate Sedley

Severn House Large Print
London & New York

This first large print edition published 2009
in Great Britain and the USA by
SEVERN HOUSE PUBLISHERS LTD of
9-15 High Street, Sutton, Surrey, SM1 1DF.
First world regular print edition published 2009 by
Severn House Publishers Ltd., London and New York.

Copyright © 2009 by Kate Sedley.

All rights reserved.
The moral right of the author has been asserted.

British Library Cataloguing in Publication Data

Sedley, Kate.
  The dance of death -- (Roger the Chapman mysteries)
  1. Roger the Chapman (Fictitious character)--Fiction.
  2. France--History--Louis XI, 1461-1483--Fiction.
  3. Detective and mystery stories. 4. Large type books.
  I. Title II. Series
  823.9'14-dc22

  ISBN-13: 978-0-7278-7800-7

Except where actual historical events and characters are being described for the sto
of this novel, all situations in this publication are fictitious and any resemblance to
persons is purely coincidental.

Printed and bound in Great Britain by
MPG Books Ltd, Bodmin, Cornwall.

One

I was speechless.

This is not a condition that afflicts me often. My daughter, Elizabeth, will tell you that I am a garrulous old man, and that one of the reasons she encourages me to write these chronicles is to keep me quiet and to prevent me from boring her and my grandchildren with reminiscences. My son and stepson, when they come to visit me with their families, are more charitable and even, on occasion, encourage my recollections. But as Elizabeth points out, I don't live with them.

However, to return to our sheep, as the French say. (Heaven knows why, but there you are!) I was bereft of words. Indignation and shock rendered me dumb. Anger stopped my tongue. I was unable to find words to express my feelings. In short, as I've already remarked, I was speechless.

Not for long, mind you, but long enough to push back my stool with an almighty scraping of wood on stone, rise to my feet with such violence that I almost upset the table at which Timothy Plummer and I were sitting, and stride to the window, flinging open the casement with an equally outraged gesture, meant to indicate the state of my mind as I stared out moodily over the Thames.

It was a beautiful, sunny, mild October afternoon, and the river was even busier than usual with what seemed to be hundreds of small craft plying up and down and across the water like so many restless water-beetles. Among these small boats, the carved and gilded barges of the great and the good, the genuinely important and the self-important glided upriver to Westminster like swans among ducklings, bright with banners, velvet cushions and the vivid liveries – scarlet, deep blue, amber or emerald – of their oarsmen. A forest of masts and tackle bristled along the wharves, while the great cranes swung bales of cargo from ship to shore or shore to ship, depending upon arrival or departure.

Almost immediately below me, I could see the water-stairs of Baynard's Castle, the London home of the Dowager Duchess of York and the present temporary lodging of her younger son, the Duke of Gloucester. I could guess that he was champing at the bit to get home to Yorkshire, to his wife and little son, but King Edward refused to let him go until his brother's recent victory over the Scots, the recapture of the border town of Berwick and its return to English dominion, had been suitably celebrated with pageants and services of thanksgiving. These had occupied most of the past fortnight and were the reason I had remained in London instead of returning immediately to my wife and children in Bristol. I had sent a note to Adela by a friendly carter, warning her to expect me sometime within the next few weeks and assuring her of my safety after my great adventure. It had been my original intention to part company with the army after it reached Nottingham – where, indeed, it began to break up and the southern levies to scatter, the northerners having already left us – but Timothy Plummer had urged me to make the journey to London. Even so, I might have refused and followed my own inclinations, but for a very flattering message from the duke himself, requesting my presence at the victory celebrations.

Now, of course, I knew why.

I turned my head and glared at Timothy Plummer. 'You bastard!' I said softly. 'You cunning little toad! You snake! You...! You...!' Imagination failed me. I was too angry to think straight.

The spymaster general smiled placatingly. 'There's no need to upset yourself, Roger. A little trip across the Channel, what could be nicer? A few days – well, let's say a little longer, just to be on the safe side – and then you'll be back again and perfectly free to go home.'

I gritted my teeth. 'I'm going home tomorrow,' I said. 'I've written to Adela to say I'm coming. She and the children are expecting me.' (Not that the latter would be bothered.)

'Er ... I'm afraid not.' Timothy suddenly looked guilty.

'What do you mean, you're afraid not?' I could sense treachery in the air and my guts were beginning to tie themselves in knots.

My companion did his best to look contrite, but only succeeded in looking smug. If I could have laid hands on my cudgel at that moment, I swear I would have rammed it down his throat. Well, I would have tried.

'I–er–I had your letter to Mistress Chapman intercepted. The carter was persuaded to hand it over in exchange for a small gratuity. I'm sorry, Roger, but Adela doesn't even know that you've returned from Scotland yet.'

'She'll know the war's over,' I retorted hotly. 'Bristol gets news just as fast as London, you know. She'll be thinking about me, w–wondering where I am.' The enormity of what he had done choked me and made me stutter. I took a deep breath. 'I've already done one favour for the Crown and come very near to being killed for my pains, and now you're asking me to do another. In case it's slipped your mind, Master Plummer, I'm a pedlar by trade – I repeat, a pedlar! – not one of your spies. My answer is no! I will not go to France!'

Timothy grimaced. 'If I've sunk to being "Master Plummer", then you must be annoyed.'

'Annoyed?' I could barely get the word out. 'Annoyed! I'm furious! Or I would be if I

8

were going.'

The spymaster sighed. 'I'm afraid you've no choice, my friend. This is an order from the king. He was so pleased with your work in Scotland that he wants to make use of your services again.'

'I didn't do anything in Scotland except come close to being murdered. What will happen this time? I'll probably be found floating face down in the Seine.'

I turned back to the window, once more staring down at the water-stairs. A woman now stood there, whether old or young I was unable to tell as, despite the warmth of the day, she was enveloped in a cloak with the hood pulled up. Maybe there was a cold breeze, as there so often was, blowing off the Thames. She made no move to hail any of the passing boats, so I presumed she was waiting for someone, and sure enough, even as I watched, one of the covered boats – price twopence instead of a penny – came across river from the Southwark bank and berthed at the foot of the steps. A young man sprang lightly out, handing over his fare to the oarsman with something of a flourish, as if to prove that money was no object – he could afford to protect himself against the sun as well as the rain – and ran quickly up towards her, smiling and holding out his hand.

He was very nattily dressed in a dark blue tunic, particoloured hose and shoes with pikes of a sufficient length to be caught round his knees with fine gold chains. To complete

9

this outfit, he wore a peaked cap, which sported a long blue feather. Altogether, he fell into that category I have always thought of as 'the smart young gent', very pleased with himself and his appearance, and not caring who knows it. The lady greeted him with a chaste kiss on one cheek, but her back still being towards me, I was unable to see if her glance was approving or no, or whether she admired him as much as he obviously admired himself. Before I could even begin to work out the relationship between them, Timothy's voice had recalled my wandering attention.

'Roger, I'm sorry but you have no choice in this matter. The king has issued his orders. I promise that you'll be in no danger and that it won't be for long.'

I swung round and returned to the table, leaning on my hands and bending over it until my face was within inches of his.

'You're a splendid liar, Timothy,' I snarled. 'I suppose you have to be in your sort of work, but you don't convince me, not one little bit. I know your promises of old. Your mind's as twisted as a coil of rope and I wouldn't trust you beyond that door over there. In fact, not so far. All right!' I straightened up and flung out a hand. 'I can guess what you're going to say: you came to my rescue in Scotland. But it was only by the merest chance that you were in time. And that wasn't supposed to be a dangerous mission, either, was it?' Bile choked me again and

I sat down heavily on my stool.

'Look,' Timothy said, taking advantage of my enforced silence, 'you may not believe me, but I'm genuinely sorry about this. If it were up to me, you'd be on your way home tomorrow with the money in your purse that you've been promised. Well, that at least will be paid to you, and you certainly won't lose by this present mission. And what you have to do is quite simple and straightforward.'

I snorted derisively and was about to express my scepticism out loud when a thought struck me. Of course! The whole thing was ludicrous. I once more leaned across the table and gripped my companion's wrist.

'You do realize, don't you, that I can't speak French?' I gave a great shout of laughter. 'I'm not going to be any good to you if I can't speak the language, am I? Have you considered that?'

Timothy looked uncomfortable, but not, as I naturally assumed, because he had overlooked an obvious fact. 'You won't have to speak French,' he said, avoiding my eyes.

'Won't have to speak French?' I repeated. 'Then whatever good am I going to be to you? And, furthermore, with my height, fair hair and blue eyes I'm simply going to shriek, "Englishman" at everyone I meet. Dangerous in itself. You know how our neighbours across the water love us! Like a rat loves poison.'

Timothy cleared his throat and squirmed a bit on his stool. He also looked embarrassed. I wondered what was coming.

'As a matter of fact, none of that will matter. You're travelling as an Englishman and using your own name.'

I stared at him blankly for a moment or two before eventually finding my tongue. 'In God's name, what use is that going to be to you?'

He chewed his thumbnail before answering. 'The truth is, Roger...' Again he hesitated.

'I should be grateful for the truth,' I snapped.

'The truth is–' Timothy took a deep breath, like a man plunging into a tub of cold water – 'the truth is, you're accompanying someone else who *can* speak French. A lady. You will pose as her husband, her English husband.'

'What?!' I couldn't believe my ears.

'Your job–' now that the murder was out, Timothy was gaining in confidence – 'is to look after her and see to her needs as if she were indeed your wife.'

Slowly I rose to my feet. 'Oh, no!'

'Oh, yes! Those are the orders, Roger, and there's no gainsaying them. And if you're thinking about Mistress Chapman, there's no reason why she should ever know. She isn't even aware of your present whereabouts. You could still be making your way back from Scotland. You've dropped out of sight and out of time as far as she's concerned. With regard to the lady you're taking to France,' he hurried on, not giving me a chance to speak, 'as her supposed husband, you'll have, of course, to share a bedchamber with her wherever you

12

stop for the night. Possibly the same bed. Well, yes, definitely the same bed if you are both to avoid suspicion. But what happens ... What I mean is...' His tongue seemed to tie itself in knots and he eventually fell silent, drumming his fingers on the table top.

'Nothing is going to happen,' I answered quietly but firmly, 'because I'm not going. The king can find someone else to play out this little charade.'

Timothy sucked his teeth as if considering the matter, then sadly (the hypocrite!) shook his head. 'No. His Highness has commanded your services and will accept no one else's. I apologize again, old friend, but there is nothing I can do.'

'Stop calling me your "friend"!' I shouted, bringing my fist down with a thump on the table. 'Sweet Virgin!' I straightened my back and took in air like a drowning man reaching the water's surface. 'You're asking me – all right, the king is asking me – to squire a woman to France, posing as her husband, and to share the same bed with her for goodness knows how many nights. If this isn't an invitation to commit adultery, I don't know what is!'

'Not if you're a faithful husband,' the spymaster retorted smugly. 'And I hope, Roger, that you've always been that.'

Which showed how much he knew. I recollected with acute discomfort an amorous episode the previous year with a cosy little armful in Gloucester by the name of Juliette

13

Gerrish. Until then, I had thought myself immune to the physical charms of other women. Now I knew better.

I walked back to the window. The man and woman had disappeared. The landing stage was empty. Typically, the warmth of the autumn afternoon had suddenly vanished and there was a spiteful rumour of winter in the air. Clouds chased one another overhead, broken by only momentary gleams of sunlight, cold as steel.

'So what is she like, this woman I'm to escort to France?' I asked harshly. 'Old? Young? Pretty? Plain? Or downright ugly with a face like a pig's backside? Probably the latter. That would be your idea of a joke.'

'All the better for you if she had.' Timothy grinned. 'It would curb your baser instincts, if they're what you're afraid of.'

'You haven't answered my question.'

There was a pause: then my companion said, with more than a touch of evasiveness, 'You'll find out, all in good time. I'm just relieved that you seem to have accepted the situation.'

'Don't be too sure.' I heaved myself away from the wall against which I had been leaning and faced him once more. 'I've a good mind to try to speak to my lord of Gloucester. He's here, in the castle, and has always shown himself sympathetic to me in the past.'

'Ah! Now!' Timothy smiled benignly. 'It's odd that you should say that, Roger, because I have instructions to take you to see the duke this very evening. His Grace has half an hour to spare before attending yet another banquet of thanksgiving, given by the lord mayor.'

'Oh? And what does he want to see me about?' I demanded belligerently. 'Prince Richard, I mean.'

Again Timothy looked discomfited. 'He wants you to undertake a special mission for him while you're in Paris. Paris, by the way, is your eventual destination. I don't think I've mentioned that.'

'There's a great deal you haven't mentioned,' I retorted wrathfully. 'This is a bit like peeling an onion: there's always another stinking layer underneath.' I returned to the table and sat down yet again, folding my hands on the table top and staring at him across the wine- and food-stained boards. I made a great effort to speak calmly. 'So let's begin at the beginning, shall we, "old friend"? Why am I – and, of course, my fair travelling companion – being sent to France in the first place? Am I allowed to know the reason?'

Timothy breathed an obvious sigh of relief, sensing my capitulation. 'Let's have some wine,' he suggested, and, going to the door, opened it and yelled for a server. 'We might as well be comfortable,' he added, 'and it's still an hour or so until supper. I don't know about you, but I could do with a drink.'

Ten minutes later – the service was prompt in Baynard's Castle – Timothy poured us both a second mazer of a wine that he assured me,

15

aware of my ignorance, was one of the best in the castle cellars. This information did nothing to reassure me. On the contrary, it only increased my uneasiness. If the lackeys had orders to treat us like honoured guests, there was a reason for it. 'Flattery' and 'bribery' were two of the words that immediately sprang to mind; 'softening up' were two more. I liked none of them.

Suddenly realizing how thirsty I was, I had tossed back the first cup of wine with an abandon that had made my companion wince, but he had forced himself to keep pace with me for the sake of good fellowship. Now, however, he urged me to savour the second with more decorum.

'We don't want to get drunk, do we?' he said. 'We need our wits about us.'

'I'd very much like to get drunk,' I snapped. 'Oh, don't worry – I won't. Just get on with what you were going to tell me. Why does the king want me to go to France...? But wait a minute!' My worst suspicions were suddenly aroused. 'You must have regular spies in Paris. Why aren't you employing one of them to do whatever needs to be done?'

'Ah! Yes!' Timothy recruited his strength with another gulp or two of wine, forgetting in his agitation to give it the respect he claimed it deserved. 'The unhappy fact is...'

'Go on,' I encouraged him grimly.

'Well, sad to say, we need a ... a fresh face in Paris to ... er ... to replace poor Hubert Pole, who...'

16

'Who what?'

'Who met with an accident,' Timothy finished in a rush. 'Have some more of this excellent Rhenish.' He refilled my mazer with a generous hand, ignoring his recent injunction to me not to get drunk.

'What sort of accident?' I pushed the cup aside, untouched.

'He ... er ... Well, strangely enough, he was found drowned in the Seine. The poor fellow must have slipped and fallen in.'

'Slipped and fallen in, my left foot!' I exclaimed with unusual restraint, adding caustically, 'Such a quiet river, the Seine, by all accounts. I don't suppose there was anyone around to pull him out ... Now, suppose you tell me the truth.'

'It did happen at night,' Timothy explained hopefully.

'Of course it did. And I expect this Hubert Pole was just enjoying a quiet nocturnal stroll, minding his own business, no threat to anyone.' I sat up straight on my stool, clasping my arms across my chest defiantly. 'You can find someone else, Timothy. I'm not going.'

'You won't be in any danger as long as you follow instructions. One of the reasons it has been decided to send you and the lady as husband and wife is that a married couple is less likely to arouse suspicion. In any case, you aren't being sent to winkle out closely guarded state secrets. In all probability, the information wanted by King Edward – if,

17

unfortunately, what he fears should prove to be true – will be common knowledge by Christmas.'

'In that case,' I interrupted angrily, '*why* are we going?'

'His Highness wishes to be forearmed.'

'About what?' Although my tone of voice was still forbidding, I relaxed my posture a little.

Timothy was quick to notice it and breathed more easily himself. 'You know, of course, that negotiations have been proceeding for some time for the betrothal of the Princess Elizabeth to the young Dauphin of France.'

'No.'

My companion, taken aback by this flat denial, looked his astonishment. 'You must do,' he protested.

'I've been otherwise occupied,' I snapped. 'Toiling up to Scotland, for example, and then nearly being murdered. Or had you forgotten?'

'But ... Oh, well, never mind. Just accept my assurances that this is so. There's been a flurry of diplomatic activity between London and Plessis-les-Tours for months. Ever since February, in fact.'

'Plessis-les-Tours?'

'It's where King Louis mainly resides these days. A château on the Loire. In fact, the rumour is that he has withdrawn there permanently with the French court. He has never liked Paris.'

'So? Princess Elizabeth is going to marry

the Dauphin. That seems simple enough. English princesses have married French princes before now, and vice versa.'

Timothy shrugged. 'Unfortunately, rumours have been reaching us of late of a change of heart by Louis. There's talk – nothing substantiated as yet, but the information is from trusted sources – that he is ready to repudiate the English alliance and marry his son to Maximilian's daughter, Margaret. Worse still, it's said that Burgundy is ready to make peace with France and that this marriage will be a part of the peace terms.'

I absorbed this information in silence. There was no need for Timothy to spell out exactly what this would mean for England. The Duchy of Burgundy had been our closest ally for many years now, and, equally important, if not more, the chief customer on mainland Europe for our wool exports. King Edward's own sister, Margaret, had been the third wife of the late Duke Charles, but his death five and a half years ago had left only one child, Mary, the daughter of his first marriage, and she had married Maximilian of Austria. Immediately, Louis had moved to bring back the duchy – for many decades now a palatinate, owing little but lip-service to the French Crown – to a fiefdom under France's control. Maximilian and the dowager duchess had appealed for England's support in vain: King Edward refused point-blank to jeopardize the substantial annual pension paid to him by King Louis ever since the Treaty of

19

Picquigny, seven years earlier. Even the disapproval of his own people, expressed in shouts and insults whenever he showed his face in public, had failed to change his mind. He had sown the wind: now, it seemed, he was about to reap the whirlwind.

I shrugged. 'What did His Highness expect when he left Burgundy to struggle on against France alone? It was surely inevitable that Maximilian would eventually be forced to make peace. And after the death of his wife, I imagine that what little remained of the will to fight went out of him.' (Mary of Burgundy had died the preceding spring after a fall from her horse.)

Timothy regarded me approvingly. 'I'll say this for you, Roger,' he conceded generously, 'you're never such an ignorant fool as you look.' I thanked him acidly, but he ignored me and continued, 'Mind you, I wouldn't argue with you on that score: nor would a lot of other people. But that's not our business. Our business is to carry out the king's commands, which are that you and the lady in question go to Paris and try to discover the truth of the matter. Separate rumour from fact.'

Before I could reply, there was tap at the door of the room in which we were sitting and Timothy rose, pushing back his stool. 'Ah! This must be the lady herself,' he muttered, giving me an oddly apprehensive glance. He braced his shoulders and went to let her in.

20

Two

I did not recognize her immediately. She was wearing a long blue cloak with the hood pulled up, and for a brief moment I wondered if she was the woman I had noticed earlier, at the top of the water-stairs. Then I dismissed the idea. She was surely somewhat taller, and the other woman's cloak was brown.

Timothy stepped forward to greet the new arrival. 'Mistress Gray,' he murmured, bending gallantly over her extended hand. He indicated me. 'You ... you ... er ... remember Master Chapman.'

The lady gave a gurgle of laughter and shed her cloak to reveal a slender, willowy form in a plain dark red woollen gown, the colour of garnets, and ornamented with nothing more than a simple leather girdle and a solitary gold chain about her throat. Her long white fingers were innocent of rings. The fair, wavy hair, which curled luxuriantly over a small, neat head, had been coaxed into a silver net at the nape of her neck, but had obviously, at some time, been cut short like a boy's, and, if loose, would, I reckoned, be barely shoulder-length. A pair of large violet-blue eyes regarded me appraisingly.

21

'Of course,' she said. 'How could I forget him?' Her voice had an underlying lilt to it, slight but unmistakable, that transported me straight back to Scotland.

And that was when I knew her, the moment the scales dropped from my eyes.

Now, it's one thing to be rendered speechless once in a while, but twice in the same day is too much. I made inarticulate gobbling noises as I backed away from her, overturning my stool as I did so, and gestured furiously with my hands as though to ward off the evil eye; all of which seemed to afford her the greatest amusement, but angered Timothy, who could plainly foresee another interminable argument with me.

I finally found my voice. 'Oh, no!' I exclaimed savagely. 'Oh, no! There is nothing on earth will persuade me to go to France – indeed, to go anywhere – with her!'

The spymaster's mouth set in a grim line. He had evidently done with trying to cajole me. When he spoke, it was with the voice of authority, reinforced by royal command. 'You've no choice, Roger. I thought I'd made that perfectly clear. Mistress Gray is your travelling companion whether you like it or not. If you refuse, I shall have no alternative but to place you under arrest.'

'That bitch tried to murder me!' I shouted. 'You know damn well she did! And you expect me to go jaunting through France with her?'

That did, at last, wipe the smile from Eloise

Gray's face. She managed to look both offended and horrified at once.

'Roger!' she protested. 'You don't really believe, surely, that I would have harmed you?'

'You gave a very good imitation of being prepared to cut my heart out,' I yelled, and was conscious that my teeth were drawn back over my lips in a wolfish grimace. I was disgusted to feel my heart pounding like that of a woman.

Eloise took a step towards me and I moved even further away until I fetched up against the wall, my hands, cold and sweating, pressed against the stones.

She sighed. 'This is ridiculous. How can I convince you that I intended you no hurt? If Master Plummer here had not arrived in time, I would have found some other way to save you. I promise! It was never my intention to allow that murdering band to carry out their fell design.'

I looked at Timothy. 'Is she telling the truth?'

I could see by the expression on his face, fleeting though it was, that he was considering whether or not to lie. In the end, however, he decided on the truth as being the wiser course.

'I don't know,' he admitted. 'I wasn't in league with Mistress Gray, if that's what you're asking. But I know of no reason to disbelieve her.' All the same, there was a shifty gleam in his eye.

'When I left Scotland,' I pointed out, 'she was under arrest with the others on a charge of sorcery. I assumed that she'd gone to the flames by now.'

For a moment, my blunt speaking brought Eloise up short and she blenched. She made a sign, but, watching her closely, I would have been willing to swear that it was not of the Cross. Some pagan symbol, perhaps? Timothy seemed to notice nothing: his eyes were fixed on me. I met the lady's limpid gaze and decided that I might have been mistaken. Surely such a beautiful face could never be a mask for evil: she must have been led astray by her erstwhile companions. And although I was not altogether convinced by this theory, common sense and fairness told me that it could indeed be true. I relaxed a little and Timothy, quick to observe it, permitted himself a brief smile.

'The fact is, Roger, that during my questioning of Mistress Gray, I discovered that she would be of greater use to us alive than dead.'

'Us?'

'To His Highness the King, and therefore, of course, to me. The first news of Hubert Pole's death, and the early rumours of a possible *rapprochement* between King Louis and Duke Maximilian reached me while we were still in Edinburgh.'

'I see ... And where does His Grace the Duke of Gloucester figure in all this?'

I saw alarm flicker in the spymaster's eyes as

he said hurriedly, 'No, no! This mission is for the king. It has nothing to do with Duke Richard. If you thought I said to the contrary, you must have misunderstood me.'

I knew, and he knew, that there had been no mistake. I was to have an audience with the duke that very evening. What I hadn't realized until that moment was that it was to be a secret from my travelling companion. Why? Was it that Timothy really didn't trust her, or was it that this special errand I was being saddled with was so dangerous that the fewer people who knew about it, the better? My uneasiness and sense of foreboding increased and I cast around frantically in my mind, searching for some way that I could escape. What was to stop me from simply leaving Baynard's Castle and London this very afternoon and melting into the countryside, making my way home to Bristol by all the byways and unfrequented roads that I knew so well as a pedlar? Nothing was the answer, except that I would be pursued, or, most likely, I would arrive home to find myself being arrested on my doorstep and hauled off to prison in front of my wife and children. There was absolutely no possibility of being allowed to flout the might of authority.

I shrugged and eased myself away from the wall, walking back to the table, where I refilled my mazer with wine and sat down, stretching out my long legs so that neither Timothy nor Eloise Gray could pull up a seat too close to me. Not, I think, that Timothy would have tried. He knew, even if the lady did not, that I was in such a cold fury that he would do well to keep his distance until my anger had abated somewhat.

Instead, he addressed himself to the task of placating me. He invited Eloise to take his vacated seat and fetched himself a joint-stool from beside the empty fireplace, sitting down somewhere between us. Then he poured wine for the two of them, casting me a reproachful look for my lack of manners.

'Mistress Gray's mother,' he announced, 'was French. Eloise speaks the language fluently.'

Well, I supposed that explained some part of her usefulness, although not all by any means. Timothy must have at his disposal a number of people fluent in the French tongue who could just as easily have been despatched on this foray across the Channel. So I waited expectantly, at the same time being careful not to display the slightest sign of interest. I studied the scuffed toes of my boots, waggling my feet up and down.

'Oh, stop sulking, you great oaf!' the spy-master roared, his patience snapping.

Both Mistress Gray and I jumped, and I turned my head to stare at him. He had gone quite red in the face and looked ready to murder me. Something about his appearance forcefully, and unreasonably, struck me as funny and I began to laugh. After a moment's hesitation, Eloise joined in, although I could tell that she was unsure exactly what I found

26

so amusing. For his part, Timothy was so relieved that the atmosphere had lightened he forgot to take umbrage and beamed at the pair of us, rather like a parent whose children had suddenly decided to be good.

'That's better,' he said approvingly, 'so I'll continue. As I was saying, Roger, Mistress Gray speaks French as a native, learned at her mother's knee. In addition, she has family connections in Flanders.' He paused, obviously to give added weight to what was to follow. I waited expectantly, but unfortunately, when the information came, it meant nothing to me. 'One of her distant cousins,' Timothy continued impressively, 'is Olivier le Daim.'

I raised my eyebrows politely and waited some more.

'Olivier le Daim!' Timothy repeated impatiently.

It was Eloise who came to my rescue. She gave a tiny gurgle of laughter, no doubt at my bewildered expression, and said, 'I don't suppose Master Chapman has ever heard of him, sir. Outside of France – indeed, beyond French court circles – he would be very little known.' She smiled at me, deliberately setting out to charm. 'This cousin of my mother's – cousin in the third or fourth degree, I forget which, but distant – was a barber by trade, and eventually – don't ask me how or when – became barber to King Louis. King Louis, however, found that Olivier had other talents, such as successfully organizing the royal

27

baggage wagons when the court moved from one place to the next. No easy task, I imagine. So my cousin was promoted and put in charge of all the king's journeyings around the kingdom. In short, he has become a great favourite and close confidant of His Highness. A few years ago, he was sent as royal envoy to the Flemings of Ghent, and nowadays entertains visiting dignitaries to Plessis whom the king cannot be bothered to see for himself. From being a mere barber, he is now a great man.'

I snorted. 'He wants to watch his back, then. Nobodies who become kings' favourites are usually hated and very often pay for it with their lives. We had a good example of that in Scotland only a few months ago, as you know as well as I. When King Louis dies, your precious cousin could find himself dancing on air at the end of a rope.' (Prophetic words, as it turned out the following year, but that has nothing to do with the present story.) 'Anyway,' I went on, 'what has Master le Daim got to do with this mission to France that you and I are undertaking?'

'I've had word,' said Timothy, 'from Lord Dynham, the deputy governor of Calais, that Monsieur le Daim will be in Paris very shortly – probably sometime next week – on a mission for King Louis to the city goldsmiths. If Mistress Gray can introduce herself to him as a kinswoman, she may be able to find out King Louis's intentions with regard to Burgundy and the English marriage between the

28

dauphin and the Princess Elizabeth, straight, as it were, from the horse's mouth.'

'And are you sure that Lord Dynham's information is reliable?'

Timothy got to his feet. 'It usually is. A great many people pass through Calais on their way home from the Continent, and, unlike most rolling stones, they gather moss. Calais is a hotbed of gossip, not all of it idle. Now!' He smiled paternally at Eloise Gray and myself, looking so pleased with himself and so condescending that the toe of my boot itched to make contact with his backside. 'I shall leave you two to get better acquainted in your new roles as husband and wife. Take a walk. Visit the shops. But, Roger, remember, I need you back here at Baynard's Castle by suppertime. My lord of Gloucester,' he explained glibly to Eloise, 'wishes to thank Roger personally for accompanying the Duke of Albany to Scotland.' Whether or not she believed this, there was no means of knowing: the elfin face gave nothing away. Timothy went on, 'Tomorrow, Roger, you must be fitted for some new clothes.' At my indignant protest, he eyed me up and down and responded sharply, 'You can't go to France posing as a prosperous haberdasher looking like that. And you will need extra baggage and some samples of cloth to give credence to your story.'

'And what is my story?' I demanded belligerently. 'Until this moment I wasn't even aware of my new calling.'

He patted my shoulder. 'Everything will finally be decided upon in the morning. You will both please meet me here, in this same chamber, immediately after dinner, when the details of your journey and of your ... er ... "marriage" will be agreed between us. The tailor will also be present to measure you, Roger, for those clothes I spoke of.'

A moment later, he was gone, whisking himself out of the room before I could raise further objections or subject him to any more of my ill humour.

'Coward!' I shouted, but the door had already closed behind him and I found myself addressing solid oak.

I turned back to my companion, eyeing her askance.

She laughed. 'You needn't worry, Master Chapman. I don't require your escort around London. I have sufficient knowledge of the streets to be able to take care of myself. I was here with my lord of Albany two years ago.'

'Just as well.' I glowered as she rose to her feet and prepared to depart. But nevertheless she intrigued me, and I detained her by the simple expedient of asking another question. 'Your mother may be French, but I'd swear there's Scottish blood in you somewhere. Your father?'

She sat down again. 'Yes. Maman was French,' she agreed. 'She died five years ago. Both my parents are dead, and you're right – my father was indeed Scottish. He was a member of King Louis's Scots Guards and died fighting for him, when I was four years old, at the battle of Montlhéry.'

'Montlhéry?' I queried, coaxing my tongue around the name, not without some difficulty.

'Oh, you probably wouldn't have heard of it,' she said. 'It was a battle fought against the king's own subjects, who wanted to depose him in favour of his brother Charles.' She added scornfully, 'They called themselves the League of the Public Weal,' and spat on the floor in a most unladylike fashion. 'Common good? They had no thought of the common good! It was pure ambition and greed. I know! My mother told me all about it when I was old enough to understand. Burgundy was one of them. The late duke, Charles of Charolais, as he still was then, fought on behalf of his father, Duke Philip.' She leaned towards me, suddenly deadly serious, her great violet-blue eyes burning with righteous wrath. 'Do you know that after he became king – that was the year I was born – Louis bought back Picardy and the Somme towns from Burgundy for four hundred thousand crowns? But then Duke Philip regretted the deal and decided he wanted them back again.'

'Don't tell me,' I interrupted, 'I can guess what's coming. Philip wanted them back *and* to hang on to the money as well. Am I right?'

She gave a mirthless laugh. 'Of course you are. So he formed this league with all the other malcontents – the dukes of Brittany,

31

Berry, Anjou, Calabria, Bourbon and I don't know how many others – all pretending that they were acting in the public interest and that it would be better for the country if they put Charles instead of Louis on the throne.'

'And did Louis win at ... at this place you mentioned?'

'Montlhéry? Sadly not. My father died in vain.' Then her little face brightened, losing its bitter look. 'But King Louis got the better of them all in the end, not by force of arms, but by cunning and sheer strength of will.'

I chewed my thumbnail thoughtfully. 'And now it would seem that he intends to bring Burgundy to heel by marrying his son to Maximilian's daughter.'

'We don't know that for certain,' she said quickly. 'That's what we're going to France to find out.'

I agreed. 'But I don't suppose it's King Louis's intentions we're being sent to discover, but Maximilian's. I have no doubt whatsoever that Louis will happily repudiate the English alliance in favour of the Burgundian. He would be a fool not to. And once Burgundy is a spent force, no longer a thorn in France's side, well then...'

'Well then what?'

'It will be farewell to that annual pension that King Louis pays to King Edward so promptly every year.'

'Why?'

'Because it's been paid for the past seven years on the understanding that England would refrain from going to Burgundy's aid in any conflict she had with France. Which is exactly what has happened. In spite of all the pressure on him from nobles and commoners alike, the king has steadily refused to send an expeditionary force to help Maximilian in his struggle against the French, with the result that he looks likely to have cut off his nose to spite his face.' I grimaced. 'My own guess is that this mission you and I are being sent on is a sheer waste of time. Any fool with half a brain could predict that Louis will choose the Burgundian marriage. He has everything to gain from it and nothing at all from the English alliance. Indeed, he'll be the richer in more ways than one for breaking with King Edward.'

Eloise raised an eyebrow. 'You think we're being sent on a fool's errand? I agree with you about King Louis, but you said yourself that it's Maximilian's intentions that are the more important, and what we have to find out.'

I snorted. 'My dear girl, I've just told you that anyone with half a brain could foretell what Louis will do. Well, anyone with the other half must surely harbour very few doubts concerning Burgundy's reaction. He's appealed to us, his closest ally, in vain. He's in a fair way to being beaten to his knees. His wife, who commanded his subjects' loyalty, is dead and their child too young to be a rallying point. He's an Austrian, a stranger, which many of the duchy's people resent. He can either wait for his lands to be overrun or he can rescue a little dignity from the situation by marrying his daughter to the dauphin and making a peace of sorts with King Louis. An idiot could work it out.'

My companion looked thoughtful. 'So, as you rightly ask, what is the purpose of sending us to Paris? My cousin Olivier, although a very shrewd man as I understand it, can only tell us what we already know.'

'Guess,' I corrected her. 'As for the rest,' I went on scornfully, 'our superiors, those set in authority over us, don't need reasons for squandering money. The discovery that you and this Olivier le Daim are in some vague way related to one another is a heaven-sent pretext for Master Plummer to arrange a secret mission for us into France. It makes him look as though he's busy protecting the safety of the realm. Our wonderful spymaster general, ever vigilant!'

She laughed. 'You sound like a man with a grudge.'

'I am. I should be on my way home now to my wife and family, none of whom I've seen for months. Instead, that little runt has enmeshed me in one of his precious schemes, which, as far as I can see, is a waste of time.' I poured what remained of the wine into my mazer, tossed it off and felt slightly better. 'However, there's nothing I can do about it, so I'd better resign myself to making the best of a bad job. At least it doesn't seem as though it'll take long, not if this cousin of yours really is going to be in Paris some time soon. Mind you,' I added gloomily, 'a dozen things could go wrong or he could simply change his mind.'

'A possibility,' Eloise agreed, smiling. 'Because it won't, of course, be Olivier who changes his mind, but the king. And Louis is a great one for altering his plans at the last moment.'

I regarded her curiously. 'You speak of him – the king, that is – as if you were fond of him. I noticed it before.'

She rose from her stool and smoothed down her skirt. 'I've never set eyes on him, so I can hardly be fond of him, but I admire him greatly, as my parents did.' She looked at me defiantly. 'You appear to find that odd.'

I shrugged. 'Most people seem to dislike him. I've heard him described as devious, cunning, crafty. Someone compared him to a spider sitting in the middle of his web, spinning his schemes. I saw him once.' She looked surprised. 'From a distance, you understand. I was at Picquigny. A very unprepossessing man and not dressed at all like a king.'

'No.' She smiled reminiscently. 'My mother said he had no interest in clothes and was always attired like one of his lowlier servants. But an extremely clever man. According to Maman, when he became king, France was a nation torn apart by a dozen rival factions, after the long years of war with the English. But when you were finally kicked out–' she gave me a cheeky grin, tinged with malice –

'Louis set about unifying the country again by any means at his command. And he has done so. If you're right, Burgundy will be brought to heel very soon ... Now, I must be off. As I mentioned, I've no need of your company. I can look after myself.' She moved towards the door, then with her hand on the latch, glanced back over her shoulder. 'Why does my lord of Gloucester want to see you?' she asked.

'What?' The question caught me off guard. 'Oh ... Didn't you hear what Timothy said?' What the devil had he said? Something about Duke Richard wanting to thank me. 'He ... er ... he wishes to express his gratitude for my—my care of the Duke of Albany in Scotland.'

I don't suppose she believed the story for a moment, but the mention of Albany and Scotland made her take herself off in a hurry with the promise to see me in this same room the next morning, after dinner, if not before. I made no immediate move to follow her, but sat for a while longer, staring into space, thinking.

At first, Eloise's admiration for King Louis seemed to me to sort ill with her undertaking of the present mission, but after a very few minutes mulling it over, I considered it less strange. To begin with, she didn't really have a choice but to comply with Timothy's and his royal master's wishes. Being convicted of sorcery and witchcraft meant being burned at the stake. She must know she was lucky to be alive and would throw no rub in the way of remaining so. Secondly, our mission was in no sort damaging or harmful to either the French king or his country.

In fact, the more I thought about it, the more unnecessary it seemed and the more my anger increased. It appeared to me that I was being made a fool of. Well, perhaps not a fool precisely, but that I was being kept in London against my will for no very obvious reason. But in that case, I told myself, there must surely be a hidden motive. In spite of what I had said to Eloise Gray, I couldn't really believe that either Timothy or, more particularly, the Duke of Gloucester would despatch me to France simply to bring back information that would probably soon be common knowledge. God forbid that I should be as cynical as that!

I had been told that my role was passive, that I was being sent in order to afford Eloise protection and to add to her disguise as an ordinary traveller. A woman alone would be too conspicuous and open to all manner of unwelcome advances from predatory men. But I was beginning to wonder if the opposite were not really the truth: if she were not *my* protection and *my* disguise. But against what? Or whom? What was this secret mission that I was to undertake for Prince Richard? And it was to be kept secret even from my companion. Now why?

My head was aching and I became conscious of a crick in the back of my neck. I was also aware of how rigid my shoulders had become, and I got to my feet, stretching my arms in order to ease the tension. I walked over to the window again, pushing the casement a little wider and breathing in the stale odours of London: fetid water, fish, seaweed, the smells of a hundred cook-shops, the blood and guts of the Shambles and the stink of the drains, full to overflowing by this time in the afternoon. The noise, too, the cacophony of a myriad voices and rumbling traffic, interlaced as it was with the constant chiming of bells, smote my ears, reminding me, in case I was in any danger of forgetting it, that this was a capital city, the hub of the country and one of the largest trading ports in the whole of Europe. But Paris, I had been reliably informed, was even bigger, noisier and of far greater importance. After the comparative quiet of Scotland that had embraced me for the past few months, I wasn't looking forward to my enforced visit.

Two people came out of the castle and stood at the top of the water-stairs just below me. I recognized them as the couple I had seen earlier: the young – at least I presumed she was young – woman, still cloaked from head to foot and with her back towards me, and her escort, as debonair and jaunty as ever. The blue feather in his hat positively quivered in the sunlight, the sun having recently deigned to show its face again.

'Wagge! Wagge! Go we hence!' the man yelled at a passing boat, and the boatman, on the lookout for a new fare, immediately row-ed to the foot of the steps. My smart young gent ran lightly down, blew a kiss to his lady with the tips of his fingers and was rowed away upstream. The woman watched for a moment or two, then turned with a swirl of her cloak and disappeared once more in-doors.

I turned from the window. Before I came back for my meeting with Timothy, and then with His Grace of Gloucester, I had visits of my own to make, old acquaintances to be looked up and friendships renewed.

Three

I emerged into the hustle and bustle of Thames Street and, by way of Fish Hill, Trinity Street and the Walbrook, found myself at last in the Stock's Market, from where it was only a few minutes' walk to the Leadenhall and Cornhill. It being the middle of the week, I guessed that my old friend Philip Lamprey would be working, so I made first for the market, where the noise was a little less insistent than outside, but not by much. The stalls, each with its own haggling, shouting crowd surrounding it, were so close together that it was impossible to force a path between them and I had to use the main aisles, pushing and shoving aside the press of people, loudly cursing and being as enthusiastically sworn at in return.

At the end of half an hour, tired, sweating profusely and with my temper in shreds, I had failed to locate Philip and his second-hand clothes stall. My attempts to question other stallholders as to his whereabouts had met either with blank stares or impatient waves of the hand, indicating that I should be off about my own business and not wasting honest men's time with foolish questions.

'What? What d'you say? Can't 'ear you!'

I repeated my question.

'Oo? Oo'd you say? Oi! You there! Stop 'andling them goods if you ain't buyin'. Thievin' baggage! I knows your sort! Sorry!' This last to me with a desperate shrug of the shoulders. 'Lamprey? ''Aven't seen 'im fer a sennight, maybe longer. Where? Where'd I see 'im? No, I ain't got no white soap, mistress. It's Bristol grey or nothing.'

Frustrated, fuming and out of sorts with the entire human race, I finally decided that, for some reason or another, Philip was not working that day, so, apostrophizing him as a lazy bastard, I quit the Leadenhall and made my way to the one-roomed daub and wattle cottage he and his wife shared in a back alley of Cornhill. I recognized it immediately, in spite of not having visited the Lampreys for some

40

time, but as I approached, I experienced a sudden premonition that all was not well. The door stood slightly ajar, but there was nothing in that. Jeanne was the friendliest of souls and kept open house for her neighbours, yet I had a sense of the place being empty. There was no smoke issuing from the hole in the roof, no indication of any movement within, no singing, none of the domestic busyness I always associated with Philip's young and pretty wife.

Uneasily, I rapped loudly on the door. There was no answer, so I knocked again. And again. Nothing happened. Cautiously, I pushed it wider and went in.

There was no one there, nor had there been for several weeks, I guessed. The ashes on the hearth were cold, almost dust. The pot hanging over it from its rusty hook was thickly coated inside with the remains of what had probably once been a stew, but was now quarter of an inch deep in mould and alive with maggots. The bile rose in my throat as I recoiled from the nauseating sight. The bed, pushed against one wall, had been stripped of bedding, and fleas chased one another merrily across the straw mattress; the curtain hanging at the single window showed signs of mildew. Everything was in a state of neglect, having been abandoned where it lay. I wondered what in heaven's name could have caused Jeanne and Philip to leave their home to the dirt and the rats, one of which had emerged from its hole and was sitting brazenly in the middle of the floor, scratching for crumbs of rotting food among the stale rushes. I kicked out at it with my foot, but was ignored.

I heard a noise behind me and swung round, my hand going to the haft of my meat knife, which was stuck in my belt. I hadn't brought my cudgel, not thinking I should need it. And nor did I. The woman who stood in the doorway, regarding me with round, suspicious eyes, was elderly with furrowed cheeks and strands of wispy grey hair escaping from beneath her cap. When she spoke, I could see that she was missing a number of teeth.

'Who are you? What d'you want?'

'I'm looking for Jeanne and Philip Lamprey,' I said, my hand dropping back to my side. 'I'm a friend.'

'Ho! A friend, is it?' She made no attempt to step beyond the threshold. 'Not so much a friend you know what's come to them, then. I'll tell you to your head, there ain't nothin' t' steal in here, master. Anything worth takin' has been took since 'e went, and that's more 'n a month gone. Them around here don' let good stuff go t' waste. An' why should they?' she added belligerently. 'Life's hard. You gotta snatch what comes your way.'

'I don't want to steal anything,' I retorted angrily. 'I told you, I'm the Lampreys' friend. I live in Bristol and recently I've been abroad – Scotland – so I haven't been able to see Master and Mistress Lamprey for some while. Where are they? What's become of them?'

The woman gnashed her gums together and subjected me to another hard stare, but then she seemed to accept my story. It was a comfort to know that at least I didn't look like a villain and could pass for an honest man.

'She died in childbirth, her and the child – oh, back in August 't would be, round 'bout Lamastide. It were a boy, too, jus' what they both wanted.'

'Jeanne dead?' I interrupted, horrified, unable for the moment to take it in. *'Dead?'* I repeated.

'Milk fever,' the woman confirmed. 'Jus' the way my eldest girl went when she had her third. Sudden like. One minute sittin' up talkin' as right as you please, the next out of her wits, poor soul. And dead within three days.'

'Oh dear God,' I groaned. 'And what of Philip? He thought the world of her.'

'Aye, he took it hard. Didn't leave the cottage for weeks after she and the babe were buried. Didn't eat, didn't sleep – well, not much – didn't work. Didn't cry even, least-ways not that I saw. Just lay in here, on that there bed, curled up, knees drawn up to his chin, not speaking. Us neighbours did our best t' rouse him, brought him food and drink – brought him some o' my best home-made beer and rabbit stew – but he refused t' touch either. Don' think he even knew it were there.

43

Worn away to a thread he were in the end. Never had much meat on his bones t' begin with. Then, all of a sudden, 'bout three weeks ago, he up and vanished. No one knows where. Jus' disappeared. Took nothin' with him that anyone could see. Nothin' but what he stood up in. My own feelin',' my inform-ant added, with a comfortable settling of her shoulders, 'is that he's drowned himself. Couldn't live without her.'

Her words confirmed my own fears. I didn't want to listen to any more. I thanked the goodwife and stumbled blindly out of the cottage and back into the general hubbub of Cornhill, feeling like a man who has been mortally wounded. What made matters worse was that I had been, albeit briefly, in London in May, and had even toyed with the idea of going to see the Lampreys, but had per-suaded myself that I couldn't spare the time. The truth was, of course, that I had been in a vile mood about my enforced journey into Scotland and been no fit company for anyone. Now, however, I blamed myself for not having overcome my ill humour. At least I would have seen my friends and known about the child.

The next thing I can remember with any clarity is standing beside the great conduit at the end of Cheapside and the beginning of the Poultry, staring around me, completely in a daze. My mind refused to function prop-erly; all I could think of was that Jeanne and most probably Philip were dead. It felt as

44

though a door had slammed shut, locking me away from a part of my life that I had taken for granted: two friends who were always there even if years elapsed between our meetings.

'You all right, master?'

The voice, that of a carter who had stopped to water his horse at the conduit (forbidden by law, but what of that? To your average Englishman, rules are only made to be broken) brought me back to my senses.

'Yes ... yes. Thank you.'

'Well, if you say so, though you don't look it.' He spoke with rough sympathy, adding acutely, 'I'd say you've had a nasty shock. What you need, friend, is a drink. Oh, not that stuff,' he went on, as I cupped my hands and scooped up some water. 'You want a cup of good ale inside your belly. Settle your guts.' With which sage advice he mounted the box of his cart, jerked on the horse's reins and rattled off towards West Cheap.

The man was right. I needed something to calm my nerves and shake myself back to normality. At the moment, nothing seemed real and I was aware of a general feeling of weakness, a sort of trembling in my bones that made me ashamed of myself. I was a big, strong man of thirty – along with Duke Richard I had passed that milestone three weeks back, on the second of this month of October – and here I was behaving like a sickly schoolboy. I took a deep breath, braced my shoulders and looked about me for the nearest alehouse.

And there, almost opposite to where I was standing, was the entrance to Bucklersbury and the inn of St Brendan the Voyager. I had stayed there on at least two occasions and counted the landlord, Reynold Makepeace, as a friend of mine. I conjured up a picture of him, short, stocky, bright hazel eyes, sparse brown hair, his large paunch covered by a leather apron and always delighted to welcome old customers. A presence infinitely comforting and just what I needed. I plunged across the road, oblivious of swearing carters and the imprecations of mounted men-at-arms and self-important messengers, and into the narrow mouth of Bucklersbury, where the upper storeys of houses and shops on either side overhung the street, meeting almost in the middle.

The Voyager was situated just before the junction with Needlers Lane and appeared to be even busier than I recalled at this time of day. I squeezed myself on to a providentially empty stool at the common table and stared around, hoping for a glimpse of Reynold, but there was no sign of him. I decided that he was most probably in the parlour attending in person to the more select of his guests. He would arrive to restore order in the ale room in just a few minutes.

There was no doubt in my mind, as I tried to catch the eye of a passing pot boy, that the present set of customers were a far more raucous bunch than they used to be. There

46

was a rough element among them that Reynold would never have tolerated in days gone by, and I wondered if times were hard that he put up with them now. A brawl had broken out in one corner of the ale room between a man with a broken nose and another with a patch over one eye, whose tunic bore witness to the fact that he was a careless eater, and who was being vociferously encouraged by his friends to 'black the bugger's daylights'.

I waited confidently for Reynold to appear, breathing fire and brimstone, in order to have the troublemakers ejected. Nothing happened. In the meantime, I at last managed to order a cup of ale, which, when it came, tasted flat and stale. After only three sips, I pushed it away, disgusted.

I turned to the man on my right. 'Where's Landlord Makepeace?' I asked, raising my voice to be heard above the increasing din.

'Who?'

'Reynold Makepeace, the owner of this place.'

Before he could reply, a slatternly looking, red-haired woman wearing a dirty apron and with her cap askew had entered the ale room and was screaming at the two antagonists to sit down and behave or they would be thrown out without more ado. To reinforce her words, a couple of very large gentlemen, also red-haired and obviously her sons, each with fists like hams, had followed her in and were indicating their readiness to carry out her

47

wishes. The would-be combatants duly subsided and peace, of a sort, reigned again.

I felt a touch on my arm. The man on the other side of me, a quiet, pleasant-spoken fellow, said, 'You were asking about Landlord Makepeace. It must be some while since you were last here, friend. You plainly haven't heard.'

'Heard what?' I asked, my heart sinking into my boots.

'Reynold was killed some year and a half ago. Stabbed to death, here in this very room.'

'Stabbed? Here? In the Voyager?'

My companion nodded. 'I don't know how long it is since you were last in these parts, but the area has been going from bad to worse for a long time. Far more thieves and beggars and pickpockets than there used to be, and foreign seamen making their way up from the wharves. You know how it is. Someone discovers a place by accident and the word spreads. Anyway, to cut a long story short, Reynold was trying to separate the contestants in just such a sort of brawl as was threatening a few moments ago, and unfortunately got in the way of a knife that was being brandished about. Died within hours.' He broke off, laying a concerned hand on my arm. 'Are you feeling unwell, sir? You're looking a very funny colour. Here, drink some of your ale.'

'No! No!' I pushed his hand away and staggered to my feet, holding him down on

48

his stool when he would have risen with me. 'There's nothing wrong. I mean, I'm not ill. It's just that this is the second piece of bad news – appalling news – that I've had within the past hour. Please don't come with me. I shall be all right once I get away from this place.'

Having made my way outside, all I could do, for several minutes at least, was to lean against the wall of the inn breathing heavily and trying to control the renewed shaking in my limbs. Above my head, the inn sign, St Brendan in his cockleshell boat, swung and creaked in the late afternoon breeze just as it had always done, giving the illusion that nothing had changed. But everything had changed and in so short a space of time. Jeanne Lamprey was dead and her baby stillborn, Philip was missing, and now Reynold Makepeace had gone, stabbed to death in his own ale room, where his word used to be law.

Suddenly, I forced myself away from the wall and started half running, half lurching through the crowded streets – the Walbrook, Dowgate Hill, Elbow Lane and so into Thames Street – instinct guiding my feet back to Baynard's Castle. I was like a man possessed, seeing no one, hearing nothing, until, without in the least knowing how I got there, I found myself sitting on the edge of the narrow bed in the tiny, cupboard-sized room that had been allotted to me for the duration of my stay in the castle. At this point, it occurred to me, quite irrelevantly, that I should have been suspicious from the moment I was given a private chamber and not put to sleep in the common dormitory, along with the scullions and spit-turners and other general dogsbodies who kept the life of the household running smoothly. Such favouritism should have been a warning that something more was required of me. For the present, however, I could concentrate only on the loss of three friends.

Perhaps it was too much to claim Reynold Makepeace as a friend, but as an acquaintance I had valued him highly and until today had regarded the Voyager as a home from home and a safe haven from the perils of the London streets when staying in the capital. Now that refuge was gone, along with Philip and Jeanne Lamprey, whose cottage door had always been open to me and where I was welcomed as a brother.

Someone was rapping on my own door with an urgency that suggested whoever it was had been knocking for some time. I got up and opened it to find Eloise Gray standing on the threshold.

'It's suppertime,' she said. 'The trumpet sounded ages ago. I thought to find you in the servants' hall before me. Is anything wrong? It's not like you to neglect your belly. You're not sick, are you?'

I shook my head. 'I'm not hungry.' When she looked her astonishment, I blurted out the sorry story, feeling foolish, but at the

50

same time needing comfort.

I should have known better than to expect it, I suppose, from a woman who had played a man's role for so long and whose companions I had, in some part, helped to destroy.

'Dear me!' she said brightly when I had finished. 'Well, you can't count this Philip Lamprey as a death, nor the child, so you'll be bound to hear of a third one within a day or two. Are you coming down to supper? You surely don't mean to starve yourself on account of a couple of people who, on your own admission, you haven't seen for years. Besides, I seem to remember you have an audience with His Grace of Gloucester this evening. You need to fortify yourself for that. You don't want to risk an empty belly rumbling as you make your obeisance, now do you?'

There was something in what she said, and her brisk, unsympathetic attitude had the effect of making me pull myself together, aware that I was perhaps indulging my grief to an unwarranted degree – or that it would seem so to other people. I was not mourning family, only two acquaintances whose existence had made very little difference to my life. I braced my shoulders and managed a smile.

'You're right,' I admitted. 'I'll come right away if–' I forced myself to say it – 'you'll give me the pleasure of escorting you down to the hall.'

She put her hand on my arm. 'I don't think

we need hurry,' she laughed. 'It's probably more of that disgusting brown pottage that we were fed at dinner. I suspect Duchess Cicely of being a thought parsimonious. These religious women very often are. They have little time for the pleasures of the flesh.' We had arrived at a narrow, twisting staircase and had to descend in single file. Eloise paused two steps down and, turning her head, glanced up at me, a malicious smile lifting her pretty lips. 'Although I understand it wasn't always so. Rumour has it that Her Grace of York was far from despising earthly pleasures in her youth.'

'What exactly do you mean by that?' I spoke more sharply than I intended and added in a milder tone, 'I've never heard any ill of her.'

Eloise continued her descent, talking over her shoulder as she did so. 'I daresay you might not. But my lord duke–' she meant Albany, of course – 'let slip odd things now and again. Being of kin, he was probably privy to family secrets.' We had by now reached the bottom of the staircase and were traversing a passage, where daylight had already given way to torchlight as a fading October sun gave up the unequal struggle to filter through infrequent arrow slits. My companion chuckled. 'Didn't Her Grace once offer to prove King Edward a bastard?'

'Oh, that!' I shrugged. 'I recall hearing something of the sort. But if I remember rightly, it was a long time ago, when the king first revealed his secret marriage to the queen. The duchess was apparently so incensed, so furiously angry, that it's generally reckoned she would have said anything in order to overset it. The marriage, that is. And so far as I know, no such proof was ever forthcoming.'

It was Eloise's turn to shrug. 'Well, I suppose it would take more audacity than most women have to admit that she had cuckolded her husband, for whatever reason, or however worthy she considered the cause. But why should she not have been telling the truth and then thought better of it? I believe she was extraordinarily beautiful when she was young. Wasn't she called the Rose of Raby?'

We descended another flight of stairs and now we could distinctly hear the clatter and chatter of the kitchens and the servants' hall, a din that would soon engulf us, making rational conversation impossible.

I said quickly, 'Beauty and immorality don't necessarily go hand in hand.'

Eloise smiled enigmatically, but, maddeningly, made no answer, moving rapidly ahead of me with a sudden burst of speed that left me behind.

Timothy Plummer was waiting for me when, an hour or so later, I re-entered the little chamber overlooking the water-stairs. So much had happened since I quit it earlier that it seemed like a different room, a different day.

I had not enjoyed my supper. As Eloise had

predicted, it had been the same pottage as at dinner with a few more vegetables added, followed – for those who wanted it – by coarse barley bread and goat's cheese. I had given my portion to my neighbour, a young page who looked as if he were perpetually hungry – as no doubt he was, poor child.

But it wasn't just the food, unpalatable as it was, that robbed me of my appetite. The memory of my friends' deaths lay like a bruise on my spirit. Not only was it grief for Jeanne and Philip Lamprey and for Reynold Makepeace, but Eloise's careless words that I would be sure to hear of a third death within a short space of time had suddenly made me anxious for news of my family. What was happening to them, to Adela, to the children, during my long absence? One of them could have died and I wouldn't know. I should be on my way home to them by now, but here I was on the verge of being sent even further afield, to France, and not allowed to send a message to enquire after their well-being. The bile rose in my throat and almost choked me. I began to rehearse in my head just what I was going to say to Duke Richard when I at last came face to face with him. As for that little stoat Timothy Plummer...

'Why that grim face?' the little stoat enquired as I took my seat opposite him at the table. 'You look as if you've lost sixpence and picked up a groat. For God's sake, man, what's the matter with you now?'

'I want to go home to my wife and children,' I snarled, 'not be packed off to France play-acting the role of husband to an evil little baggage I wouldn't trust further than I could see her.'

Timothy sighed heavily. 'I thought you'd reconciled yourself to that fact. I'll be truthful with you, Roger—'

'Do you think you can?' I sneered.

He chose to overlook this interruption, continuing smoothly, trying not to let his annoyance show, 'I don't know, as I believe I've already mentioned, whether Mistress Gray would have killed you or not if I hadn't turned up in time, but I give you my word that she is absolutely no danger to you now. Why should she be? Ask yourself that. The circumstances are completely different. She no longer has a motive, so stop talking like a fool. If that's your only objection—'

'It's not, and you must know it's not.' I had myself under control now, keeping my tone level and the peevish note out of my voice. I leaned forward on my stool, my arms folded on the table. 'Let's leave aside the fact that I am being used, as I have been used for the past four, five months. Let us also ignore another inconvenient fact – that I am not one of your spies and have never been officially recruited for the job – and finally let us consider whether or not Duke Richard, being the man he is, would force me to leave my home and family to run my head into danger on his behalf if you were not constantly reassuring him of my willingness to do so. Oh, I admit he might be disappointed in me, feel that I had betrayed him in some way or another, but I doubt very much if he would absolutely insist or throw me into prison for disobedience. It's not in his nature to be unjust.'

'He trusts you—' Timothy was beginning, but I waved him to silence.

'And,' I went on ruthlessly, 'I hold you primarily responsible for this present jaunt, which, as far as I can tell – and it might interest you to know that Mistress Gray agrees with me – appears to be totally unnecessary. The information that Eloise can wring from this cousin of hers is no state secret and is bound to be common knowledge on this side of the Channel almost as soon as it is known in France. Moreover, even a fool unversed in politics like me can predict what King Louis's decision will be. And whatever else I think about you, Timothy, and in spite of anything I've ever said to the contrary, I have never thought you lacking in wit.'

The spymaster bowed ironically (not an easy feat when you're sitting down). 'I suppose I should be grateful for your good opinion,' he said, 'however grudgingly given. But if you don't think me stupid, then give me credit for not sending you on a fool's errand. You know very well, because I have told you, the reason for this present meeting and for your audience this evening with Duke Richard. This is a mission within a mission. Your ostensible reason for accompanying Mistress Gray to France is merely a cloak for a secret

– and I emphasize "secret" – undertaking for His Grace. And before you say anything else, yes, I admit my first thought was of you because the duke and I are both agreed that you are the only man we can fully trust. You have not only, in the past, proved your loyalty to my lord, but you seem to me to have a genuine affection for him. Is that not so?'

I couldn't deny it. The king's sole surviving brother was a man who either attracted or repelled people; they either loved him or hated him. I had, from the first moment of seeing him, and aware that we had been born on the very same day, been one of the former.

It was my turn to sigh. 'So what is this commission?'

For answer, Timothy reached into the breast of his tunic and brought out a folded paper, which he passed to me. 'Read it,' he commanded.

I did so in mounting horror and, when I had mastered its contents, drew a slow, deep breath. I stared at Timothy across the table.

'But this is rank treason,' I whispered.

Four

Throughout my life, I have frequently observed that whenever I have been reminded of some past event, long forgotten, a further reference to it occurs within days. Or, in this case, hours...

I repeated, 'Treason.' My heart began to pound and I felt breathless. I was in a state of shock, not the first shock I had received that day, but this was by far the worst.

Timothy shifted uncomfortably and avoided my gaze. 'It depends how you interpret the word "treason",' he said at last. 'If it's treasonable to want to right a wrong, then I suppose you could call it that.'

I barely heard him. 'I've always thought my lord of Gloucester so loyal to his brother.'

That brought my companion's head up with a jerk as he fixed me with a gimlet eye. 'And so he is,' he answered fiercely. 'And so will he always be as long as Edward lives. But you saw for yourself, last May at Fotheringay, how ill the king was then, and you've seen him again these past weeks. You can't have failed to notice the deterioration in him even in that short time. There's no reason why an injustice should be perpetuated if he...'

Timothy broke off, but I was able to finish the rest of his speech for him in my head. If Edward died, there was no reason for the Duke of Gloucester to extend that lifelong loyalty to his nephew – who, on his mother's side, was one of the hated Woodvilles – if what he suspected should prove to be fact.

'Why doesn't the duke just ask his mother for the facts?' I demanded bluntly. 'The duchess once offered to declare Edward a bastard, as I was reminded only a short while ago. If it was indeed the truth, what's to prevent her doing so again?'

'Not "again",' Timothy corrected me. 'The duchess never actually lived up to her word, if you remember. It was a threat that was never carried out. And you could argue,' he went on, repeating almost verbatim what I had said earlier to Eloise, 'that she was so furious she would have said anything at the time to prevent Elizabeth Woodville becoming queen.' He grinned. 'I'm sorry, Roger. You're not going to wriggle out of this trip to France so easily.'

'But the stupidity of it!' I exclaimed. 'The expense!' That surely should be an argument to appeal to Timothy's heart and pocket. 'When all my lord of Gloucester has to do is ask his mother to confirm or deny the accusation she made all those years ago. As possibly the rightful king—' But here I stopped, frowning. 'What about Clarence's son, the young Earl of Warwick?'

'Barred from inheriting on account of his
59

father's attainder. And for God's sake, keep your voice down! You're not wrong when you say that this could be interpreted as treason.'

Frightened, I lowered my voice to a whisper. 'And Clarence's daughter?'

'Same reason, of course. Besides, what dolt would want a woman on the throne? We nearly had one once, and look what an unmitigated disaster Matilda was all those centuries ago.'

'You still haven't answered my query,' I hissed. 'Why doesn't the duke ask his mother for the truth?'

'I haven't enquired,' Timothy snapped back. 'It's not my place. I just carry out my orders. At a guess, I'd say it's not the sort of question a man wants to ask his mother. "Did you cuckold my father while he was away fighting the French?" Especially if the rumours are true and the man concerned wasn't even a member of the nobility, but a common archer.'

'There are rumours, then?'

'There are always rumours,' was the brief riposte.

Silence reigned for a moment or two while I studied the paper in front of me once again. The more I read it, the more I could see the desperate need for secrecy, even from my travelling companion. If Duchess Cicely's claim had been a lie, prompted by nothing other than anger at Edward's clandestine marriage, and if the king was truly her eldest son by her husband, the late Duke of York, then what I was about to get involved in was in very truth high treason, and enough to get me hanged, drawn and quartered. I broke into a cold sweat.

'You realize I'm putting my head in a noose?' I demanded. 'I have a wife and children dependent on me. I have every right to refuse.'

Timothy nodded. 'His Grace knows that and would do everything in his power to protect you if things should go wrong. It's why he wants to speak to you himself.'

'To over-persuade me, you mean. To assure me that it will all be as simple as falling off a log.'

'There's no need to take that tone. Believe me, the duke fully appreciates the risk you're running on his behalf. But as I said, you're the only person he trusts completely. And you must see that this is something he needs to know. If King Edward is really a bastard...' The spymaster gestured with his hands.

'Then, of course, his children have no claim to the crown,' I finished. I tapped the paper, realizing as I did so that the deaths of Jeanne Lamprey and Reynold Makepeace had been almost completely driven from my thoughts. Dabbling in treason focuses the mind wonderfully. 'So, who is this man I have to find? This Robin Gaunt? What is he like, and where does he live?'

Timothy looked guilty, always a bad sign. 'Well, we know he probably lives in Paris. He did ten years ago, at any rate.'

Oh, marvellous! Paris is one of the largest, most highly populated cities in Europe and here was a man who possibly might live there.

'What street?' I asked coldly.

'Ah!' Timothy smirked and tried to put a brave face on things. 'We don't actually have that information.' He added hurriedly, 'He is English.'

I expelled my breath in silent fury. 'It says here that he was one of the Duke of York's men-at-arms when York was governor of France in the early forties, but that he stayed on after the English withdrawal because he'd married one of Duchess Cicely's French tiring-women who didn't want to leave. Doesn't it perhaps occur to you that by this time he also might speak French like a native?'

'He still has an English name.'

I let rip with a string of oaths that even put Timothy to the blush – 'Really, Roger!' he protested – and he could be pretty foul-mouthed when he put his mind to it, I can tell you.

'Do you seriously understand how impossible this is?' I fumed, fairly spluttering with rage. 'You know I can't speak French. You've forbidden me to take Mistress Gray into my confidence. Yet you expect me to wander all over Paris on my own – and how I'm to do that without arousing her suspicions, I've no idea – searching for a man who might not even live there any more, and if he does, is quite likely no longer distinguishable as an

Englishman. You're mad!'

'You'll manage,' Timothy assured me winningly. 'You always do.'

'Bollocks!' I stormed. 'I suppose you can't even tell me what this Robin Gaunt looks like?'

'Ah, now there we might be able to help.'

'Dear God, a miracle! Don't tell me! Some ancient codger who knew Gaunt forty years ago, when they were soldiers together in France, but who hasn't set eyes on him since.'

'Well, yes,' Timothy admitted, plainly unnerved by my perspicacity. 'One of my agents only tracked him down the day before yesterday. We haven't spoken to him yet – we thought it best to leave that to you – but it's definite that he fought alongside Robin Gaunt and was garrisoned in Rouen with him. His name is Humphrey Culpepper and he lives in Stinking Lane, just off the Shambles. At least he'll be able to give you some idea whether Gaunt was tall or short, fat or thin and if he had blue eyes or brown. I'm informed that Culpepper's hair is grey now, so it's probable that Gaunt's is, too.'

'Do you really think,' I asked wrathfully, 'that a soldier would have any idea of the colour of another soldier's eyes? Especially after forty years! Your idea of military life needs some revision, old friend.'

'Well, he may be able to tell you something useful,' Timothy snapped, exasperated, and knowing, I suspected, that my anger was justified. He was nobody's fool and could appreciate as well as I could that I was being sent on a well-nigh impossible mission.

He got up. The evening had drawn in while we were talking and it was nearly too dark to see one another clearly, but he wouldn't send for candles: he didn't want anyone else in the room.

'What do I do with this?' I queried, indicating the paper on the table and also rising to my feet.

'Put it away, but for the Lord's sweet sake keep it safe. No one must be allowed to set eyes on it but yourself. If anyone were to read those questions that you must put to Gaunt and his wife, it wouldn't take them long to work out what it's all about. And I don't need to tell you, Roger, to watch yourself. If any Woodville agent gets a whisper of this, I wouldn't give much for your chances.'

'Thank you.' I bowed ironically. 'It's always good to be reassured. And what do you reckon the chances are of a Woodville agent getting to know about this mission of mine? How much do you trust the men you employ? Can you guarantee they are all completely loyal?'

Timothy tried to look affronted. 'Of course!'

I knew what that meant: no, but I'm not admitting as much. Well, who could blame him? He, too, had his loyalties until they were proved to be misplaced.

'I'd better take you to see the duke,' he said, 'or it will be time for him to dress for the mayor's banquet. Put that paper away for now, and later, I suggest you try to learn its contents off by heart and then destroy it. Do you have a good memory?'

'Good enough.' I wasn't going to relieve his mind by telling him that, from boyhood, my memory had always been excellent with almost total recall of people, incidents and places. (Even in old age, memory is my greatest gift or I wouldn't be able to write these memoirs. My children would probably inform you that I make half of it up as I go along. But what do they know?) And in this case I felt that Timothy was right. Better by far to make an effort to commit my instructions to memory than to be caught with them in my possession. For the time being, I folded the paper into its creases and put it in the pouch at my belt with the rueful reflection that it was rather like pocketing a live coal.

Duke Richard was alone when I was eventually ushered into his presence. There had been some delay, Timothy and I being forced to wait in an ante-room while His Grace, a loving parent, had said goodnight to his bastard children, my lord John and the lady Katherine. The boy accompanied his father everywhere, a handsome, bright, intelligent youth with a ready smile for everyone (very different, people whispered, from the delicate, legitimate son who stayed mostly in the North with his mother). Lady Katherine was slightly older, a beautiful girl of very nearly marriageable age, visiting the duke while he was in London. They had both wished Timothy and myself a charming 'Goodnight and God be with you' as they passed where we sat. Then a page appeared and called my name.

I raised my eyebrows at Timothy, but he shook his head.

'No,' he muttered. 'I thought I told you. My lord wishes to see you alone.'

The duke was seated beside a leaping fire, wearing a long chamber robe of amber velvet, his slippered feet stretched towards the flames. Candles had been lit, sending ripples of orange and gold licking across the walls, a draught making one of them splutter until it was suddenly extinguished in a puff of clouded blue smoke. A small table, close to the duke's chair, supported a flask and two goblets of fine Venetian glass, glowing blood-red in the half-light.

As soon as I entered, the duke rose from his seat, hand extended. I knelt and would have kissed it, but he withdrew it, smiling.

'No, no, Roger! Get up, man. I was going to shake your hand. I owe you a great deal, more than I can ever repay, from the time of our very first meeting. You have just endured a long and arduous trip to Scotland at my and the king's behest – and not without its dangers, I'm given to understand – and here I am asking you to ... to...'

'Commit treason, Your Highness?' I thought

66

it best to get things straight from the beginning.

I must have spoken more sharply than I realized because his hand fell back to his side and he flinched. He sat down again in his chair and indicated that I should take the one opposite him, on the other side of the hearth. After a moment or two while he stared into the fire with its glowing caverns and ash-fringed logs, there was a silence so profound that I could hear the popping of resin in the wood. Suddenly panic-stricken, I wondered what was to be my fate, and whether my outspokenness had really landed me in serious trouble at last.

Nothing happened, however, except that the duke finally raised his eyes, regarding me steadily, a half-smile curling the corners of his thin lips. 'Some might see it as such, I suppose, but rest assured that my loyalty to my brother has never wavered, nor will it do so, as long as he lives. I love him too much.' The smile deepened. 'When I was a child, I thought him the most splendid being I had ever seen, over six feet tall and as fair as a Nordic god. I would have gone to the ends of the earth for him. I still would. But...' Another silence, then he asked abruptly, 'Master Plummer has explained the matter to you?'

'More or less, my lord. He didn't really have to. My–my instructions made everything plain to me. By one of those odd coincidences, I had been reminded of your lady mother's ... er...'

'Outburst? At the time of Edward's marriage?'

'Yes, as Your Grace says. Outburst. Strangely enough, I heard reference made to it only an hour or so ago, so that when I read what you had written–' I tapped the pouch at my belt – 'I ... well, I understood.'

A servant, who must have entered the room unobserved by me, slid out of the shadows and poured wine from the flask into the two goblets, presenting one to the duke on bended knee and handing me the other with much less ceremony. Indeed, to my annoyance, a little of the wine slopped on to my sleeve. I glared and received a smirk in return. Duke Richard, who had gone back to staring at the fire, waved a hand in dismissal. The man made himself scarce.

'So, Roger!' As the latch clicked, my royal host returned his gaze to me. 'You think me capable of treason?'

I swallowed some wine to give myself courage and leaned forward. 'My lord,' I said desperately, 'if you believe the Duchess of York to have been telling the truth all those years past, why do you not ask her to confirm or deny it now?'

He nodded. 'It would seem the obvious course, I agree. But a great deal has happened in my mother's life over the past eighteen years: eight grandchildren – I am referring here only to the offspring of the king and queen, you understand – and her strong affection for the eldest of them, my niece,

Elizabeth. Also, I suspect that the duchess's deepening religious experience would inhibit her from repeating the accusation. Further-more–' he smiled wryly – 'it's no easy matter to ask your mother if she was unfaithful to your father.'

'I don't see that,' I argued, the wine making me bold. 'She has only to say, "No, I was so angry at the time that I made it up. Of course it isn't true."'

Duke Richard set down his half-empty goblet. 'But how would I know if she is telling the truth now?' he asked quietly. 'As I've said, nearly two decades have gone by. Circum-stances have altered. And remember, she didn't implement her threat eighteen years ago when her rage was white-hot.'

The fire leaped and crackled. I leaned even closer, resting my elbows on my knees. 'But what if, my lord, when you ask her, your lady mother admits that what she avowed back then was in fact true? You would have your answer.' And I should be spared a fool's errand to France, I thought.

The duke gave a short laugh as though he knew what I was thinking. 'To set your mind at rest, Roger, I have come as close as a duti-ful son dare to begging her for confirmation of her words.'

'And Her Grace has denied them?'

He sighed. 'If only she had. No, my mother remains evasive, easily turning aside a ques-tion that is not quite a question and which she is confident I shall never ask openly or force her to answer unequivocally.' He smiled conspiratorially, inviting me to share his exasperation. 'You know how women enjoy mystifying us men, not wishing to say yea or nay but not wanting to let us off the hook that easily, either. They like to keep us in suspense. It makes them more interesting.' He added hastily, 'I mean no disrespect to my mother. I owe her a son's love and obedience, which she will always have until the day she dies. It's just that she's ... a woman!'

From all this, I gathered that the duke had not asked the duchess for a direct answer to a direct question, that he might have tried to prise the truth out of her by indirect ones and that Duchess Cicely was saying nothing one way or another. But what did strike me most forcibly, although it was more by the tone of his voice than by what he had actually said, was that Duke Richard desperately wanted his mother's eighteen-year-old accusation to be true. Why?

The reason, I supposed, was obvious: if his beloved brother really was no son of the late Duke of York, but the bastard of an archer, then he, Richard of Gloucester, was rightful heir to the throne of England and not the half-Woodville brat at present called the Prince of Wales. (Indeed, he was already the rightful king.) He had to know the truth: rumours and suspicion were no good to him. But how was he to discover it after forty years if the one person who knew the answer refused to reveal it?

I wondered how long Timothy Plummer had been in the duke's confidence. Long enough, obviously, for his agents to have tracked down a man who had served under the Duke of York's command in France all those years previously and who, moreover, had a wife who had been one of the duchess's tiring-women in Rouen, where King Edward had been conceived and born.

But 'tracked down' was hardly the term to use. This useless bunch of so-called spies had merely heard of a man who had once lived in Paris and were unable to say if he were living there still. Nor could they describe him, apart from the fact that he was English and his dame French. At least I had a name, Robin Gaunt, although, heaven knew, he might well have changed it to something more Gallic in the intervening forty years.

I must have been looking grim, for the duke suddenly leaned over and seized one of my hands between both of his.

'Roger, forgive me for asking you to do this. I'm perfectly well aware that you haven't yet been home to your wife and children. Believe me when I say that neither they nor you will suffer financial hardship in your absence. But you realize how delicate a matter this is and there is no one else that I can trust with it.'

'Timothy Plummer?' I suggested drily.

He shook his head. 'He can't be spared: I need him on other work. And you are completely unknown in France. You can travel as Mistress Gray's husband and it will be the perfect disguise.'

'And yet she's to be kept in the dark regarding my mission. Without her to speak French and translate for me, I'm likely to prove a broken reed, and so I warn Your Highness. And how I'm to escape from her for maybe hours at a time, and without arousing her suspicions, I'm not sure.' I added daringly, 'Perhaps, my lord, you have a suggestion?'

The duke smiled and gave me the same answer as Timothy Plummer: 'You'll manage.'

I sighed, keeping my temper. 'I can only hope,' I retorted acidly, 'that the confidence you and your spymaster profess to have in me is not misplaced. I give Your Highness due warning that, in this instance, I may fail you.'

He released my hand and rose to his feet. I followed suit. 'I refuse even to contemplate your failure. You will find this Robin Gaunt for me and find out what he knows.'

'And if I do but he knows nothing, my lord? What then?'

He shrugged, the gesture showing up the slight unevenness of his shoulders, caused by the overuse of his sword arm from a very early age. 'Let's not anticipate defeat,' he said. 'Godspeed, Roger. I shall hope to see you the week after next when you return.' He must have noticed my dismayed expression, because he laughed. 'Don't worry. If you haven't returned by the time I leave for the North, make your report to Master Plummer and he will send an express messenger to

72

Middleham.' He rubbed a weary hand across his forehead. 'And now I must dismiss you. I have to dress for this banquet.' He grimaced ruefully. 'Truth to tell, I feel a fraud. You and I both know how little credit can be attributed to me for what is being hailed as a great victory over the Scots. We got Berwick back and a part of the Princess Cicely's dowry, but we failed completely to put Albany on the Scottish throne. There was no great battle. The old enemy was not defeated.'

'None of that was your fault, my lord,' I protested. 'The Scots lords were ready with their own plan long before we crossed the border.'

'You think so? You think it was planned?'

'Possibly. They're a crafty nation. Your Grace has no cause to demean what you achieved. As you say, Berwick is English again and with luck will remain so.' I began to sidle towards the door. 'Her Grace of Gloucester and Prince Edward are both in good health?'

A shadow crossed the thin, careworn face. 'As well as they ever are, I thank you. I know I should bring them south for the winter months, but...' He trailed off and shrugged again.

Once more, I was briefly conscious of the disproportion of his shoulders, but then the illusion of lopsidedness was gone. He rang a small silver hand-bell that was on the tray with the flask and goblets and, to my astonishment, stepped forward and embraced me.

'You've been a good friend and servant to

73

me, Roger, over the years and I wouldn't have you think that I'm ungrateful. Don't let this mission to France worry you. If things should go wrong – which I by no means expect – I shan't let them hail you off to the gallows.'

Which was very pretty talking, I thought to myself, provided the duke didn't first find himself dead by poisoning or a mysterious accident. Or if I didn't. Because if the queen's family did happen to get even the merest whisper of what I was about, I'd be far more likely to end up in some Parisian alley with a dagger in my back than find myself arraigned for treason. That would mean a trial with witnesses and evidence, and the Woodvilles wouldn't want that: it would bring everything into the open. Secrecy and no questions raised in people's minds were the better option. I recalled the Duke of Clarence's obscure death in the Tower – drowned, the rumour had it, in a butt of malmsey wine. He had had a trial of sorts – I had been present at it, amongst the spectators – but it had amounted to little more than a shouting match between him and his elder brother. And it had ended abruptly with nothing really resolved: no explanation of why the king, after years of enduring brother George's vagaries and betrayals, had suddenly decided to be rid of him. Had Clarence also been digging around in this particular bed of worms? Had it occurred to him that if their mother's story were indeed true, and Edward were really a bastard, then he was the rightful

74

king? Loyalty to his brother wouldn't have stayed his hand, as it stayed Prince Richard's...

My uneasy thoughts were interrupted as I realized the duke was bidding me goodnight. The servant who had poured the wine for us was again in the room, waiting to show me out. I knelt and kissed my lord's hand, catching his eye as I rose to my feet. His expression was wry and he gave me a half-guilty smile.

'God be with you, Roger,' he said. And, almost as if it were forced from him, 'Good luck.'

There was no answer to that. I bowed, swung on my heel and left the room.

Five

Outside the chamber, I found the lackey who had earlier served the wine waiting for me. I raised my eyebrows in enquiry.

'I'm to conduct you to your room, master.'

I shook my head. 'There's no need. I know where it is.'

'I'll accompany you,' he insisted stubbornly. 'The duke's orders. I've to see you're comfortable and to bring you your all-night.'

I shrugged. 'Oh, very well.'

He followed me silently along the narrow

passages and up the twisting stairs until we finally reached a row of five single cells close to the men servants' dormitory. Once or twice I made an attempt at conversation, but my efforts were met either with silence or a grunt, so I gave up, saying nothing more until I came to a halt outside the first door of the five.

I turned to face him. 'This is it.'

He nodded. 'I'll remember.' He hesitated, then said with more warmth than he had displayed so far, 'If you wish to come down to the common hall later on, you'll likely find some games of chance being played – fivestones, three men's morris, hazard, that sort of thing – among those of us not on duty. A few will even wager on the outcome of a game of chess. You'll come to the chapel for prayers, of course, when the bell rings.'

'I'm in no mood for playing games,' I said abruptly, then added, to show I meant no ill will, 'I've had bad news today. I'd rather be alone.'

'In that case–' the man stepped back a pace – 'I'll see you get your all-night and leave you to your own company.' And he made off down the stairs.

I sat down heavily on the edge of the bed, a straw-filled mattress placed on a stone ledge and covered with three rough grey blankets. The pillow, however, was stuffed with feathers, and a linen sheet had been interposed between blankets and mattress. I supposed I was lucky – I was being afforded special treatment – but it was nothing like the comfort I enjoyed at home, where I ought to be, and my grievance returned in full force. My grief for Jeanne Lamprey and Reynold Makepeace also surfaced again and I found tears welling up and running down my cheeks before I could check them. Moreover, the stuffiness of the little room was beginning to make my senses swim. I almost decided to visit the common hall and distract myself with some cheerful company, but somehow could not bring myself to do so.

The opening of the door heralded the arrival of my all-night, a ewer of wine, a mazer, a large hunk of bread and a leather bottle that proved to contain water. The young boy who brought the tray drew my attention to it. 'I put it on meself,' he confided. 'Gets 'ot up 'ere, it does. These rooms are like a bake'ouse oven, I'll tell you. An' wine don't allus quench yer thirst.'

I thanked him with real gratitude. He gave me a sympathetic wink and withdrew. I moved the tray and its burden from the end of the bed, where the boy had placed it, to a shelf just inside the door. This, together with a wooden armchair, that looked as if it had seen better days and had been dragged in to give the room some semblance of added comfort (a forlorn hope!) comprised the rest of the furnishings. Luxury was not for menials, I reflected bitterly, recalling the richness of the ducal apartment and also what travelling with the Duke of Albany had meant over the past few months.

It was too early to sleep properly, so I stretched out on the bed and tried to doze, but the castle was still too alive, echoing to the sounds of distant laughter and raised voices. I sat up again and swung my legs to the floor, my feet tapping a tattoo against the cold stone. Now, suddenly, I felt fidgety, bored and bad-tempered all at the same time. I knew that if I just sat and thought, grief and longing for home would engulf me once more and that desperation might make me do something extremely foolish, such as rushing headlong to the duke and telling him to find someone else to do his bidding.

I stood up and reached for the bottle of water, removing the stopper and swallowing half the contents at one go. Then I sat down again and drank the rest slowly, savouring the clear, refreshing taste of the Paddington springs, whence it came, piped into the city's conduits. I felt a little better and was once more toying with the idea of descending to the common hall when I remembered Timothy's suggestion that I commit the duke's instructions to memory before disposing of them. I took the paper from my pouch, then got up and lit the candle, which was on the shelf beside a tinder box, dragged the chair into its circle of light and settled down to read and reread the neat, meticulous writing of John Kendal, Prince Richard's secretary, until I could recite every word without once referring to the text. When I had done this three times in a row, and then done it a fourth and fifth time, just to be certain, I held the paper to the candle-flame and watched it burn to ashes, which I scrunched beneath my heel as they floated to the ground.

I decided I deserved a reward and, raising my arm, lifted down the mazer without getting to my feet. But when, lazily, I attempted to do the same with the ewer, I only succeeded in hitting it off the tray. It fell with a crash of metal against stone, the lid flying open and the wine spilling across the floor in dark red rivulets, making little islands and peninsulas on the flags. Cursing myself for a fool, and a clumsy fool at that, I picked up the jug to see if any wine was left, but all my shaking produced only the merest dribble in the bottom of the cup. Disgustedly, I replaced everything on the shelf and retired to the bed, leaving the puddle of wine to dry overnight or seep away between the pavers.

I realized that the castle was quiet at last, only the shouts of the watchmen punctuating the silence. It had taken me longer than I thought to learn by heart the list of questions that I must eventually put to Robin Gaunt if ever I managed to find him. Perhaps this Humphrey Culpepper would be able to provide me with some valuable information, but I very much doubted it. It was all too long ago: forty years.

I stood up, stretched and undressed, pulling off my boots and then stripping slowly, feeling the cold night air from the slit of a

79

window on my bare skin. I threw my clothes on to the chair in an untidy heap, opened the door briefly while I peed into the corridor, then, suddenly overwhelmed by fatigue, climbed into bed and fell immediately asleep.

In my dream, both Jeanne Lamprey and Reynold Makepeace were seated in my kitchen at home, assuring me that they were not, after all, dead and that I did not have to go to France. It was all just a silly joke perpetrated by my family. Adela and the children, who had not been present a moment ago, were now seated on the other side of the table, nodding and doubled up with laughter, pointing their fingers and shouting, 'April fool!' I kept trying to tell them that it wasn't spring but autumn, but no one would listen to me. A strange man then appeared, saying that he was Robin Gaunt, all the time dodging behind the others so that I was unable to see his face. I yelled at him to stand still, but he only laughed and kept on moving.

Suddenly, I was wide awake, staring into the darkness and conscious of another presence in the room. I raised myself on one elbow, still trying to free my mind from the cobwebs of sleep.

'Who...? What...?' I muttered, my voice thick in my throat.

There was a violent imprecation, then a sudden rush of movement and the opening of the door, letting in a draught of stale air from the passageway. I struggled out of bed, the cold of the flagstones striking up through the soles of my feet and shocking me into wakefulness. But I was too late to catch a glimpse of the intruder. The flickering torches in the wall sconces illuminated the corridor, to right and left, silent and empty. The only noise came from the adjacent male dormitory, a faint cacophony of snores and groans that disturbed the men's sleep. Cursing, I stepped back inside my narrow cell, pulling the door shut behind me.

I lit the candle and looked around. My clothes, which had been thrown across the chair, now lay in a heap on the floor, and on top of the pile was my pouch. This had been freed from my belt and was open, the flap bent back to give a groping hand better access, and my breeches, shirt and jerkin had been turned carefully inside out as if to ensure that they contained no concealed pockets. Someone, I reflected grimly, had been searching for the Duke of Gloucester's instructions, and but for my boredom of the previous evening, they would have been found. Thankfully, I blessed Timothy Plummer's foresight.

Something moved near my foot, and such was my state of nerves that I jumped nearly out of my skin. I spun round and lowered the candlestick nearer the floor just in time to see a mouse scrabbling wildly to find its feet, its little claws scraping the stones. It was acting as if it were drunk, its whiskers all wet, and I suddenly realized the reason. It must have been licking up some of the spilled wine and was now paying the penalty for its greed. But even as I watched, it staggered, fell over, twitched violently for a second or two, then lay still. My heart pounding uncomfortably, I crouched down and prodded it with my finger. There was no response. It was dead.

I reached out a finger and dipped it in a half-dried puddle of the ruby liquid, then cautiously raised it to my lips. There was a slightly strange taste to it, but that, of course, could be nothing more than the taint of damp and mildew from the flagstones. It wasn't in itself proof that the wine had been drugged, but the evidence of the mouse seemed to point that way. If a strong soporific had been used, it might well have proved too much for a little rodent. I ruled out poison. That would have been stupid, indicating at once that there were others anxious to learn of the duke's intentions, others who suspected that my and Mistress Gray's journey to France was a cloak for another, more secret mission. But thanks to my clumsiness, I had failed to drink the wine and so been alerted to possible danger. Nor were the unknown 'they' any the wiser.

I picked up my clothes, laid them on the chair again and got back into bed, shivering with cold. If I caught an ague on top of every-thing else, I should have a few harsh words to say to Timothy Plummer. On reflection, I would have more than a few harsh words to say to him in the morning. I lay for a while, straining my ears, but I doubted anyone would risk a return visit, especially as whoever it was had probably satisfied himself that what he was looking for was no longer among my possessions.

But why did I naturally assume that my visitor had been a man? It might equally as well have been a woman. I had been too drugged with sleep to have any clear idea of the intruder's sex, yet a certain sense of bulk persuaded me that the presence had been male. But who? Who, apart from Timothy and the duke, knew of my secret instructions, and, above all, who could possibly have been aware that I was carrying them in my pouch?

I had a sudden picture of myself the previous evening with the duke. I was saying something, something about 'when I read what you had written', and tapping my belt ... And the servant, who had entered unobserved by me, was there, pouring the wine, the same servant who had insisted on accompanying me to my room so that he might know where I was housed...

A Woodville agent? He had to be! I could at least provide Timothy with a description, although I doubted that morning would still find the man in the castle. He would slip out at first light to report his failure to his superiors, and if he had any sense, he wouldn't come back. On the other hand, he might underrate my intelligence. Plenty of people had done that before now. To their cost.

Eventually, I drifted into an uneasy sleep, a

tangle of nightmarish dreams that again featured Reynold Makepeace and Jeanne Lamprey and a whole host of grinning skeletons who were dancing round and round me in a ring.

I awoke the following morning with a crick in my neck and feeling far from refreshed. By the time I had finished dressing, I was in a foul temper, angry with all the world and ready to take offence if someone so much as looked at me the wrong way. Sensing my mood, I was given a wide berth at breakfast by the duchess's servants, so I seized the opportunity to look around at the neighbouring tables to see if I could spot the wine-server of the previous evening, but there was no one resembling him that I could make out – at least, not enough to say positively, 'That is the man.' My guess was probably correct: he had already left the castle.

A page came to tell me that Timothy wanted to see me as soon as I had finished eating. 'The same room as yesterday, overlooking the water-stairs.' The boy nodded towards my plate, indicating the half-eaten oatcake. 'Don't you want that?'

I shook my head and he leaned over and grabbed it, cramming it into his mouth all in one go.

'Don't they feed you in this place?' I asked. 'It's as dry as last week's bread.'

He grimaced. 'Her Grace doesn't believe in too much indulgence of the flesh.'

Not now, I thought, not now she's an old woman, but in the past ... that might well have been a different story.

I found the spymaster waiting for me, impatiently pacing up and down the room. He rounded on me as I entered. 'Where have you been?'

'At breakfast,' I snapped. 'And pretty poor victuals they were, too. That's beside the point. I overslept, but there was a reason for it.'

'It had better be a good one.'

'Oh, it is,' I said, seating myself on one of the stools. 'The best.' And I told him what had happened.

Timothy cursed softly under his breath. 'Would you recognize this server again?'

I pursed my lips. 'I might, although there was nothing outstanding about him. Couldn't you ask the duke? His Grace might know who he is.'

My companion snorted derisively. 'I don't suppose the duke even glanced at the man's face, and even if he did, he wouldn't know his name. He doesn't recognize half his own servants, let alone his mother's. But why do you think this fellow suspected you?'

I explained and received a tongue-lashing for my pains.

'You must be more careful,' Timothy ended, but then sat down beside me and patted my arm, probably being able to tell from my expression that I was in a right royal rage. 'However, I suppose it wasn't really your fault,' he added placatingly. 'And at least it's put us on our guard. We know now that the Woodvilles have got wind of something, but thanks to the fact that you had already committed the paper's contents to memory and then destroyed it, they still don't know what it is we're after.'

I was in no mood to be buttered up and asked abruptly, 'Where do I find this Humphrey Culpepper, then? Stinking Lane, did you say?'

Timothy nodded. 'It's off the Shambles. The first turning after Pentecost Lane as you come from West Cheap.'

'Which house?'

'The third one on the left.'

I was surprised and showed it. 'Not like your men to be so precise,' I sneered, getting a little of my own back. 'They must have been having one of their better days.'

Timothy scowled. 'None of this is a joke, Roger. It's damnably dangerous.'

'Oho!' I exclaimed. 'The truth at last! Of course it's dangerous. I told you yesterday we were dabbling in treason. It's all very well saying that the duke will protect us. He may not be able to. He could be in the Tower – or worse.'

Timothy's irritation was written large on his face. He was under great strain, and suddenly it showed. 'That's enough of that sort of talk.' The corner of his right eye had developed a twitch. 'Now listen to me carefully. Make sure that no one is watching you when you enter

Culpepper's house and be certain it's him when he answers the door. He's a widower. Lives alone. An old man, over sixty, as you'd expect. Grey hair, thickset. None too keen on using the communal pump.'

'You mean he stinks more than normal?'

'We-ell ... yes. But it's another way of identifying him. Here, take this token.' The spymaster pushed a bone disc, with the emblem of the White Boar carved on one side, towards me. 'If he jibs at letting you in, show him this. But not unless you have to. Then ask him for a description of Robin Gaunt. That's all you want. Nothing more. Don't enter into conversation with him.'

'And if he can't remember this Robin Gaunt, or perhaps won't say unless I tell him why I wish to know?'

Timothy sighed, the lines of weariness about his eyes seeming to increase. 'Then I'll have to have him brought in for questioning. Frighten him a bit. But I don't want to do that unless it's necessary. His neighbours are bound to get wind of it, and the last thing I want is to draw any attention to him.'

'But isn't he going to discuss my visit with the neighbours anyway?'

'The man who's been keeping an eye on him these past few days reports that Culpepper doesn't like company and speaks to very few people. Other people tend to avoid him.'

'The smell must be worse than we thought,' I commented with a grin, then wished I hadn't. Timothy looked for a moment as though he might burst into tears.

'I've warned you, Roger, that this is a serious matter. Don't make a jest of it.' He rose to his feet. 'I shall expect you back here after dinner, when Mistress Gray will join us. Now, off you go, and for God's sake, take care. Make sure you're not being followed. If anything – anything at all – arouses your suspicions, come back and try again tomorrow.'

Half an hour later, I crossed West Cheap, strolled through the goldsmiths' quarter and bore right into the Shambles.

I had been able to smell it from some way off, the stench assaulting my nose from the second I entered Old Change. Up close, it was even more pungent, the cobbles slippery with blood and the central drain piled high with discarded animal bones and offal. Mind you, there was less waste here than in many other parts of London. There wasn't much of any beast that couldn't be used; eyes were a great delicacy, as also were brains, very tasty, like the innards, stewed with an onion, and some meat could even be scraped off the ears. A whole sheep or cow's head could make several meals and feed a family quite cheaply, as I well knew. Adela was nothing if not a thrifty housewife. I had often enjoyed a pig's cheek, although I have to admit to a certain queasiness about eating eyes.

Stinking Lane more than lived up to its name, the houses on either side being extremely close together and the smell from the

Shambles getting trapped between them. There were other aromas, too; poor drainage meant that urine and faeces were mixed with rotting vegetables and the other detritus of daily life. (Urine and faeces? I'm becoming too nice in my old age. 'Pee' and 'shit' were words that would have served me well enough once.) Twice the soles of my boots slipped on the slime of the cobbles as I counted three cottages up on the left-hand side. I took a step back and surveyed the frontage.

There was only one window, located on the ground floor, and that was shuttered. The door, too, was inhospitably closed. I hammered against the wood and waited. Nothing happened.

I hammered again, louder this time, but again no one answered. A third endeavour produced the same result.

I felt suddenly angry and kicked the door violently, but my irritation was really directed more at Timothy and myself. Why had it not entered our heads that Culpepper might be out? Why had we expected him to be sitting there, awaiting our pleasure? He wasn't even aware of our existence.

Refusing to accept defeat, I knocked a fourth time. The door of the next hovel was wrenched open and a young woman appeared, waving a broom with fell intent.

'Stop makin' that fuckin' noise, can't you?' she hissed. 'I've just got my baby off to sleep, an' now you come along, wakin' the dead with yer rattling and bangin'.'

'I'm looking for Master Culpepper,' I said. 'Do you know if he's in?'

'No, I don't,' the woman answered viciously, but keeping her voice low. 'I'm not 'is bloody keeper.' She relented slightly. ''E were there first thing this morning, 'bout an hour ago. I do know that 'cos I saw 'im, throwin' 'is rubbish into the drain. Gone out, I reckon. But 'e won't be long. 'E never is.'

I thanked her and apologized for the disturbance, hoping I hadn't wakened the child. She grunted, but gave me a nod of acceptance before whisking herself inside again and closing her door.

I decided that it would be worthwhile to wait around and return in half an hour or so, but as there was nothing in Stinking Lane or the Shambles to interest me, I decided that I might as well walk as far as St Paul's. If memory served me aright, there was usually some sort of entertainment going on in and around the church or churchyard. I swung on my heel and, as I did so, saw a young man on the other side of the lane, walking in the opposite direction, going towards Aldersgate. I probably wouldn't have thought twice about him, had it not been for the jaunty blue feather in his hat.

I knew him at once. The arrogant gait, as he picked his careful way across the slimy cobbles, and the self-satisfied smirk half seen on his face both told me that this was the same man I had noticed yesterday on the water-stairs at Baynard's Castle. With a guilty start,

I remembered Timothy Plummer's admonition to keep my visit to Master Culpepper's house as secret as possible. Instead of which, I had made enough noise to alert one of his neighbours and had then indulged in a loud-voiced conversation with her that, in this very narrow street, could probably be heard for quarter of a mile around. I cursed myself royally for the fool that I undoubtedly was. My anger and resentment were making me careless, and that could endanger my own life as well as those of others.

How long, I wondered, had Blue Feather been there? Was he, as he seemed to be, just passing by, or had he been standing opposite, unnoticed by me, for some little time, listening to my exchange with Humphrey Culpepper's neighbour? I shrugged fatalistically. There was no point in pursuit: he would tell me nothing to any purpose even if I accosted him, and I would only draw attention to myself and put him on his guard. If, that is, he had anything to be on guard about. The chances were, it was mere coincidence that I had remarked him two days running – although I couldn't quite bring myself to believe this. At least I had one advantage over the stranger; he didn't know that I had spotted him the previous day and would therefore have no reason to think that I might be suspicious of him.

On this consoling thought, I made my way across the Shambles, down Ivy Lane into Paternoster Row and from there into St

Paul's Churchyard. After a moment or two's hesitation, I decided to pay a visit to the library housed in the east quadrant of the north cloister, which I recollected from a previous visit as being a particularly fine one. The north cloister provided further entertainment in the shape of the lawyers who congregated there day after day, either touting for business or discussing with their clients ways and means of circumventing wills that did not favour them, or how to upset the land title of some relative whom they considered to have usurped their place, or how to get an annulment for a marriage that was beginning to pall. But today, although the north cloister was as packed as ever by these gentlemen, resplendent in their striped hoods and gowns, they failed to arrest my attention. What did was the series of paintings around the walls: a depiction of *The Dance of Death*, the grinning skeletons writhing and cavorting as they carried off their unwilling victims one by one. Perhaps it was because of the deaths of Jeanne Lamprey and Reynold Makepeace that they caught my eye and made me stop to stare, cold fingers of foreboding stroking my spine.

However we tried to cheat it, death was always lying in wait for us from the moment we were born. Young or old, male or female, king or commoner, it was there, its crooked, bony finger beckoning us on, all unknowing to our fate, leering at us with empty eye sockets, out of the dark.

Six

'Chilling, isn't it?' asked a voice behind me.

I spun round to find Eloise Gray standing at my elbow, her eyes fixed on the wall paintings in front of her. She took a step backwards in order to see them better, almost colliding with a fat little lawyer fussing along the cloister in pursuit of a client who appeared to be getting away. He glared furiously at Eloise, but she remained oblivious of his displeasure.

'What are you doing here?' I demanded angrily, but she ignored me, too.

'*The Dance of Death*,' she murmured. 'The French call it *La Danse Macabre*, and the original of this is painted around the cloister walls of the Cemetery of the Innocents, in Paris. The story is that your late king Henry saw it when he was in the city for his coronation and ordered it to be reproduced in St Paul's.'

Coronation? Then I recalled that Henry VI, at the age of ten or thereabouts, had been crowned king of France, the only English monarch – so far – to achieve that much coveted goal. Although I glanced once more at the wall with its deadly message that the grave is what eventually awaits us all, I now had other things on my mind. Firstly, what was Eloise doing there? Had she been following me? And secondly, if her presence was accidental, how did I get rid of her without arousing her suspicions? It would be the ten o'clock dinnertime in just over an hour, and after that we both had a meeting with Timothy. The obvious course was to return to Baynard's Castle and eat together, but I had to return to Stinking Lane and speak to Humphrey Culpepper. What plausible excuse could I offer my fair companion for avoiding her company that would not make her curious?

Fortunately for me, Eloise made her own excuses. 'You're here to browse in the library, I suppose?' And when I nodded with apparent enthusiasm, she gave a little grimace. 'Poor entertainment,' she said. 'I shall return to Cheapside and look again at the goldsmiths' shops. It's what I've been doing for most of the morning and it was only with the greatest reluctance that I tore myself away. Being so close to St Paul's, I couldn't resist coming to look at *La Danse Macabre*, just to see if it was indeed a copy of the one in Paris.' She treated me to a dazzling smile. 'And now that I've satisfied myself on that score, I shall go back and tantalize myself by staring at all the beautiful jewellery that I covet but can't afford to buy.' To my astonishment, she reached up and kissed me on the cheek, at the same time gurgling with laughter. 'If you could only see your face! There's no need for

94

such an outraged expression, I assure you. I'm just practising for when we're pretending to be husband and wife. I'm sorry you don't approve, although I'm certain Master Plummer would.'

She gave me no chance to answer, but whisked round and was soon lost to view among the crowd of lawyers and their clients, leaving me staring after her, not knowing quite what to think. Had she been following me, or was the meeting as unplanned as she would have me believe? Whatever the answer, it demonstrated how difficult it was going to be to avoid her even in a city as large as Paris, because in every town there is a hub of activity, a central area frequented by the vast majority of its population –a town, if you like, within a town – where, during the day, the press of people is greatest and where you are more likely to run across somebody you know.

I reminded myself that time was getting on, and only waiting until I felt sure that Eloise was safely back in Cheapside, I returned to the Culpepper house by way of Paternoster Row and Ivy Lane. As I approached it, my heart sank. There was the same sort of lifelessness about it as there had been about the Lampreys' dwelling yesterday, indicating that no one was at home. I knocked, all the same, but with a gentle tattoo so as not to rouse the neighbours. There was no answer and I cursed roundly under my breath. Then I shrugged. If Humphrey Culpepper was out, there was nothing to be done and I should have to try again tomorrow. I had tried my best and Timothy couldn't ask for more.

On the other hand, knowing him, he probably could: he was always an unreasonable little bastard. And it was with that thought in mind, as I turned to retreat thankfully from Stinking Lane, that I noticed a narrow alleyway, about shoulder-width, running between Culpepper's house and the one on its left as I faced it. I hesitated, but only for a moment, then trod softly between the two cottages to find myself in another alley, which ran along the back of all the dwellings on that side of the lane. I turned right and stared at the rear of Culpepper's house, where, surprisingly for such a mean hovel, there was a back entrance, a door made of rough planking that was ominously swinging open on its broken hinges.

My breath caught in my throat. Even before I investigated, I knew that I was going to find nothing good in there. My heart pounding uncomfortably, I pushed aside the broken planking and went inside.

It was a two-roomed cottage with a narrow staircase in one corner rising to the second storey. The floor of the living room was of beaten earth without even a scattering of rushes. The furniture was minimal: a table, a stool, some shelves on which cooking utensils were stacked, a water butt and a rough, patently home-made armchair drawn near to the hearth, where a pile of sticks stood ready for lighting beneath a pot already partially filled with water. On the table stood a wooden bowl of dried oatmeal, ready to be made into porridge, alongside a plate and beaker. Plainly, Master Culpepper had prepared his breakfast before, or just after, going out to dispose of his rubbish in the common drain, when he had been spotted by his neighbour. But he had never made his meal, so what had happened to him since then?

The whole house was permeated by the stench from the Shambles, so it was the activity of the flies that first arrested my attention. I would have expected them to be congregated downstairs, where food was kept and where crumbs had dropped between the cracks in the table top, but the buzzing came from overhead, and I noticed five or six circling at the head of the staircase, far more of the creatures than one would normally find in late October. My heart began to thump again as I cautiously mounted to the upper room, treading as gently as if I were walking on eggshells.

Now the smell of fresh blood assailed my nostrils most powerfully, making me flinch. There was nothing in the room except for a clothes chest and a bed, both of which I could just make out in the gloom, for this upper storey had no window and relied, even in daytime, either on candlelight or on the faint glow that came up from the living quarters downstairs. All the same, I could see that the cloud of flies was hovering and settling on something sprawled across the bed. Instinct told me at once what it was – or, rather, who it was – but I had to be certain. I returned to the ground floor and lit a candle, which I found on one of the shelves, together with a tinderbox, and then went back upstairs, holding the flame aloft with a hand that trembled.

Humphrey Culpepper – for who else could it possibly be? – lay face upwards, his throat cut neatly and cleanly from ear to ear. It was beautifully done, if one can ever say such a thing about murder, the head almost severed from the body, but the sight made me retch and I almost dropped the candle. I clutched the bedpost for a moment or two, feeling dizzy, then managed to pull myself together, angry at such weakness. I forced myself to look around, taking in the details.

Humphrey Culpepper lay with his head towards the top of the stairs and was dressed in hose, shirt and boots, his right arm through a sleeve of his jerkin. I reckoned that after going outside to the drain, he had come upstairs again to finish dressing before going down once more to light his fire and make his porridge. He was sitting on the further edge of his bed, his back towards the staircase, and had neither heard his murderer entering the cottage nor creeping up to kill him. At his age, he was likely to be somewhat deaf, a probability of which his assailant had taken full advantage. Completely unaware of being in any danger – for what did he know of the machinations of Timothy Plummer or that I was on my way to interrogate him? – Culpepper had been seized from behind and despatched, with all the skill and precision of a butcher, to meet his Maker unshriven, which meant that he would have to spend a longer time in Purgatory. A cruel fate and one that made me angry, not merely with whoever killed him, but with Timothy and myself.

The thought of Timothy brought me up short. As a law-abiding citizen, it was my duty to raise the alarm, and I had almost been on the verge of doing so, but what if I were to fall under suspicion for the murder? The goodwife next door would confirm that I had been making enquiries about Master Culpepper earlier in the morning, and although I had no doubt that I would be cleared in time, the investigation would draw just the sort of attention to me that the spymaster and Duke Richard were anxious to avoid. No; although every fibre of my being called out for justice on the person who had committed this atrocity, I knew that I had no choice but to get away from there as quickly as possible, without being seen, and report back to Timothy at Baynard's Castle.

My demand for an interview with Master Plummer produced the information that he was at present unavailable, being closeted with my lord of Gloucester.

'Splendid!' I said to the supercilious steward who was regarding me as though I were something slimy that had just crawled out of the wall. 'I'll see the duke as well, then. It'll kill two birds with one stone.' The steward raised haughty eyebrows and curled his lip, but I kept my temper. 'You'll be sorry if you don't take my message to His Grace,' I said coldly, in a voice every bit as disdainful as his own. 'He will not be pleased. In fact, he'll probably be very annoyed.'

In the event, I was the one who found himself in hot water.

'Will you stop drawing attention to yourself like this, Roger?' Timothy demanded furiously. 'You can't insist on access to a meeting between my lord duke and myself without arousing people's curiosity, and that's the last thing we want at the moment. I'm due to see you, anyway, after dinner.'

I could tell by the duke's frown that he agreed with his spymaster, but once I told them what had happened, they were both too concerned to be angry.

'And you got away from the house without being seen?' Timothy asked anxiously.

'As far as I know,' I said. 'I went down the back lane behind the cottages that comes out into the Shambles. After that, I lost myself in the crowds.'

'No one could have noticed you from the other houses?' the duke put in.

I shook my head. 'The only windows are at the front, and as far as I could tell, most of the residents keep their shutters closed because of the stink.'

'Stinking Lane lives up to its name, eh?'

Prince Richard gave a little half-smile, but immediately sobered again. 'This means that someone knows something,' he muttered, looking at Timothy and twisting the ring on the little finger of his left hand round and round, as he always did when troubled.

'Not necessarily, my lord,' Timothy protested. 'There's no proof that this murder has any connection with Roger's mission. It might simply be a revenge killing – a personal grudge settled in a violent way.'

'You don't really believe that,' the duke answered quietly, 'and neither do I.' He glanced at me with a rueful grin. 'And I'm sure Roger here doesn't, either.'

'It would be too much of a coincidence, Your Highness,' I said firmly.

Timothy looked as if he might be ready to do murder himself, but all he said was, 'Whoever did the deed must have been covered in blood. It might be worth a few judicious enquiries to find out if anyone in Stinking Lane noticed a person in bloodstained clothing.'

I laughed. 'That could be difficult. You won't find many men around the Shambles district who *aren't* wearing bloodstained clothing.'

Timothy gave an embarrassed laugh. 'I suppose not,' he agreed.

The duke, who, up until now, had been standing warming his hands at the fire, threw himself back into a cushioned armchair with a muttered curse. 'If this man Culpepper,' he said, 'has been killed by a Woodville agent, how on earth did they find out what I'm up to?'

I raised sardonic eyebrows at Timothy, who reddened and looked highly uncomfortable. Obviously, he had so far failed to acquaint Duke Richard with my previous night's experience. This he now proceeded to do with much self-blame for not having mentioned it earlier.

The duke looked furious, realizing, as he must have done, that Timothy had been intending to keep the incident quiet had not circumstances forced him to reveal it. As usual, though, he kept his anger in check, never, to my knowledge, berating one of his officers in front of a second person; and for someone who undoubtedly had the Plantagenet temper, I have always thought this consideration for others one of his most endearing traits. (And whatever our present lords and masters would have you believe to the contrary, he had many.)

'Do we know the name of this server? Has he been found?'

The spymaster looked even more unhappy as he haltingly explained that the man appeared to have fled the castle as soon as he possibly could. 'But I still do not see, Your Grace, how he could have known anything about Culpepper.'

'Maybe not.' The duke pushed a lock of dark hair back from his forehead. 'But the moment he reported to his superiors, some-one would have been set to follow Roger and keep an eye on what he was up to. When he knocked on the door of Master Culpepper's house, it would have been noted.' He frowned. 'If only you hadn't gone away, Roger, but stayed to watch the house, there would have been no opportunity for anyone to enter and murder this poor man.' He added repressively, 'However, it's done, and there's no good to be gained by apportioning blame.'

I remembered the smart young gent with the blue feather in his hat and knew that I ought to mention him. Feeling disinclined to draw further attention to myself, however, I kept quiet. With luck, the duke might decide to abandon his enquiries for Robin Gaunt.

But luck, as usual, was against me. After further discussion between him and Timothy, it was agreed that the Woodvilles could have no real knowledge of my true mission in Paris and that my trip in the company of Eloise Gray, posing as her husband, and her meetings with Olivier le Daim, would provide sufficient cover to conceal my main purpose.

'And it's still by no means certain,' Timothy pointed out eagerly, 'that the murder of Humphrey Culpepper is in any way connected with Roger's visit to him.'

Duke Richard conceded the fact, but without, I thought, any great conviction. 'What was the man's use to you?' he asked.

Timothy explained, 'We know him to have fought alongside Gaunt at Pontoise and to have been a part of the Rouen garrison. We hoped for some description of our friend –

103

enough to say whether he is short and stout or tall and thin.'

The duke nodded. 'Perhaps the name Gaunt itself is descriptive,' he suggested. 'It may have been a nickname. Perhaps he was thin and haggard-looking. It's little enough to go on, I agree, but worth consideration.' He glanced at me with raised eyebrows.

I made no answer, but Timothy hurried to fill the breach. 'It's most certainly worth a thought, Your Grace,' he smarmed, his eyes furiously signalling to me to contribute my groat's worth. But I maintained a stubborn silence, signifying my disapproval of a scheme whose success hinged on such a lack of practical knowledge.

Duke Richard accepted this with a wry smile and prevented Timothy from bullying me into submission by announcing that it was the dinner hour and he knew that I was always hungry. 'Roger's a good trencherman,' he laughed. 'And with that great frame to feed, it's small wonder.' He rose to his feet, giving me a hand to kiss, at the same time delaying Timothy's departure by laying the other on the spymaster's shoulder. There were evidently things they had to discuss that my arrival had interrupted. 'I'm relying on you to do your best, Roger,' he added.

I bowed. 'I always endeavour to do that, Your Grace.' I realized I sounded offended.

The duke kept his grip on my hand, pressing it strongly. 'I know,' he said, 'and I appreciate it, the more so when I'm aware that I don't have your wholehearted approval.' He laughed again as he released me. 'Timothy's trying to look shocked, pretending he believes I have a mandate straight from God.' The dark eyes twinkled. 'He knows it's not true, of course, just as we do.'

The duke's caustic sense of humour, always so unexpected in someone who outwardly seemed so serious, caught me off guard as it had a good many times in the past and completely won me over. It was, I decided, the secret of his charm, a side of himself he revealed only to those whom he liked and trusted, and explained why men accorded him either their deepest devotion or their instant dislike. I have always been one of the former. (And that admission is another reason why these chronicles must never be made public in my lifetime.)

I was about to take my leave when Duke Richard, regaining his grip on my hand, turned to Timothy and asked, 'Who are we sending to France with Roger and Mistress Gray as their bodyguard?'

I blinked in surprise: this was the first intimation I had had that Eloise and I were to be afforded any sort of protection.

Timothy replied promptly, 'John Bradshaw, Your Grace. He will travel as their servant.'

'Ah!' The duke nodded his approval. 'The very best.' He smiled at me. 'John Bradshaw is one of my most trusted agents. A fine man, and one who has done me great service in the past.' He looked again at Timothy. 'Is he privy as to why Roger is going to Paris?'

The spymaster shook his head. 'Not precisely, my lord. He knows, however, that Roger has ... er ... has business other than simply posing as Mistress Gray's husband, and that it maybe necessary, on occasion, to distract the lady's attention while Roger slips away to make his enquiries.'

'You don't think it would be better to put John in the picture?'

Timothy pursed his lips judiciously while he considered the matter. Finally, he shook his head. 'My own feeling, Your Grace, is that the fewer people who know the true nature of this mission, the less likelihood there is of the secret getting out. And Bradshaw would be the first to agree with me. But I will say this. If ever you feel, Roger, for whatever reason, that you need to confide in him, you have my permission to take Jack Bradshaw into your confidence. He won't let you down, I promise.'

'And when do I get to meet this paragon?' I asked, my tongue running away with me, as usual.

The duke's lips twitched, but Timothy frowned angrily. He would have liked to utter a stinging reproof, but obvious royal amusement kept him silent. 'At our meeting after dinner with Mistress Gray,' he snapped. 'You haven't forgotten it, I hope. You are to be measured for some more suitable clothes than those you are wearing.' He eyed my own with disparagement.

'You aren't having these clothes specially made, are you, Timothy?' the duke asked, suddenly anxious. 'Roger's and Mistress Gray's departure should not be postponed too long. It's already late October and winter storms will soon be causing problems in the Channel. Besides, there is Olivier le Daim's visit to Paris to be considered, the ostensible reason for their going.'

'No, no!' The spymaster waved dismissive hands. 'The tailor will provide the necessary clothing from his warehouse.' He smiled evilly. 'Our little party should be in Calais by Friday evening. A night there and then on to Paris.'

'Good! Good!' The duke pressed my hand for a second time. 'Once again, Roger, let me express my deepest gratitude to you for undertaking this dangerous commission for me.' The quizzical look came back into his face. 'And don't say what I'm perfectly aware you'd like to say: that you don't suppose you had any choice. I know how your mind works by now. Well, perhaps you didn't, but that doesn't make my gratitude any the less sincere. Now, go and have your dinner. I can hear the trumpets braying. And let me commend your good sense this morning in leaving that poor man's corpse for others to find and not getting involved yourself. Stay within the castle precincts for your remaining time here. I don't want you recognized.'

'Your Grace.' I bowed and withdrew, wondering more than ever how dangerous this forthcoming visit to France might prove.

I was faintly surprised, after a dinner of tasteless pottage and dry bread, to find not only Timothy but also Eloise already waiting for me in the room overlooking the water-stairs. I had looked for Eloise in the dining hall but failed to find her. However, she appeared sleek and well fed. Timothy, on the other hand, had the irritable expression of a man who had been forced to give up his mealtime for work.

'Where have you been?' he rapped out as I entered. 'You're late.'

'I was late going for my dinner,' I answered, giving him a level look. I opened my mouth as if to say more.

'Yes, yes! All right!' he interrupted quickly. He turned towards another man, whom I had not noticed, standing by the table, his young apprentice by his side. 'This is Master Taylor, the tailor. Get your jerkin off and he can begin measuring you. Mistress Gray won't mind seeing you in your shirt, I don't suppose.'

Eloise smiled serenely. 'Not at all,' she said, but crossed the room and stood looking out of the window all the same.

I reflected that if we were going to play at being husband and wife for the next few days – or possibly a week – she would have to get used to seeing me in a state of undress, as I would her. This last thought hit with a

108

suddenness that made me blush, something I rarely do.

The tailor and his apprentice set to work, pulling me about and prodding me in the sort of places I prefer not be prodded in, the former calling out figures that the latter wrote down in a book in a sprawling and somewhat crooked hand. Timothy looked on anxiously.

'Will you have anything to fit him, Master Taylor? He's rather on the large side.'

'Lord bless you, sir,' the tailor retorted huffily, 'I've stuff in my warehouse would fit a giant or a dwarf. I assume you want the best quality as this gentleman is to wait upon the king?'

Wait upon the king? What now? Fortunately, before I could voice a question and bring the vials of Timothy's wrath down upon my head, I realized that this was a story simply for the tailor's benefit to explain his and my presence here.

'Oh, the very best,' I said without giving Timothy the time to reply. 'Two of your most expensive outfits. A man must have a change of clothes if he is to wait upon the king.'

The spymaster eyed me malevolently, but made no comment. No doubt he would have a quiet word with the tailor afterwards.

At last, they had finished with me and I was able to resume my old jerkin. I saw the tailor regarding it askance and heard him mutter something to his apprentice. The next moment, however, he was all smiles again and bowing himself out.

'Both outfits will be delivered by tomorrow morning at the latest, Master Plummer,' he mouthed obsequiously, his nose almost touching his knees, 'in good time for Master ... er ... to try them on and any necessary alterations to be made.'

'Splendid.' Timothy beamed before adding tartly, 'Tonight would be even better.'

The tailor bowed again, but I could tell by the look on his face that he had no intention of working late or losing sleep over a mere hiring job (for I didn't suppose for a moment that I would be allowed to keep my fine feathers once they had served their purpose). Silently, I applauded his independence.

He had barely left the room, his apprentice scurrying behind him, when a sharp rap on the door was followed immediately by the appearance of a square-faced, square-bodied man whom I judged to be in his late forties or early fifties. He had powerful arms and thighs, but apart from that, there was nothing to distinguish him from any other well-built man you could pass half a dozen times a day in the street without particularly noticing him. He had brown hair, bluish-grey eyes, big hands and feet, encased in good leather gloves and boots, was clean-shaven and alto-gether suggested that here was a person to be relied upon in a difficult situation.

'Ah! John!' Timothy turned to Eloise and me. 'This is John Bradshaw, who will be act-ing as your bodyguard and servant. He speaks French—'

'Well, let's just say that, if absolutely necessary, I can make myself understood,' John Bradshaw interrupted, his eyes twinkling. 'It wouldn't be any good you people thinking that I can parlez vous with the m'soos much better than you can.'

'My mother was French,' Eloise informed him coldly. 'I speak the language perfectly.'

The spy swept her a deep bow. 'My apologies, mistress.'

Unsure as to whether he was mocking her or not, Eloise maintained a dignified silence, but her general demeanour was hostile. I hoped to God that they weren't going to rub each other up the wrong way for the rest of the time we had to spend together. More than ever I cursed that long-gone day when I had rescued Timothy from the importunate pie-man and first become entangled in the Duke of Gloucester's affairs.

Seven

I slept badly that night. My dreams were muddled, stupid. People came and went in them without rhyme or reason. At one point, Philip Lamprey distinctly told me that Jeanne was not dead, nor the baby, but that they were living in some other part of London because they were afraid of being killed like Reynold Makepeace. At another, Eloise and our new acquaintance Master Bradshaw were having an almighty quarrel about who could speak French better. (Although their threatened animosity had in reality come to nothing, and, in spite of my apprehension, they had parted the best of friends; for which happy state of affairs we had to thank Timothy, who had united the couple in good-natured derision of me and my total inability to grasp even the rudiments of any language other than my own.) On yet another occasion, I was in the kitchen at home, attempting to explain to Adela why I was unable to remain with her and the children as I was on my way to Gloucester to seek out Juliette Gerrish, who was about to give birth to my child.

This was when I awoke, drenched in sweat, my heart pounding as though I had just run up a long flight of steps.

'Dear God, dear God, let it not be true!'

I found I was praying aloud, my lips were dry, and my throat was parched. I got out of bed, my legs trembling beneath me, and poured some small beer from the flagon on my all-night tray into the beaker and then tore a crust from the accompanying loaf. While I chewed on this, and to clear my head of the miasma of unwelcome dreams, I strolled over to the narrow window and opened the shutter. The bright, frosty sky, peppered with stars, told me that it was getting colder even before the chill night air stroked my bare skin. I shivered and leaned out to close the shutter again. It was then that I realized my chamber – if one could dignify it with such a name – must be somewhere directly above the room where my meetings with Timothy were taking place. For there, below me, were the water-stairs and beyond them the river, faintly silvered under a waxing moon.

Someone was walking up the steps, as a boat, with muffled oars, pulled silently out towards midstream. I had no idea what the time was, but there was a sense of the city sleeping, and the cries of the night watchmen, although faint and far off, came to my ears with a clarity born of silence. It was the dead hours of night, I felt sure of that. So who was entering Baynard's Castle in such secrecy? And why?

I tried to make out the contours of the shadowy figure, but dared not risk drawing attention to myself by leaning out of the window too far. And whoever it was moved swiftly, seeking the shelter of the castle walls as quickly as possible, shifting with an agility that suggested someone small and light on his – or her – feet. Man or woman? I found I couldn't say. Often I got a feeling about the sex of someone seen from a distance – the outline, the way a person moved would provide a clear hint – but not tonight. The glimpse had been too brief, too nebulous. It had also, for some reason I was unable to fathom, disturbed me. Foolish, of course!

How was I to know the comings and goings of a place as big and as complex as Baynard's Castle? Servants rose early, long before dawn, to make sure that all was in readiness for their masters and mistresses when the sun eventually rose above the horizon. Maybe the early morning visitor was a scullion or a serving maid sent out on some urgent errand, or even a lackey who lived at home in the city arriving for the start of yet another working day.

Somehow or another these explanations failed to satisfy me, even though I knew I was being foolish. As compensation, I watched the boat until it was little more than a speck on the opposite shore, coming to rest on the mudflats, where its owner left it, disembarking, climbing the steps and disappearing, a tiny figure, into the Southwark stews.

I became aware that I was still trembling, no longer from the effect of uneasy dreams, however, but because I was frozen to the very marrow. Hastily, I closed the shutter and crawled back into my, by now, stone-cold bed, where I resigned myself to lying awake, shivering, for the rest of the night.

The next thing I knew, of course, it was day, a morning of heavy frost and needle-sharp sunlight, the houses on the distant Southwark shore nothing more than a grey shadow lost behind a shimmering veil of amber-coloured mist. Everywhere was brilliance and sparkle, from the glittering rooftops to the sun-spangled water-stairs. I had opened the shutter before pulling on my clothes in an effort to free my dream-clogged mind from the clinging rags of sleep. The cold air was better than a draught of wine.

I made my way downstairs to the common hall for breakfast. Dried oatmeal and salted herring, washed down by more small beer, made me thankful that my stay in Baynard's Castle was limited, and I could only pray that, in my disguise of a moneyed gentleman, food and lodgings provided on the forthcoming journey would prove to be of the best (although I had little doubt that Timothy would be exhorting us all to economy before we left).

The morning was young, and it was some hours yet to my next meeting with the tailor in order to try on my new clothes. I recalled guiltily that the duke had ordered me to stay within the precincts of the castle until my departure, but I was restless and not in the mood for doing as I was told. The underlying resentment at my enforced absence from home was still there, gnawing away at my vitals and making me scornful of compliance towards those whom I considered responsible for my present situation. Disobedience and rebellion were in the air.

As soon as I had finished eating therefore, and happily not having seen any sign of Eloise Gray, I made my way outside to the water-stairs and hailed the first passing boat. It happened to be one of the covered twopenny ones, but I didn't want to wait longer than I had to.

'Southwark,' I said briefly, stepping in.

I disembarked at roughly the same spot where I had seen the mysterious boatman land some hours previously. I climbed what I was certain were the same steps from the foreshore and looked about me.

I was no stranger to Southwark, that sprawling borough which was a part of London and yet outside the city's jurisdiction. It was, on the one hand, a criminal's paradise, a maze of waterfront streets, teeming with vice of every sort, the home of more brothels, both female and male, than a man could dream of. There were bear-baiting pits, cock-fighting rings and the stews, all paying rent to the Bishop of Winchester, which was why the whores were known as 'Winchester geese'. The bawdiest of entertainments took place at the outdoor theatres, and many buildings had never been repaired since Jack Cade's rebellion thirty-two years before. But on the other hand, Southwark was not all drunkenness and lechery and rowdy pleasure. Some of the taverns, like the Walnut Tree and the Tabard Inn (made famous by Master Chaucer in his tales) were highly respectable, while many of the clergy, including a couple of bishops and several abbots, had large houses in the vicinity of St Thomas's Hospital and the Church of St Mary Overy.

My previous business on this side of the river had, I regret to say, all been among the seamier denizens of Southwark. Today, however, I was looking for a more respectable sort of man. I collared the first boatman I saw just as he was about to descend the steps to the strand.

'Do any of you fellows work at night?' I asked. 'Through the night, that is, not just after dark.'

The man, tall and bald with a broken nose, regarded me suspiciously, but seemed a little reassured by my shabby clothes. 'You ain't from these parts,' he said by way of answer.

'No. I'm from the West Country. Somerset,' I said impatiently. 'Well, do you?'

'Do I what?'

'Know of any boatmen who work all night?'

'All right! All right! Keep your breeches on. Why do you want to know?'

I breathed deeply. I had forgotten how wary these people were of 'foreigners'. 'I might have need of one, that's all.'

Suddenly, my companion grinned and tapped the side of his nose. 'Oho! Like that, eh?' What exactly he thought I was up to, I had no idea, but it was obviously something nefarious. 'Well, good luck to you, friend. There is one fellow who'll row you across river at any hour you like. Jeremiah Tucker's his name. But he'll charge you double rates if it's after curfew.'

I nodded. 'Fair enough. He's taking a risk. Where do I find him?'

The bald-headed man scanned the fore-shore, where a number of boats were lined up at the water's edge. He waved a large hand at

117

one of them. 'That's his, over there. The one with the blue canopy.' A faint frown puckered his forehead. 'He's late this morning. It ain't like Jeremiah to oversleep.'

'Maybe he had a client last night,' I suggested.

'Aye, p'r'aps he did. But it don't usually make him late for work the following morning.'

'So, where do I find him?' I asked again.

Once more suspicion gleamed in the slightly protuberant eyes. Then he shrugged. 'I suppose if you ask around enough, someone'll tell you, so it might as well be me. You don't mean him any harm, do you?'

'Not the least in the world. I just want to ask him a question.'

'We-ell...' The boatman considered me for a moment longer before deciding in my favour. 'You don't look like anyone in the pay of the law.' I abstained from pointing out that if I were indeed a lawman, I shouldn't be strutting around in my best Sunday-go-to-church clothes. But there! He had the brawn. What did he want with brains? He went on, 'Jerry Tucker lives a couple o' streets back from here, near a tavern called the Rattlebones. Just ask for him. Most people hereabouts know who he is.'

I thanked the man profusely and watched him descend the steps, to where a queue of folk had already formed alongside his own boat, before turning away from the wharf. Another enquiry, two minutes later, of a baker, plying his early morning trade, elicited the fact that the Rattlebones was just round the nearest corner.

'But you won't get much service there this morning. There were a nasty murder there last night.'

'Oh?'

The baker nodded. 'Will Tanner, one of our locals, were stabbed to death in a quarrel. God knows what it were about, but the little bastard what did it got clean away in spite o' the hue and cry.'

The story reminded me of Reynold Makepeace, and the baker and I spent ten minutes or so deploring the lawlessness of the London and Southwark streets. But time was pressing and I had to return to Baynard's Castle before I was missed. I asked for Jeremiah Tucker and was told the fifth house from the Rattlebones on the left.

I turned the corner, walked past the tavern, giving it a curious glance as I did so, counted five houses along, and was just in time to catch a plump woman, erupting from the cottage like a bat out of hell and screaming at the top of her voice, in my arms.

'What is it? What's the matter?' I asked.

She continued screaming. I shook her hard, but to no avail. Other people were emerging from their houses, attracted by the noise. Afraid that they would get the wrong impression, I slapped her, putting the full force of my right arm behind the blow.

'What's the matter?' I yelled again.

She made a gobbling sound.

A man stepped forward from the little crowd that had now gathered around us, and clapped the plump woman on the shoulder. 'Marjorie, tell us what's the matter,' he urged. He looked at me. 'Is this fellow molesting you?'

The woman shook her head vigorously while I uttered a furiously indignant denial. Sweet Virgin! Was I beginning to look like a man desperate enough to force my attentions on middle-aged goodwives?

'What is it, then?' the man persisted, while the rest nodded encouragement.

The plump woman gave another despairing moan. Tired of this, I pushed her gently into the arms of her friends and strode into the cottage with a determination that belied my growing fear – almost a certainty – of what I was going to find. My presentiment was all too soon proved correct. A man whom I presumed to be Jeremiah Tucker was stretched out on the beaten-earth floor, face upwards, his throat neatly cut from ear to ear – a good, clean stroke with which I had seen slaughtermen in my native Somerset kill cattle. It was Humphrey Culpepper all over again.

My breath caught in my throat. A vision of that terrible wall painting in the north cloister of St Paul's entered my head: *The Dance of Death*, the *Danse Macabre* of the French, the grinning skeletons dragging away their victims one by one ... With an effort, I pulled myself together. I must get out of here and quickly. I had defied the duke's orders only to find myself in another imbroglio in which I seemed destined to play a leading part.

I leaned down and quickly touched the unfortunate Jeremiah Tucker's face and hands He was stiff and cold. This murder had taken place some time ago, but once again I had been making enquiries about the dead man. I glanced around. The one-roomed cottage was small and, in general, ill maintained, but the shutters of the single window opened silently on recently oiled hinges. My luck was in and I was out – both legs over the sill – of that window and running along the backs of the houses into the next street, plunging deeper into the maze of narrow alleyways until I was far enough away to risk descending to the foreshore, where I signalled to a cruising boatman looking for a fare. A short time later – although it seemed like an eternity – I was back within the walls of Baynard's Castle, sitting on the edge of my bed in my tiny room, desperately trying to control the trembling of my limbs.

Once I was more myself, I stretched out on my bed, linked my hands behind my head and tried to make sense of what was going on.

There had to be a connection between the deaths of Humphrey Culpepper and Jeremiah Tucker. The coincidence of two men having their throats cut within a day or so of each other was nothing extraordinary in a city like London, or indeed in any city, but the chances of them both being despatched in an identical manner – so neatly and with such precision – were far greater. The odds against that happening were impossibly short. Furthermore, both victims were linked – although they did not know it – with Baynard's Castle, for if Jeremiah Tucker was not the boatman who had dropped off the mysterious visitor at the castle's water-stairs in the early hours of the morning, then I'd never trust my instincts again.

According to my bald-headed friend, Tucker was a boatman willing to flout authority and work during the hours of night, carrying, no doubt, many thieves and robbers across from Southwark to London to ply their trade under cover of darkness, and then to ferry them home again. And yet the fact that Bald Head had only mentioned one man didn't mean to say that there weren't others...

I drew a deep breath, swung my legs over the edge of the bed and sat upright, telling myself not to be a fool or to be seduced into following false trails. The fact that the one man mentioned was now dead – and dead in exactly the same circumstances as Humphrey Culpepper – spoke for itself. He had to be the man whose progress I had watched back across the river some six or seven hours earlier. Someone had been waiting for his return to the Southwark side, followed him home, knocked and been admitted. Why? The most probable answer to that question was that he was supposed to be the payer, the man who had brought the money now that the mission had been successfully accomplished. But instead of bringing silver, he had brought merely a knife, and when the boatman's back was turned, had seized him and cut his throat, swiftly, cleanly, so that the poor man had known only a momentary fear before he died. That, at least, was something.

This time, however, the blood that drenched the attacker would not have been so easily disguised as it had been near the Shambles. But then, it was dark; fewer people would have been about, and those who were were minding their own shady business, disinclined to pry into that of others. A quick plunge into the murky waters of the nearby Thames – not something I should have cared to do, but you couldn't be fussy if you'd just killed a man – and much of the blood would have been washed off. Or maybe the murderer had gone prepared with a change of clothing.

All of which, of course, posed the questions: who had been landed at Baynard's Castle and why was his – her? – arrival to be kept so secret that it was worthwhile to kill a man? It was at this point that I began to realize the seriousness of the situation I was in. The murder of Humphrey Culpepper had not appeared so frightening on its own; the old man might or might not have been killed in order to prevent my having any contact with him. But if his death was linked to that of the boatman, as it so plainly was, then truly ruthless forces were against us. This had to be the work of someone who would stop at nothing.

It was my duty to inform Timothy and Duke Richard of the second murder straight away, but the thought was daunting. To begin with, I would be forced to admit that I had flagrantly disobeyed the duke's order, flouted a royal command. Secondly, I had been seen and, with my height and West Country accent, inevitably noted at the scene of a second crime and, doubtless, my description passed on to the authorities. And, of course, to anyone else who was interested. The duke and his spymaster general would be furious, to put it no higher. I should be in for a very uncomfortable half-hour (another under-statement). I might even find myself facing punishment. So, in the end, after careful consideration, weighing up this and that, I decided to say nothing. It was more than probable, almost a certainty in fact, that the murder in Southwark would be thought of insufficient importance to come to the Duke of Gloucester's ears, or even Timothy's – just another killing among the many that occur-red every night south of the Thames.

I slid off the bed and stretched, feeling calmer for having arrived at a decision, no matter how craven it might be. I justified it by telling myself that I hadn't asked to be put in this situation and that, on top of everything else, I didn't deserve further recriminations and the discomfort of royal disapproval. What the duke and Timothy didn't know wouldn't hurt them, and I could be extra vigilant and on my guard throughout the coming journey.

It was dinnertime. The trumpets were sounding. I straightened my tunic, ran my fingers through my hair and descended to the common hall.

It was later than I intended when I finally made my way to the room overlooking the water-stairs. I had lingered over my dinner, debating with myself as to whether or not I was being criminally foolish in not divulging the latest development to Timothy and the duke, but, in the end, came to the same conclusion as before. Coward that I was, I was not prepared to bear the brunt of their wrath. I would just have to take extra precautions on my travels.

The tailor and his assistant were waiting for me, as was an irate spymaster general.

'I was just going to send someone to look for you,' the latter spat, 'and haul you up here by the seat of your breeches.'

The apprentice giggled and I gave Timothy a nasty look.

'Am I not to be allowed time to eat, then?' I demanded. 'I notice Mistress Gray hasn't arrived yet.'

'She won't be, at least not for a while.' Timothy smirked. 'As you will be trying on your new clothes, I thought it best to spare your blushes.'

This time, the tailor laughed as well. I

ground my teeth and bit back a withering retort. (Or I would have done if only I could have thought of anything withering enough in time. No doubt something would occur to me later, when the moment had passed.)

For the next half-hour, I was stripped naked, then pulled and prodded about while I was eased into two sets of new clothes, both of which felt alien and uncomfortable on my large body, used as it was to old, ill-fitting garments that moulded themselves to my shape. A fine cambric shirt was the foundation for two pairs of hose, one dark blue and the other brown – I had stipulated fiercely against any particoloured nonsense – and two woollen tunics, one a pale green adorned with silver-gilt buttons, which I hated on sight, and the other, nearly but not quite so bad, of a deep yellow. I was also equipped with a warm, all-enveloping cloak made from camlet, that mixture of wool and camel hair that is so good at keeping out the winter cold, and, finally, a brown velvet hat, sporting a fake jewel on its upturned brim. My feet being on the big side, I was allowed to keep my own boots, with the proviso that I cleaned them of their usual mud and grime.

'Will he pass as a gentleman, do you think?' Timothy asked dubiously.

The tailor gave a confident affirmative. 'My clothes would make a gentleman of anyone,' he said.

I thanked him solemnly, but he merely nodded, accepting the compliment at its face value. Timothy, on the other hand, grinned.

One set of clothes, together with a second shirt, were duly stored away in a small travelling chest, while I was handed the others, ready for me to wear the next day.

'You'll be starting early,' Timothy informed me, when the tailor had been paid and bowed himself and his apprentice out, not without some mutterings under his breath about the niggardly rates paid by the state. 'You'll be a night on the road to Dover, then, the weather being fair, cross to Calais, which you should reach by Friday evening. Accommodation has been reserved for you and Mistress Gray – Mistress Chapman I should say – when you get to Paris.' He turned towards the door as it opened. 'Ah! Here she is now.'

But he was mistaken. It was not Eloise who entered but John Bradshaw, looking, I thought, somewhat defiant, like a man about to do battle. He nodded at me before addressing himself to Timothy.

'I told you yesterday,' he began abruptly, 'that I needed help on this journey. I can't keep my eye on Madame Eloise while Roger here is about whatever it is he has to be about as well as see to everything else.'

'And I told you I can't spare anyone,' Timothy retorted angrily. 'We're short of men as it is.'

Bradshaw grunted. 'I know you did. So I've taken it upon myself to hire someone of my own.'

There was a pregnant silence. Then Timothy burst out, 'You've done *what*?'

The other man flushed slightly but stood his ground. 'You heard me.'

The spymaster general appeared to be struck dumb. Finally, he managed to gasp out, 'Have you taken leave of your senses?'

John Bradshaw scowled. 'I'm not a fool. This is a man I know and trust. We were soldiers together longer ago now than I care to remember. I'd trust him with my life.'

'I daresay. But what about other people's lives?' Timothy demanded, breathing hard.

I nodded my agreement in no uncertain fashion. Mine was one of those lives he was talking about.

'You of all people,' Timothy continued, his voice shaking with barely suppressed fury, 'should know that you can't do this sort of thing, Jack. I need to know about this man. The duke – who will not be pleased – will want to know all about him from me, and he'll be deeply disappointed. He was only saying yesterday to Roger that you were one of the best, if not the best, agent we had. And now for you to go and do something as ... as fucking stupid as this, it's unbelievable! For the Lord's sake, man! Hasn't it occurred to you that this old friend might be a Woodville spy?'

'Well, he ain't,' John Bradshaw replied positively. 'He hasn't got the brains for it, for one thing. For another, he's no interest in anything at present. He's a lost soul. His wife – woman a lot younger'n him – died in child-

128

birth a few months back, and the little 'un was stillborn. Half mad with grief he is. Used to keep an old clothes stall in Leadenhall Market. He's abandoned it. Abandoned everything. Just roaming the streets with the beggars. Used up all his money on drink. Fell in with him last night in the White Hart, one of the waterfront taverns, sobered him up and heard his story. He doesn't know anything but that I'm accompanying a Master and Mistress Chapman to France and that we need another man to help with the horses and baggage. He'll meet us tomorrow morning at the White Hart in Southwark. His name,' Bradshaw added, 'is Philip Lamprey.'

But I had already guessed that.

Eight

I had known it, of course, from almost the first sentence of John Bradshaw's description. There couldn't possibly be two men in London who had once been soldiers, kept an old-clothes stall in Leadenhall Market and recently lost wife and child.

'That's all very well, Jack,' Timothy was beginning, when I interrupted him, addressing myself to the other man.

'I'm afraid Philip will have to know a bit

more than you've told him, Master Bradshaw. He's not only a very old friend of mine, but he also knows my wife. He'll realize at once that Mistress Gray's an impostor.'

There was a moment's complete silence before Timothy swung slowly round to face me. 'You're acquainted with this man?' he asked incredulously, but not without a certain amount of relief.

'Been friends for years.' I nodded. 'As a matter of fact, I went to visit him the day before yesterday. That was when I found his cottage empty – abandoned – and a neighbour told me what had happened to Jeanne and the baby. She told me, too, that Philip was dumb with grief and had disappeared some weeks later. If you want me to vouch for his character, I'll willingly do so. Everything Master Bradshaw has said about him is true. Philip would have neither the inclination nor the nous to be a spy. He's never had any particular loyalty to anyone but himself and Jeanne.'

Timothy heaved what sounded like a thankful sigh. 'Then that's what I shall tell the duke – that this man, Philip ... Philip...'

'Lamprey,' John Bradshaw and I supplied in unison.

'Like the fish,' I added, then puckered my brow. 'Didn't one of our kings die of a surfeit of—?'

'Yes, yes!' Timothy cut in testily. 'No need to show off just because the Glastonbury monks gave you an education. As I was saying, I shall tell Duke Richard that I have hired this man on the recommendation of both yourself and Jack here and that you can each vouch for his integrity.'

'What you mean,' John Bradshaw growled, 'is that if anything should go wrong – which it won't – Master Chapman and I will take the blame, while your reputation will still be as pure as the driven snow.'

'Well, that it won't be,' Timothy snapped. 'The duke will be angry enough that I've hired an extra man for this journey and not discussed it with him first. Particularly as it means we shall have to let this Lamprey into our confidence a little way. But just remember, the pair of you, that Lamprey knows only that Mistress Gray goes to see her cousin Maître le Daim to discover King Louis's intentions towards Burgundy. And don't you,' he hissed, turning to John Bradshaw and pointing an accusatory finger, 'ever, ever take it upon yourself again to do anything like this without my knowledge. Because if you do, master spy though you may be, you will leave His Grace of Gloucester's service just as fast as I can kick you downstairs.'

'Not very fast, then,' the other man retaliated, his pleasant features flushing a dull red. But I could guess from his defiant attitude that he knew he had overstepped the mark and that Timothy's anger was justified. He was about to add something else when Timothy waved him to silence with an abrupt motion of one hand.

131

'Mistress Gray,' he mouthed, although I had heard nothing.

But sure enough, a moment later the latch lifted and Eloise came in, smiling her prettiest smile; not, I was certain, for my benefit – she had long given up trying to impress me – but for Master Bradshaw's.

Timothy at once put her in the picture regarding the new addition to our party, a fact that she accepted with the least possible show of interest. She was far more concerned with examining my new clothes, turning over the set that was folded up on the table and opening the travelling chest to look at the rest.

'Oh, Roger,' she gurgled, 'what peacock's feathers! It will almost be a pleasure to be seen with you. What are you wearing tomorrow? I see, the brown hose and green tunic, and of course the cloak and hat, which are also brown. Here! Let me recommend the yellow with all that mud colour. It will cheer it up and make a splash of brightness on what seems set to be another dull day.'

She removed the yellow tunic from the chest, but I firmly replaced it. 'I shall decide what to wear,' I said pettishly. 'You are not my wife.'

'No, but she has to pretend to be,' Timothy put in, 'and the sooner you begin practising your roles, the better it will be. Do as Mistress Gray – no, as Mistress Chapman – tells you, Roger.'

John Bradshaw gave a throaty chuckle. 'And

you'd both better stop calling me Master Bradshaw. Remember I'm your servant. Jack's the name. Start using it now so you'll be used to it before we get on the road.'

'Very well ... Jack!' Eloise simpered nauseatingly. (I found it nauseating, at any rate, although John Bradshaw seemed to find nothing objectionable in it.) She looked at me. 'By the way, I've been informed that supper will be early this evening. The kitcheners, cooks and scullions want everyone out of the common hall by the hour of five at the very latest. They need to use it as an extension to the kitchens. It seems Her Grace of York and the Duke of Gloucester are entertaining Earl Rivers at a banquet tonight in acknowledgement of his recent good work in Scotland, before he returns to the Prince of Wales's household at Ludlow tomorrow.'

I grimaced and avoided catching Timothy's eye. Personally, I rather liked the queen's elder brother, Anthony. From the little I had seen of him, he appeared a great deal less self-important than the other Woodvilles I had encountered. By contrast, his younger brother, Edward, who had accompanied him on the Scottish expedition this past summer, was a bumptious, self-opinionated egotist who considered that life could bestow no greater honour than being a Woodville on the one hand and a scion of the House of Luxembourg on the other. (Jacquetta of Luxembourg had married the then Sir Richard Woodville after the death of her first husband

– Henry V's brother, John, Duke of Bedford –
and borne him a large family.) I could not
imagine, however, that my lord of Gloucester
was looking forward to this evening with
anything but dismay, considering his dislike
of all his Woodville in-laws in general and the
nature of the mission I was to undertake for
him in France in particular. But I made no
comment, merely nodding to signify that I
had got the message.

Timothy then proceeded to instruct me in
all the things I should be interested in as a
prosperous haberdasher: cloth, lace, neck-
laces, combs, pins, brushes, gloves and so
forth. Pretty much like being a chapman,
really (which, I suppose, was why Timothy,
no fool, had chosen the occupation for me),
but conducting business from a nice warm
stall or shop, instead of roaming the countryside in all winds and weathers. After that, he
gave Eloise and me a little homily about not
forgetting to behave as man and wife in
public, while, at the same time, exhorting me
to recollect that I was a happily married man
in private.

'I've no intention of forgetting,' I answered
austerely. Eloise simply smiled and cast down
her eyes.

After which, there was little left to do but to
arrange the time and place at which she and
I would meet with John Bradshaw in the
morning – sunrise in the castle courtyard –
before dispersing to amuse ourselves in our
separate ways for the rest of the day. Timothy

detained me for a moment or two, holding me back as the other two departed in order to make certain that I knew exactly what it was that I had to do once we reached Paris, and that I could still remember, word for word, the questions I must put to Robin Gaunt when, eventually, I found him.

'If I find him,' I muttered.

Somewhat to my surprise, Timothy did not argue with this caveat, merely nodding, rather lugubriously, I thought, in agreement.

'Do your best,' he urged, patting me on the shoulder.

'I've already assured the duke that I shall do so.' I hesitated for a second, then asked, 'Timothy, is this leading where I think it's leading?'

'That's not for you or me to worry about,' he answered sharply. 'The likes of us do as we're told. We decide who we're for and carry out orders. For my part, I've always been the Duke of Gloucester's man from the very first day I entered his service. There's an under-lying sweetness to his nature that binds men to him – those of us who are privileged to see that side of him, that is. You've seen it, I know. You must have. In your way, you're as devoted to him as I am.'

'Yes, I am,' I admitted. 'But I don't let it cloud my judgement. There's a ruthlessness to him, as well. He wouldn't be a true Plantagenet if there weren't. He loves the king, but he hates the Woodvilles, all the more because he keeps it hidden for his brother's

135

sake. But if Edward dies while the Prince of Wales is still a minor—'

'Shush!' Timothy hastened to the door, wrenched it open and glanced into the corridor. Satisfied that no one was outside, he closed it again and came back, frowning heavily. 'For God's sake, watch your tongue, Roger! It runs away with you sometimes.'

'When we were on our way to Scotland,' I persisted, 'I overheard a very disturbing conversation between the duke and Albany—'

'I don't wish to be told,' Timothy said firmly. 'It's time—'

I ignored him. 'His Highness wanted to know what plans Albany had made concerning his nephews in the event of Albany's becoming king of Scotland. As it turned out, of course, Albany never did.'

'I've said–' Timothy raised his voice, then hastily lowered it again – 'I've said, Roger, that I don't want to hear this. And you had no business listening in on His Grace's private conversation. I thought better of you.'

'I couldn't help overhearing,' I disclaimed angrily. 'They thought I was asleep.'

'Then you should have declared yourself,' was the sententious reply, 'as a man of honour would have done.'

Riled, I snapped back, 'I didn't know spies were supposed to be men of honour. I thought that the first requirement for a spy was to be a devious little bastard.'

Timothy drew himself up to his full height,

which wasn't very high, but he could look impressive when he tried, and announced, 'I think this discussion had better end here before we both say things we shall be sorry for later.' He held out his hand with great dignity. 'In case I don't see you again before tomorrow, let me wish you good luck and good fortune. Take care of yourself, because now that the Woodvilles have got the scent of something being in the wind, even though they have no idea exactly what, there will be danger. Rely on John Bradshaw for assistance and protection. In spite of his recent lapse, he really is a good man.' Timothy snorted with sudden laughter. 'And even that lapse has turned out to be for the best. That's another thing about him. He's lucky, always has been. And luck is one of the greatest gifts that anyone can have.'

He gripped my hand tighter and then, to my amazement, embraced me. This unlooked-for gesture seemed to embarrass him more than it did me, and he resumed his acerbic tone. 'Just remember,' he admonished me as he turned away, 'don't leave the castle until tomorrow morning when you're in disguise. There might still be people looking out for you in connection with Master Culpepper's murder.'

The weary hours until suppertime stretched before me, arid and empty. I dared not risk another foray into the London streets, especially now that I could be wanted in connection with a second killing. (Just as well Timothy knew nothing about that or I would doubtless have been treated to another homily concerning my unreliability.) My little cell of a room was distinctly uninviting, so there was nothing for it but to wander around Baynard's Castle, getting in honest folk's way and irritating them beyond endurance by trying to engage them in idle conversation. When a fifth person – a pretty young girl who was carrying in great swathes of greenery to decorate tonight's banqueting tables – snubbed me, I gave up and went in the general direction of the kitchens, where surplus food might be picked up in order to assuage the rumblings of my empty belly (although I suspected there was not much allowance made for wastage in Her Grace of York's frugal budget).

The kitchens, as was usual in most noble households, were situated in the darkest, hottest part of the building, at ground-floor level and occasionally even partially underground. Summer or winter, the heat was always such that many of the cooks and scullions worked stark naked, while others, more sensitive to the danger of exposing themselves fully to hissing fat and scalding water – not to mention the occasional derogatory remarks of their fellow workers – wore loincloths underneath leather aprons.

The common dining hall was very close to this furnace, but the long trestle-boards were at present laid ready for the servants' own supper and had not yet been appropriated as extra space for laying out the banquet dishes. A few early eaters had gathered at a table in one corner and were making short work of a bowl of pottage and the inevitable hunks of yesterday's stale bread. I thought I might as well join them, but as I walked the length of the room, I became aware of a flurry of movement. A man – I was sure it was a man – who had been sitting in the shadows ducked down beneath the table and must have crawled on all fours between his companions' legs to the door leading into the kitchens. Having reached it, he suddenly straightened up and burst through, slamming it shut behind him.

His companions seemed as startled by his conduct as I was and turned grinning faces towards me as I neared the table.

'What you done to our friend that he does not want to meet you?' one of them asked.

Another said, 'He seems shit-scared of you, lad, and no mistake.'

'Who is he?' I demanded. 'What's his name?'

They all shrugged.

'Dunno,' a fat one said. 'Newcomer. Ain't seen 'im afore. Probably brought in special for the banquet.'

I wondered who the unknown could possibly be, but a moment's thought supplied the answer. It had to be the shadowy figure I had seen arriving at the water-stairs the previous night. Somehow or another, he had received word that I had been over to Southwark, making enquiries, a fact that in itself must have suggested to him that I had seen something that had aroused my suspicions. The last thing he would wish to do would be to meet me face to face.

'What does this man look like?' I asked.

'Dunno.'

'Didn't really take much notice of him.'

'Just a fellow.'

'Didn't say much. Quiet type.'

I thanked them sarcastically for their help and opened the door into the kitchens.

'Shouldn't go in there just now,' one of the men advised. 'Not when they're so busy. You might meet—'

But here the others all hushed him or shouted him down. That should have been a warning to me, but I was too intent on pursuing my quarry to take any notice, and plunged through, straight into Hell.

That was what it felt like, anyway.

There were at least three spits turning over enormous fires – three suckling pigs roasting on one, two haunches of venison on another and a whole ox on the largest. A swan had just been removed from one of the many ovens and was being carried across to a side table, where three men stood beside a great pile of the creature's feathers, ready to replace its plumage, beak and eyes. At another bench, fish were being cleaned and gutted, while one of the pastry cooks was having a fit of hysterics because two of his pies had been knocked to the floor by a passing scullion.

The whole place was a seething, chaotic mass of people, all of them screaming instructions and shouting orders amidst clouds of steam from boiling cauldrons and hissing vats of oil. I soon realized that there was very little hope, if any, of locating anyone who had run in there to hide.

But I wasn't prepared to give up that easily. I edged my way between the benches, dodged around kitchen boys who were scurrying from place to place in answer to various imperious summonses, ignored the curses that greeted my enquiry as to whether or not a stranger had recently entered the kitchens, and generally made a nuisance of myself, while all the time my belly rumbled incessantly in response to the wonderful smells emanating from pots and ovens. Finally, one of the spit-turners, friendlier than the rest, indicated a second door at the far end of the vast room and said he'd seen someone go through it minutes before.

'Not one of us,' he shouted. 'Fully dressed.'

I was by now sweating profusely, face, arms, legs, body, my clothes sticking to me like a burr to a sheep's fleece. I thanked my informant and had just turned with relief to escape from the overwhelming heat when I found my path blocked by the most enormous man it has ever been my misfortune to meet. I'm a big man myself, over six feet tall and not ill proportioned – indeed, I've grown used to being described as a well-set-up young fellow – but this man made me feel puny. He was as

141

broad as he was high, and he could top me by half a head, with muscles like young tree trunks all over his body (and as he was naked, I speak with authority). His great torso ran with sweat, gleaming in the light from the fires as he stood with arms akimbo and legs wide apart, glaring at me with small, hostile eyes.

'Get out of my kitchen!' he roared.

'I'm just trying to find—' I was beginning, but he roared again.

'Out!'

I adopted a reasonable tone. 'Now, look here—'

Before I knew what was happening to me, I was lifted bodily off my feet, slung over one mighty shoulder, carried the length of the kitchens, to the cheers of the workers, and literally thrown through the door into the common hall. The giant then returned to his own domain with the satisfied air of a man who had acquitted himself well.

In my absence, the hall had filled up with diners who had come early to supper, as bidden. The men sitting at the corner table were convulsed with laughter, and after the first stunned silence at my unconventional arrival, their mirth was shared by others. As I lay there, wondering if I were still all in one piece, gingerly flexing my limbs to make sure that nothing was broken, the hilarity gradually spread throughout the hall as the story passed from table to table.

There was a rustle of skirts and I glanced

up to see Eloise kneeling beside me.

'Are you all right?' she enquired anxiously, although I could see that even she was struggling to keep a straight face.

'Oh, very well, indeed,' I snapped, having by this time ascertained that nothing was really hurt except my pride. I should have a few ugly bruises in the morning, but that was all. Pettishly refusing her assistance, I struggled to my feet.

'You met Goliath, then,' one of the men at the corner table sniggered.

'As you see! You didn't think to warn me, I suppose?'

'Well, Rob there did,' the same man admitted, 'but the rest of us thought it would be a lesson to you not to go poking your nose in where it's not wanted.'

I breathed deeply and clenched my fists; at which point, Eloise decided it was the right moment to beat a strategic retreat, so she propelled me firmly towards two empty places at a table much further up the hall. The lackeys had started serving the meal a few minutes earlier, while I had still been lying prostrate on the floor, and my companion and I were only just in time to grab our portions of the inevitable pottage from the common bowl. As it was, we earned ourselves dirty looks from the table's other occupants, who had obviously been promising themselves second helpings. (Which showed how desperate the poor devils must have been.)

'What on earth were you doing in the

kitchens?' Eloise wanted to know, once she had blunted the edge of her appetite.

I had already foreseen the question and had been wondering what my answer would be.

'I ... er ... I was hungry,' I said. 'I thought I might pick up some titbits to eat.' True enough: it had been my original intention.

Eloise appeared unconvinced. More, she looked highly sceptical. I couldn't blame her. She was an intelligent woman and surely must have begun, by now, to have her suspicions that she was not being told the whole truth about this French mission. Timothy's reasons for seeing me alone and for my meetings with the duke would surely have a hollow ring to anyone of even average quickness of mind, and Eloise was brighter than that. She chose, however, to accept my explanation, which in itself was worrying.

'You eat too much, Roger.' She smiled.

'Not in this place!' I retorted feelingly. 'Nobody could.'

That made her laugh, a peal of mirth that lit up her face and transformed her naturally petulant, slightly sour expression into one of genuine enjoyment. With a blinding flash of revelation, I could see how really pretty she was and was conscious of a sudden stirring in my loins. Dear God! This wouldn't do! Not when we had to share the same bed for the next goodness knew how many nights. And I had already proved to myself that I couldn't be trusted with an attractive and determined woman. If Adela ever found out...! It didn't

144

bear thinking about. I shuddered. At least I knew now that I must be on my guard every minute of our nights together.

'Are you cold?' Eloise asked in surprise.

'What? Oh, no. Just ... just someone walking over my grave.'

'Don't say that,' she murmured. 'Ever since I saw *The Dance of Death* in the cloister at St Paul's, I've been haunted by its images.' She laid a hand on my arm. 'Enough! Will you come with me down to the water-stairs this evening, after dark, and watch the guests arrive? I understand they will be coming by river.'

I knew I should refuse. Here was my first opportunity to demonstrate my strength of will.

Of course I said yes.

The lights from the barges coruscated across the water, amber and white and red. Musicians played softly, strains of popular airs wafting gently towards the shore. The moon hung low in the night sky, adding to the fairy-like quality of the scene. The neighbouring wharves and warehouses had melted into the encroaching darkness, so that they were no more than faint stains on an inky cloth.

The Dowager Duchess of York, leaning heavily on an ebony stick, but still straight-backed and magnificent in black velvet trimmed with sable, received her guests accompanied by her younger son, the Duke of Gloucester, impressive in cloth of gold and yellow brocade, with jewels flashing on both breast and fingers, but looking tired and strained, I thought, in the flaring light from a myriad torches. Anthony Woodville, Earl Rivers, on the other hand appeared relaxed and smiling as he alighted from his barge and knelt to kiss the duchess's outstretched hand. He had chosen to wear royal purple, a fact that had doubtless not gone unnoticed by his hosts, and could possibly have accounted for the tightening of the muscles around the duke's thin mouth as he stepped forward, in his turn, to greet the arrivals.

That cocky little bastard Edward Woodville, who was also being honoured for his part in the Scottish expedition, strutted up the water-stairs arrayed, suitably enough, in pea-cock-blue (or a colour as near as the dyers could make it). He saluted his hostess with a flourish that would not have shamed that showy bird itself, before turning, with ill-concealed condescension, to the duke. He must know, as everyone else did, that each day brought fresh speculation concerning the king's health. Did he already see himself, as uncle to King Edward V, on an equal footing with Richard of Gloucester?

Trumpets sounded as the principal guests were conducted indoors, the remainder of their retinues left to straggle after them, a gaudy throng, chattering like so many mag-pies as they followed in their masters' gor-geous wake. Eloise and I were standing re-spectfully to one side of the steps in company

146

with other servants and people of no account who had come to watch Earl Rivers's arrival. One of the last to mount the water-stairs from Sir Edward Woodville's barge, not so splendidly dressed as some of the others and plainly one of the lesser fry, turned his head to stare at the spectators. I caught my breath.

I recognized him instantly, even without his hat.

It was the smart young gent of the blue feather.

Nine

I lowered my head and edged behind two or three of the other spectators. Although my movements were slight, Eloise turned to look at me.

'Is something wrong?' she asked.

She missed very little and her suspicions seemed easily aroused, a fact that worried me. Not only was I under orders to keep the duke's private mission hidden from her, but I realized that I was accumulating a number of secrets of my own: noticing Blue Feather in Stinking Lane the previous day; seeing a man – I was now certain it had been a man – being landed at the castle water-stairs in the early hours of this morning; my trip to Southwark

147

and the murder of the boatman Jeremiah Tucker; the fellow who had been desperate to avoid my company in the common hall this evening; now the knowledge that Blue Feather was a member of Edward Woodville's household; and, of course, the start of it all – seeing my smart young gent the day before yesterday in conversation with a woman who must be an inmate of the castle. I couldn't help wondering if I was being wise in keeping all this to myself: the answer to which was a resounding 'No!' But it was too late to do anything about it now.

It did cross my mind, however, that I might confide in John Bradshaw. He, after all, was the man responsible for my safety and well-being in the coming days, and had proved himself not to be above taking matters into his own hands when and if he considered it necessary. Nor, if I had judged him aright, was he the sort to read me a homily or stigmatize me as a stupid, lying bastard with the brains of a louse who was liable to wreck the whole carefully laid scheme. I decided I could probably do worse than make a clean breast of things to this eminently level-headed and sensible man. If I got the chance, I would do so.

I became aware that Eloise was shaking my arm.

'Roger! I asked you if anything is wrong.'

'What? Oh, no. The light from the torches was hurting my eyes, that's all.'

She didn't believe me, naturally, but she

made no further comment. In any case, by this time all the guests had disappeared inside the castle, including the stragglers, and those of us who had come out to watch were also slowly wending our way back indoors.

'Well, there won't be any games of chance in the common hall tonight, not with it being given over to the kitcheners. I suppose there's nothing for it but to go to bed.' Eloise didn't sound as if she found the prospect very alluring.

'We do have an early start tomorrow,' I pointed out. 'The castle courtyard at sunrise, with all our gear packed and ready to be loaded on to the horses.'

She grimaced. 'You and I won't find that a hardship, surely? We experienced enough dawn marches with the army during the summer.'

'How that used to upset my lord Albany.'

'Didn't it just!' We both snorted with laughter.

We had paused, without my realizing it, at the water-door of the castle, through which, by now, everyone else, both high and low, had vanished. Only Eloise and I were left, staring out over the Thames, the lights from the Woodvilles' moored barges strung like a necklace along the side of the wharf, their drowned reflections spangling the river. The night was very quiet. Every now and again the shouts of oarsmen reached our ears, but distantly, from the Southwark shore, faint and far off, while from within the castle a thread of music wound its way down the stairs and along the corridors to lie, sweet and trembling, on the evening air. It all added to the intimacy that our moment of shared reminiscence had engendered.

Eloise was standing close to me, shivering a little inside her cloak. It seemed a perfectly natural gesture at the time to put my arm about her shoulders and draw her even closer for warmth. She put up her face, the soft lips quivering, the violet-blue eyes widening in expectation, and before I knew it, I had lowered my head and kissed her. And it wasn't just a kiss. She wrapped her arms round my body, straining against me with every fibre of her being.

My first thought was, however could I have lived alongside her for months and not realized she was a woman?

My second was, what in the Virgin's name was I doing? I was a happily married man with three children, those innocent little darlings who depended on me for their daily bread (not to mention their meat, honey, comfits, clothes and other highly expensive goodies).

Frantically, I struggled free of Eloise's clinging embrace. I pushed her from me almost roughly and supported myself with one hand against the wall, breathing heavily. I saw those wonderful eyes momentarily darken with anger; then she recovered her poise.

She tossed her head and laughed. 'Oh, Roger! My dear "husband"! I can see that I'm going to have to guard my virtue with you.'

'You're going to...' I spluttered indignantly. 'I was under the impression there for a moment that ... that...'

'That what? That I was about to seduce you? Don't flatter yourself.' She spun on her heel and went inside, leaving me alone with the night and my misgivings.

I awoke from a broken, uneasy dream in that hour just before daybreak when it is still dark but there is a slight but subtle change in the light – enough to warn you that it will soon be dawn and that it is useless to go back to sleep.

It had been a disturbed night. To begin with, as if my own conduct was not a sufficient worry – my urge to bed Eloise was overwhelming – there was the added anxiety as to what her motive might have been. Adela would tell you that, like most men, I consider myself irresistible to women, but that's a wife talking and isn't necessarily true (or even meant to be believed). Second thoughts had warned me that Eloise would use her charms to try to satisfy her curiosity. She must have worked out by now that there was something she wasn't being told, whatever Timothy said to the contrary. But added to this was the sudden fear that she could be a French spy. What did we really know about her, after all? Timothy may think he was being very clever and using her for his own ends, but perhaps the shoe was on the other foot. Moreover, he only had her word that her mother had been distantly related to this Olivier le Daim. I should have to be careful to guard my tongue in her presence.

I had just, finally, been drifting off to sleep, feeling as though I had all the weight of the world on my shoulders, when the Woodvilles and their retinue began taking their leave. The chief guests and their hosts sounded relatively restrained; I was able to make out my lord of Gloucester's and the duchess's sober tones, and a voice I vaguely recognized as Earl River's held only the merest intimation of a slur. The rest of the party, however, had evidently done themselves proud, and once Duke Richard and his mother had withdrawn from the scene, the wine started to talk – and guffaw, sing, shout and generally make merry. Everyone seemed to be as drunk as a lord (except, perhaps, the lords themselves), and judging by the splash and the ensuing cries of alarm, one person at least had missed his footing and fallen into the river.

After that, I dozed fitfully until, as I say, I awoke in the stifling dark but with the knowledge that daybreak was not far off, even if the first rays of light had not yet crested the rooftops. I decided I might as well get up, knowing that it would take me longer than usual to dress myself in my unaccustomed finery. I had swung my legs to the floor before I realized that my bruises from yesterday's encounter with the Goliath of the castle kitchens had developed and stiffened nicely overnight. Riding a horse was going to be even more of a trial than usual.

By the time I was decked out in tight brown hose and green tunic over one of the cambric shirts, struggling with laces, points and buttons, I was in no very pleasant frame of mind. I stuck the hat on my head, draped the cloak over one arm, tucked my travelling chest under the other and descended to the common hall, where we had been promised an early breakfast. No one else was about yet, so I left the chest on a bench and made my way out to the courtyard for a breath of fresh air in order to clear away the cobwebs of the night.

Somewhat to my surprise, John Bradshaw was before me, just dismounting from one of three horses already saddled and bridled, two of which were in the charge of a young groom and were presumably intended for Eloise and me. (Indeed, on closer inspection, I could see that one of the saddles was a lady's.) The spy's ruddy complexion was even ruddier in the light from the wall cressets, which had not yet been doused.

He nodded to me. 'You've taken my instructions to be up early to heart, Roger. That's good. I like a man who can get up in the mornings.'

I didn't contradict him, merely indicating his horse and remarking, 'You're no slugabed yourself. Out and about at this time of day?'

He grinned. 'As you see. I thought I'd best ride across to Southwark, to the White Hart, as soon as curfew was lifted, to make certain that our friend Lamprey would be ready and waiting when we got there.'

'A wise precaution,' I agreed. 'Or that he was there at all, I suppose. A man in his frame of mind might easily have absconded.'

John Bradshaw shook his head. 'I don't think he'll do that now. A week, a month ago maybe. But a man can't grieve for ever, however great the loss.' He threw his reins to the groom with instructions to see that all three animals were fed and watered and ready for the road as soon as we and, of course, the lady had breakfasted. 'Is your box down here?' he added to me. When I said that I had left it in the common hall, he told the poor lad to fetch it and make sure that the contents were transferred to the saddlebags. 'Mistress Gray can do her own,' he chuckled. 'I daresay there are things she won't want pawed about by a stable boy.'

The groom looked offended at this lowly description, but contented himself with sniffing loudly and asking, 'And yours ... my lord?'

The sarcasm was lost on John Bradshaw, who gave no sign of noticing it. 'Already done,' he answered briefly, before turning aside and taking my arm. 'Let's see if Goliath and his men can produce anything more sustaining than cold porridge and small beer.'

Eloise had still not put in an appearance and we had the common hall to ourselves, choosing a table as near to the kitchens as possible so that we benefited from the heat on this raw late October morning. John Bradshaw's name seemed, after all, to carry some weight because we got porridge and oatmeal cakes, both piping-hot. Even the ale had been warmed.

My companion lowered his voice, leaning confidentially across the table towards me. 'I've told Lamprey as much as he needs to know about this mission, but not a word more. Well, come to that, I don't know everything myself. That's your privilege.' Was there a sour note in there somewhere? I didn't think so. John Bradshaw was too professional a man to harbour petty jealousies, a fact he confirmed almost straight away. 'And a good thing, too. In my experience, a secret shared with even one person is no longer a secret. Shared with more than one, you might as well shout it from the housetops. My job is to see that Mistress Gray is kept occupied enough to allow you time to do whatever it is you have to do.'

'And Philip's?' I asked.

'To see to the horses and generally do what he's told,' was the uncompromising answer.

I was just wondering if now was the moment to take John Bradshaw into my confidence and unburden myself of all the various secrets I was harbouring when we were joined by Eloise, ready for travelling in a green woollen gown trimmed with squirrel skin, and carrying a thick, hooded cloak of grey camlet, together with a squirrel-skin muff. Her hair,

155

growing a little longer each day, was caught up in its usual silver net.

As soon as she saw me, she gave a peal of laughter. 'You have your hat on backwards, Roger. The brooch should go at the front.'

John Bradshaw, joining in the merriment, made room for her beside him on the bench. His grey eyes signalled appreciation of her appearance as he shouted for a server to bring the lady's breakfast. Meanwhile, I bad-temperedly snatched off my hat and put it on again the right way round.

'Much better,' Eloise approved. 'I must say you look very well and nearly worthy of being my husband.' I could tell that she wasn't going to forgive me very easily for last night, and that mockery and jibes were to be the order of the day.

As she reached for the beaker of ale that John Bradshaw had poured for her, I noticed a fine gold ring on her wedding finger and, leaning forward, caught her left hand in mine. I grimaced. 'An expensive piece,' I remarked. 'Do you get to keep it when this little charade is finished?'

'As a matter of fact, it's mine.' She smiled. 'I bought it yesterday in Cheapside.' She lifted her hand closer to my face. 'You see, it's really a loving-ring with hearts engraved round the outside. I thought I'd use it instead of the cheap-looking thing Master Plummer gave me to wear. You are meant to be a prosperous haberdasher, after all. And I, presumably, am the love of your life.'

Again the little pinprick of mockery, but this time I barely noticed it. I was too busy wondering where she got her money from. She had two good woollen gowns to my knowledge, and quite likely a third, and now she had bought herself a gold ring. This sudden affluence was troubling. Could it mean that she was in fact not a French but a Woodville spy and in receipt of payment from them?

As if reading my thoughts, her smile deepened and grew more enigmatic. Then she withdrew her gaze from mine and ignored me for the rest of the time it took her to eat her breakfast, deliberately setting out to charm John Bradshaw. In this, she succeeded so well that she did not even have to ask him to carry her travelling chest out to the waiting horses; he had it under his arm before she had risen from the table. He then delicately withdrew, taking the interested young groom with him, while she transferred her belongings to her saddlebags, but he was instantly at hand to assist her to mount. While I hoisted myself stiffly on to the back of my own animal, he adjured us both to wrap our cloaks well around us as it was a chilly morning, with more than a nip of the coming winter in the air. He himself had a thick, serviceable frieze cloak to cover his servant's garb and a plain peaked hat to keep off the worst of the weather.

And so, finally, we were ready, setting forward just as a pale sun was doing its best to gild the rooftops, riding the length of Thames Street, past the steelyard, where the Hanseatic merchants were, by the sound of things, already hard at work, into the Ropery and, eventually, crossing London Bridge into Southwark.

The first leg of our journey had begun.

I don't know why I felt surprised to see Philip waiting for us in the courtyard of the White Hart Inn. Somewhere at the back of my mind, I suppose, I hadn't quite believed in his existence in this ridiculous, dreamlike situation that I found myself a part of. But there he was, as large – or, in his case, as small – as life, standing unhappily beside a brown cob and with a hangdog expression on his narrow features. His old sparkle and zest for life were completely missing, his shoulders slumped, his thin lips unsmiling. His hair was sparser and greyer than when I had last seen him, but that, at least, was not surprising: by my calculations he had to be nearing fifty, or maybe even past it. I don't think he knew himself exactly how old he was. His pock-marked, weather-beaten face, too, was greyer, the healthy tan that contentment and Jeanne's good food had given it dulled with hopelessness and grief.

'Philip!' I dismounted and walked towards him, hand outstretched, but I had to speak to him again and shake him by the arm before I could rouse him.

He blinked rapidly several times, as though

158

trying to get his bearings and his thoughts in order, before he suddenly forced a smile and responded, 'Roger!'

His voice, thank heaven, hadn't altered. It still had that rasping quality that made it sound like an old file being dragged across iron.

I tightened my grip on his arm. 'Philip, I'm so sorry ... so very sorry—' I stumbled, but he cut me short, shaking off my hand and moving slightly away from me.

'Yes,' he said abruptly, and again, 'yes.' Then, as though conscious of discourtesy, he added, with a catch in his throat, 'I understand. I know what you want to say. But don't, that's all. It's over. Done with. Finished.'

The most eloquent prose could not have affected me more profoundly and I found myself struggling to suppress my tears. I had to take several deep breaths before I had my emotions under control and could lead the way back to where John Bradshaw and Eloise were waiting, amidst all the bustle, the comings and goings of a busy inn and a new day.

'Ready?' John Bradshaw spoke briskly. 'I only want to spend one night on the road, so we've some hard riding to do before dusk. The days are getting shorter, so we'd best be on our way. Roger, ride ahead with Mistress Gray, or Mistress Chapman, as we'd better get used to calling her. Lamprey, behind, with me! From now on, we're master and mistress, man and groom. Try to remember it, all three

159

of you.'

Eloise gave him her most winning smile. Philip and I said nothing.

It was not the cheeriest of journeys. Once the noise of London was left behind, we were enveloped in the peculiar soundlessness of a winter's day. Birds wheeled silently overhead, while a sullen wind had begun stripping the trees. The people we passed were disinclined to talk – they were too cold or too busy – and John Bradshaw pressed us forward, discouraging any friendly overtures that might have been made by either side. We did stop once for a draught of cider at a cider press, but the man who served us could do nothing but moan dismally about the poor apple harvest, a result of the terrible weather that had gripped the country for the past eighteen months, causing misery and famine throughout the length and breadth of the land.

It was little better at the wayside inn where we ate a dinner of bread and cheese and drank yet more cider – Kent, like my native Somerset, being apple country, where the orchards foamed and frothed in springtime, but were now struggling to produce a decent crop of fruit. The landscape also yielded a view of oast houses, but hops, we learned had also been disastrously affected by the recent weather. In the woods and forest, we passed a number of swineherds watching while the animals they tended foraged for beech nuts and acorns among the roots of the trees, but they, too, were taciturn and meagre of speech. All but one did nothing more than grunt a reply to our greetings, and that one merely recommended us to watch out for armed robber bands and to have our cudgels at the ready.

'Food's scarce. They'm desperate men, masters. And lady,' he added, catching sight of Eloise.

We thanked him and rode on, the blown branches of the trees rattling like angry skeletons. Every now and then a watery sun broke through a growing pall of cloud, but by early afternoon, when we stopped to let the horses drink at a little stream, a dark, rough, brown streak of troubled water, we were all chilled to the marrow. Eloise asked me to look in her left-hand saddlebag for a pair of gloves she had brought with her, but John Bradshaw forestalled me.

'I'm the servant, mistress,' he reminded her. 'You must remember to ask me to perform these services.'

He seemed to take longer than I thought strictly necessary to find the gloves – a fine leather, lined with that thin, cochineal-dyed wool known as scarlet – and I wondered if he had snatched the opportunity to look swiftly through some of her belongings. Perhaps, like me, he was growing uneasy about the costliness of quite a few of her possessions.

By the time we reached Rochester on the River Medway, the great castle, set on its high chalk cliff, dominating the town, it was almost dark, and the four of us were cold, saddle-sore, ravenous and so bone-weary that we could barely speak. I don't recollect the name of the inn we stayed at – I was too tired even to notice it – but it was in the shadow of the cathedral and offered Eloise and myself some excellent fare. There was a particularly fine pigeon pie, as I remember, which at any other time would have had me calling for more, but I could barely keep my eyes open long enough to eat it. (Eloise informed me the following day that I had also swallowed two portions of fruit syllabub, but I had no memory of them.) When the pair of us were finally shown to our bedchamber by an obsequious landlord, where our saddlebags had already been bestowed, we were both too exhausted even to notice the embarrassment of our first night together in the same room, let alone the hideous awkwardness of sharing a bed. I must have stripped, because in the morning I was wearing only my shirt, and so must she in order to don her night-rail, but neither of us could recall anything about it. It was only when we opened our eyes in the morning, and stared into one another's faces, that we realized our fictional life as man and wife had actually begun.

'Well,' Eloise said, dragging herself into a sitting position and hugging her raised knees, 'that wasn't so bad, was it?' She stretched and almost immediately groaned. 'Dear heaven, I feel as though I've been kicked all over by a mule.' She frowned. 'Why? It wasn't like this when we were travelling to Scotland.'

I, too, sat up. 'It was a much longer journey but not at such a determined pace. Bradshaw is set on getting us to Dover by tonight. He's afraid the weather's going to turn nasty and the autumn gales make sailing impossible for days, maybe even weeks. I understand that most people doing the ride from London to Dover also stop a night at Canterbury, but he'll make us do the rest of the journey today, if he possibly can.' I eased my body against the pillows. 'I know what you mean.'

She giggled suddenly. 'You do appreciate that we're now the master and mistress, and can therefore order the going as we please?' she asked. 'If we say that we're not prepared to set forward until after dinner, and say it loudly in the presence of the landlord and other guests, there is nothing our "servant" can do about it. Shall we try it? It would be interesting to watch his face.'

I smiled but shook my head. 'I somehow don't think that John Bradshaw's a man to trifle with,' I advised, 'and I wouldn't attempt it if I were you.' I got out of bed, carefully pulling my rumpled shirt down around my knees for propriety's sake. 'I'm going downstairs to the pump in the yard, but I'll ask in the kitchen for some hot water to be sent up. Don't use it all. I need to shave.'

I slid between the bed curtains, closing them again behind me, and pulled on the brown hose that I had worn yesterday, then, wrapping myself in my cloak, went down to the yard, passing on my message to a pot boy whom I encountered at the bottom of the stairs. By the time I returned to the bedchamber, shivering and blue-knuckled, Eloise was in her under-shift, washing her face and neck before proceeding to her hands and arms. She indicated the gently steaming pitcher to one side of the bowl. 'There's your shaving water.'

I thanked her and went over to my saddlebags to retrieve my razor. I knew it was at the bottom of one of them. In fact, it was in the first one I opened, underneath my blue hose and yellow tunic, but as I walked slowly back across the room to pour hot water into a second bowl, thoughtfully provided by the landlord, I had a distinct recollection of packing my yellow tunic on top of the hose. I told myself not to be silly, but I was certain that I could remember seeing yellow as I had fastened the saddlebag straps. Feeling that I was making something out of nothing, I kept quiet, leaving Eloise to prattle away and giving only random answers, but as soon as I had finished shaving, I went on my knees beside the other bag, unstrapped it and examined its contents.

My spare shirt lay on top of my second-best boots – much patched and mended – just as I had packed them, but my knife, which I had carefully placed within the folds of the shirt, was lying loose at the bottom of the bag, still sheathed but most definitely not where I had put it. Had it just worked free of its own accord? That was possible, considering the jolting the saddlebags had received yesterday. Or had someone gone through my belongings while I slept? Heaven knew, my sleep had been deep enough for me to miss the Last Trump had it sounded and I felt certain that anyone could have entered the bedchamber during the night without me hearing. Or Eloise could have got out of bed and examined the bags and I should have been none the wiser.

I went down to breakfast still wondering if I were not being unnecessarily suspicious, when I was brought up short by the sight of someone already seated at a table in the ale room, eating his porridge.

It was, once again, the smart young gent of the blue feather.

Ten

He glanced up as I entered, then rose, hand outstretched. 'Master Chapman, I presume. Please allow me to introduce myself. William Lackpenny, at your service.'

Close to, he was a little older than I had thought him – somewhere around twenty-five would have been my guess, but I don't believe I ever did learn his correct age. He was good-looking in a foxy kind of way, although his reddish hair and lean features might well have contributed to that impression. The eyes, now regarding me so limpidly, were hazel.

Taken completely aback, a dozen thoughts rioting through my head, I realized that I must be looking far more surprised – shocked, even – than the situation warranted. Hastily sketching a smile, I asked, 'How–how do you know my name?'

'I'm staying here myself. I saw you and your wife and servants come in last night and asked the landlord who you were. The fact is, I'm hoping you'll grant me a favour.'

I heard the door behind me open and close again. The next second, Eloise was standing by my side, looking enquiringly, and with considerable interest, at our new acquaintance.

'Master Lackpenny, my dear, who's staying here. Master Lackpenny, my ... my wife.'

I was waiting for some start of recognition on Eloise's part, and was readying myself to distract the young man's attention, when I recollected that she would have no cause to recognize him. She had never set eyes on him until the evening before last, on the water-stairs, and even then, had he claimed her attention, which was extremely unlikely, my antics had diverted her.

'Oh, please! Not Master Lackpenny,' was the instant response. 'Friends and acquaintances never call me anything but Will.'

'And do you always make friends this quickly, Master Will?' Eloise asked coyly, simpering in a way that made me want to slap her.

He laughed but, I thought, backed off a little at this open invitation to dalliance. 'Ah, well, the truth is, Mistress Chapman, as I was saying to your husband when you came in, I'm hoping you and he will grant me a favour.'

'Of course,' she said.

'As long as it's within our power,' I amended firmly.

'Aha! A wise man!' Will Lackpenny smiled ingratiatingly. 'Your husband won't commit himself, Mistress Chapman, until he knows the nature of my request.'

'You're right, sir. He's a very careful man.' Eloise gazed at me fondly and heaved a doting little sigh. 'No woman could ask for a better husband.'

I was going to have trouble with her, I could see that.

'What is it you want, Master Lackpenny?' I demanded.

He smiled again. He smiled a lot. 'The fact is, I'm travelling to Dover and thence to France on sudden business. Foolishly – very foolishly – because I wanted to take ship before the winter weather made the Channel crossing too hazardous, I set out alone. But there are too many dangers on the road to make travelling by oneself a comfortable experience, so when the landlord told me that you and your party are also bound for Dover, I wondered if you would allow me to journey with you.'

'We shall be delighted,' Eloise confirmed without giving me a chance to say anything. 'Won't we, sweetheart?' Again she gave me that adoring smile.

'Delighted,' I agreed stiffly.

But what else could I have said in the circumstances? If, as I half suspected, he already knew who I was and why I was on my way to France, it was up to me to keep him guessing as much as possible. But if, which was equally possible, he was an innocent bystander who just happened to have aroused my wrongful suspicions, then not by word or look must I hint at being other than I seemed. One thing was certain, however: I must consult with John Bradshaw as soon as I could.

'That's settled, then.' He beamed at us. 'You'll want to be setting out as soon as you've eaten, I daresay. I'll go and make certain my horse is saddled and my gear packed. I'll see you in about half an hour in the stables.'

I can't pretend I was a scintillating breakfast companion: I was too wrapped up in my own thoughts. Eloise felt neglected.

'Thank the good Lord I'm not really your wife,' she remarked waspishly across the table, but remembering to lower her voice to a whisper, 'if you're as morose as this every morning.'

'I usually have better company,' I snapped back.

She turned white with anger, and her lips thinned in a most unattractive manner. We

168

were heading for a major quarrel and I could well imagine John Bradshaw's reaction to such a state of affairs.

I forced myself to smile and reached for her hand. 'I'm sorry. Forgive me. Such rudeness was unpardonable. It's just that ... I've a lot on my mind.'

She returned the pressure of my fingers. 'Are you worried about this William Lackpenny travelling with us? Don't be. As long as we all act naturally, he'll be no trouble. I've met his sort before. All he's really interested in is himself and other people being interested in him. A coxcomb. He won't suspect a thing.'

'Then stop trying to flirt with him,' I said acidly, then kicked myself mentally for creating dissension again.

But to my surprise, this seemed to please her.

'Roger, I do believe you're jealous.' She smiled.

Jealous? I was just about to make a stinging retort when honesty made me pause. Could she be right? Never! Or could she? She must have seen something in my face because she chuckled mischievously and rose from the table, smoothing down her skirt. Today she was wearing the garnet-coloured gown with the simple leather girdle and gold chain in which I had first seen her dressed as a woman. I had a sudden, vivid recollection of her in her boy's clothing, travelling with the army in the summer, straight and slim as a young sapling. I felt a sudden urge to take her in my arms and kiss her, but fortunately the memory also reminded me that she could be treacherous. If for no other reason, it was as well not to let her get too close to me. Or me to her: it cut both ways.

There was a knock at the ale-room door and John Bradshaw came in, looking none too pleased.

'I understand we're taking that whipper-snapper with us,' he said in a low voice. He lifted a hand. 'All right. No need to explain how it happened. Tells me he asked you out-right, so I don't suppose there was much you could do except agree. But for the sweet Virgin's sake, watch what you say in front of him. My guess is he's not such a fool as he looks. Lord!' His mood lightened. 'You ought to see the hat he's wearing. A pointy thing with a great blue feather. Behave yourselves and try not to laugh.'

With that, he was gone, except for a parting shot instructing us not to dawdle. The sun was up and he was anxious to be on the road.

I was surprised, when I at last set foot out of doors, to discover that the morning had sud-denly grown colder and that everything was beginning to freeze. I tested a puddle with the toe of my boot and found it solid ice. Trapped in its depth was a cluster of bubbles like a shower of tiny, pale green stars. My hands burned with cold as I mounted my horse and took the reins, and I drew my cloak more tightly around me. Eloise, too, was muffled to the eyes in her grey camlet cloak, the hood pulled well forward to shield her face from the wind, a pair of gauntleted gloves covering her hands. John Bradshaw wore his good frieze cloak, hat and sensible leather boots, and I was glad to see that Philip had also acquired from somewhere similarly warm garments to protect him against the bitter chill. But it was Master Lackpenny who arrested the attention. In addition to the hat that I had come to know so well, he was enveloped in a scarlet fur-lined cloak – although, on closer inspection, I recognized the fur as merely rabbit – matching boots of scarlet leather and a pair of doe-skin gloves, a tribute to the glove-maker's art. He bestrode a showy chestnut and looked altogether too fine for our party, in spite of my new clothes and Eloise's efforts at refinement.

We set off at a decent pace, and for the first stage of the journey were mainly silent. All I really remember, until we stopped eventually for a dinner of cheese and apple pasties and small beer at a remote wayside inn, was the smell of the cold air and the thud of the horses' hooves as they struck sparks from the frost-bitten earth. After we had eaten, however, and rested for half an hour, we mounted once again and continued southwards at a fair pace, although this mode of travelling necessitated frequent rests to feed and water the horses.

It was during one such pause that Eloise

said roundly we must change our plans and stop at Canterbury for the night. There was no way she could continue with our original plan to cover the forty-odd miles between Rochester and Dover in a single day. Moreover, she was unwell. We all knew what that meant, but I was appalled to find myself thrust into such an intimate situation with a woman who was not my wife. For his part, John Bradshaw was silently fuming over his inability to argue the point with her, William Lackpenny's unwanted presence limiting him to the role of servant and deferential silence.

Lackpenny, himself, agreed with Eloise.

'I must say–' he beamed at me – 'I thought you by far too optimistic to imagine you could travel from Rochester to Dover in just one day, particularly–' here he bowed gallantly in Eloise's direction – 'with a lady in the party. Don't worry. Leave everything to me. There's a cosy little inn in the lee of Canterbury Cathedral where I'm well known to the landlord. Besides,' he added, 'even if you'd reached Dover tonight, there might have been little, if any, likelihood of getting a ship first thing tomorrow morning.'

He had a point, and a good one. Furthermore, when we finally reached the coast, everything depended on the wind and the tides. There was a possibility that we could be trapped at Dover for several days.

'Master Lackpenny's right,' I said, trying to speak with the authority of the leader of the party and avoiding John Bradshaw's fulminating eye.

Again, as my servant, he could do nothing but agree, though it went against the grain with him, I could tell. However, once we had entered the town and settled into Will Lackpenny's 'cosy little inn', I think even he was relieved to be out of the wind and biting cold. When I had seen Eloise installed in our bedchamber with our saddlebags, I went in search of him, finding him still in the stables, bullying poor Philip.

'Just get on with things and keep your mouth shut,' he was saying as I entered. He turned and saw me and made a bad-tempered grimace. 'This journey is not turning out as I planned it,' he went on savagely. 'If we're not careful, Olivier le Daim will have left Paris before we even arrive. We'll have to spend at least one night in Calais and then at least two more on the road before we get there. This damn Lackpenny attaching himself to us has been a disaster. All right! All right! I agree you couldn't have refused him.'

'Besides,' I said, leaning against the door of the chestnut's stall and absentmindedly patting his rump, 'Mistress Gray is unwell. You heard her say so. The onset of the flux is always the most painful part of it, at least so Adela tells me.'

'Well, she'll have to travel tomorrow, painful or not,' he snapped back. 'Did you want something? Why did you come to find me?'

'I need to talk to you. Alone.'

He raised his eyebrows and regarded me

173

thoughtfully. 'Right,' he said. 'After supper, tell the other two you have some instructions to give me and meet me here, in the stables. We can go into one of the empty stalls. Philip, you can make yourself scarce. Go and have a drink in the ale room.'

Philip nodded without saying anything. In fact, he had said practically nothing all day yesterday or today except 'yes' and 'no' and 'thank you'. And even those meagre words had been little more than grunts. He continued to be sunk in the black despair that had gripped him ever since Jeanne's death. I went up to him and put my arm about his shoulder.

'Philip—' I was beginning, but he thrust me off.

'Leave me alone, Roger.'

I shrugged, hurt and offended.

'Very well! If that's how you want things.' I turned. 'After supper, then, Jack. Here.'

He nodded, eyeing Philip inimically. 'He'll get over it,' he said to me.

'He'll have to,' I agreed coldly, still smarting from my rebuff, and without looking at my old friend again, I returned to the bed-chamber.

Eloise was seated on the narrow window seat, still huddled in her cloak.

'I'll sleep on the floor tonight,' I said abruptly. 'Then you can have the bed to yourself.'

'What?' She stared at me for a moment uncomprehendingly. Then she laughed. 'Oh, I see,' she said. 'There's no need. Trust a man

174

to jump to the wrong conclusion.'

'It was what you implied,' I answered indignantly.

She hesitated before admitting, 'Well, perhaps. But you can be easy. I shall not be wearing the red rose for another three weeks.'

'Then why...?'

'As a matter of fact,' she began, looking uncomfortable, 'while we were eating our pasties this morning, Master Lackpenny asked me if there was any way of changing your mind about pressing on to Dover today. He not only thought it too tiring but also considered it foolish as we should be travelling the last miles after sundown, in the dark and the cold. Besides which...' She faltered to a stop.

'Besides which?'

'He was hoping to meet some friends here. Friends who are, like him – like us – on the way to France. I promised him I would do what I could. So ... I lied a little. It makes sense to stop for the night,' she added defensively, watching my face. 'We're all tired and hungry, and although we're travelling south, the weather is getting very much colder.'

'You ... you took it upon yourself to oblige Master Lackpenny?' I gasped. 'For God's sake, woman, are you out of your senses? You know how secret our mission is and that we may be short of time.'

'As to the secrecy,' she retorted with spirit, 'it seems to me it would have looked far more suspicious for us to have insisted on hurrying on to Dover tonight in spite of fatigue and the obviously worsening weather. Concerning the time, who's to say positively that Cousin Olivier will turn up in Paris at all? The whole expedition may be a fool's errand.'

She had a point – two points – I was bound to agree, and without divulging what I already knew about William Lackpenny, any argument I could offer would crumble before the force of her logic. In any case, we were here now, in this pleasant inn, in the warm and the dry, and there was nothing I could do to change the situation. When I had un-burdened myself to John Bradshaw tonight, I must discuss with him the advisability of also taking Eloise into my confidence.

And who were these people my smart young gent was meeting in Canterbury? They must surely be local, I reasoned, or he would have journeyed with them from the start, instead of by himself. Or, then again, had his solitary ride from London been just part of a well-laid plan? Had he been waiting there, at Rochester, ready to insinuate himself into our company with the plea of being on his own? My head was bursting with unanswered questions, but at least Eloise had relieved me of one worry and the prospect of sleeping on the floor for the next few nights.

It was a brief respite, however. When, after washing and changing our travel-stained clothes, Eloise and I – one of us a treat in blue and yellow, she in green – descended to the parlour for supper, we found Will Lackpenny already there, talking to a tall, thin, bearded man with a slight stoop and his much younger – his very much younger – very attractive, round-faced, blue-eyed wife. I felt Eloise's grip tighten on my arm. You could, as the saying goes, have cut her animosity towards this seductive young creature with a knife.

I don't know if Will Lackpenny noticed it or not: he certainly gave no sign of being aware of any tension.

'Allow me,' he said sunnily, 'to introduce my good friends Master Robert Armiger and his wife, Jane. They have been here since midday.'

As I extended my hand and uttered the usual platitudes of greeting, it struck me that Master Armiger was probably a good thirty years older than his spouse. His hair, brown, threaded with grey, like his beard, was thinning at the temples, and the stoop became more pronounced when he stood up. But there was an undoubted air of affluence about him, not to mention arrogance, and the way he spoke to, and about, the pretty little thing at his elbow suggested that he knew he had married beneath him. Jane Armiger, for her part, seemed in awe of her husband, as well she might be – admiring but resentful at one and the same time.

'You've come far, Master Armiger?' I asked, as the five of us took our places around the long table and waited for the landlord to bring in our meal.

'London, like yourselves. Or so I'm told by

Will here.'

His answer took me by surprise, and I turned an enquiring look on our travelling companion. He understood it perfectly.

'Master and Mistress Armiger left London a day ahead of me,' he explained eagerly. 'I ... er ... It was impossible for me to leave on Wednesday. There was business I had to see to that evening.'

And little do you know that I know what it was, I thought to myself. You had to attend Edward Woodville to Baynard's Castle. I merely inclined my head.

'You have business in France, Master Armiger?' Eloise enquired, as bowls of leek soup were brought to the table by the landlord's wife. She was followed by her husband, bearing a lordly dish on which sat one of the fattest capons I have ever seen. This he placed reverently on the sideboard and began carving it into succulent slices. The smell of the gravy alone made my mouth water.

Robert Armiger puffed out his thin chest and shook his head. The smile he gave Eloise was appreciative but condescending. I could amost hear her gritting her teeth. I chuckled silently. 'I have no need to work, Mistress Chapman.' It still gave me a shock to hear her called by that name. 'I am a man of substance. No, we go to France to visit my wife's French relatives.'

Eloise turned impulsively towards Jane Armiger, her manner, until now notably frosty, immediately thawing. 'My mother was

French!' she exclaimed. 'Was yours?'

The other woman shook her head. 'No, my grandmother, my father's mother. She was one of Duchess Cicely's sewing-women in Rouen, and by the time the Duke and Duchess of York returned to England, she had married my grandfather and so came with him.'

'Not a seamstress, you silly little goose,' her husband reproved her. His words were indulgent, but there was more than a hint of annoyance in his tone. 'A tiring-woman. Maybe even a lady-in-waiting. According to your dear mama, your grandmother tended to be vague about such things. Like you.'

Oh, yes, Robert Armiger certainly had his fair share of pride, but I suppose with a name like that, perhaps he had a right to be. One of his ancestors must have been the carrier of arms for a knight and may eventually have been entitled to bear his own. It was more than any of the rest of us could boast. Meantime, my interest in Mistress Armiger had increased fourfold. Was there any possibility, I wondered, of her grandmother ever having spoken to her about the York household in Rouen? Had any scandal concerning the duchess been mentioned? I must try to get her on her own and find out.

As we started on the capon, Robert Armiger asked the inevitable question: 'And what is your business in France, Master Chapman?'

Now for it. 'I'm a haberdasher,' I answered blandly, and hoped it sounded convincing.

179

'I'm hoping to sell some wares as well as buy new stock while I'm in Paris. My wife also hopes to see at least one of her French relations.' Which was true enough.

'A haberdasher.' There was something in the way Master Armiger repeated the word that told me he thought little of my occupation. Not that it worried me. The less I saw of him, the better. His airs and graces could give one the bellyache if one was exposed to them too long.

But it suddenly seemed that this could well be the case.

'I've asked Master Armiger and his fair wife to honour us by joining our party for the rest of the trip to France,' Will Lackpenny announced, delicately wiping gravy from his chin with the cuff of one sleeve. 'In any case, they and I were going to travel together once we had met up here, but I can't just abandon you and Mistress Chapman. Therefore the solution is for us all to ride together.' He turned to Robert Armiger. 'If that would be your wish, sir.' (Unctuous little bastard!)

'Oh, by all means!' Armiger waved his spoon nonchalantly in the air. 'As you say, Lackpenny, you can't just abandon these people.'

Eloise choked over a sliver of capon and hastily swallowed some wine. I didn't trust myself to speak. There was no need, however, for either of us to say anything. Will Lackpenny was prattling happily on, dispensing information regarding his friends.

'Master and Mistress Armiger have been staying this past week in Baynard's Castle as the guests of Mistress Armiger's brother.'

My head came up at that, and I pressed Eloise's foot warningly under the table with one of mine. Say nothing: we haven't been there, my eyes signalled to her. But I needn't have bothered. She was no fool: she had beauty and brains in equal measure.

'Baynard's Castle,' she breathed reverently. 'Did you by any chance see my lord of Gloucester? Or his mother?'

Robert Armiger gestured again with his spoon. 'My brother-in-law is a member of the Duchess of York's household,' he said grandly, and left us to draw our own conclusions.

Eloise and I both tried to look impressed and, judging by the gratified expression on our new companion's face, succeeded.

The capon had, by this time, been supplanted by an apple tart, flavoured with cloves and cinnamon, and thick cream filled an earthenwere pitcher. Eloise sighed, obviously thinking of her figure, but couldn't resist a second helping. Indeed, none of us could, and we finally rose from the table a good deal heavier than when we sat down. I concealed a grin as I remembered the fat purse Timothy had given me, with strict instructions not to spend a groat more than I had to. 'This amount is just in case of emergencies, Roger! I want most of it back, if possible. My budget is limited.' It looked as if he were going to be disappointed.

'If you will all excuse me,' I said, 'I must speak with John Bradshaw about the arrangements for tomorrow. I said I'd meet him in the stables after supper.'

I noticed Eloise glance sharply at me, but no one else, of course, saw anything unusual in this decision.

'Don't be long, then,' she admonished me in a very wifely spirit. 'When the table's cleared, we might while away the evening with a game or two of three men's morris. I see a board and counters up there on the shelf.'

William Lackpenny endorsed this proposal with great enthusiasm, in no way dampened by Master Armiger saying austerely that he would prefer to sit by the fire and read a book.

'A good idea, sir. We shan't disturb you too much, I hope, with our nonsense.'

'Meantime,' said Eloise, 'I propose taking a short walk outside, just to get a breath of air. Would you care to join me, Mistress Armiger?'

'Oh, yes, indeed. If ... That is if...' She looked timidly at her husband.

'Oh, go! Go!' he answered irritably. 'But don't start snivelling tomorrow that you have a rheum.'

'No, I won't, I promise. I shall wrap up warmly.' She smiled at Eloise. 'I'll just run upstairs and get my cloak.'

'And I must have one, too.' Eloise turned to me with a winning smile. 'Sweetheart, will you go up to our bedchamber and fetch mine

182

for me? The grey one that I've been wearing for the past two days.'

What could I say without appearing a curmudgeon? I noticed that Robert Armiger didn't offer to get his wife's cloak. But then, she didn't ask him to.

I followed Jane Armiger upstairs and I followed her down again, a neat little figure in a brown cloak.

A familiar figure in a brown cloak.

I realized with a shock that I was looking at the back of the same young woman who had waited for William Lackpenny on the watersteps of Baynard's Castle just a few days ago.

Eleven

'You *have* been keeping things to yourself, my lad, haven't you?' John Bradshaw sounded amused rather than either reproachful or condemning.

He and I were sitting comfortably together on a bale of hay in an empty stall of the inn stables, a candle in its holder placed on a ledge just above the manger and suffusing the confined space with a warm, golden glow. From neighbouring stalls came the occasional shifting of hooves or a gusty breath blown through flaring nostrils as the horses of our party and those of Master and Mistress Armiger settled themselves for the night.

Bradshaw took a swig from a leather bottle that he had produced from some capacious pocket, then wiped the neck on his sleeve and handed it to me. I took a generous gulp of some wine I had never tasted before but which seemed to run like fire through my veins and made the world at large appear a much less harsh and hostile place.

'What is it?' I asked, but my companion shook his head and shrugged. He knew no more about fine wines than I did.

'Got friendly with one of the cellarers,' he said in explanation. 'Asked him to fill the bottle with something warming for a cold autumn evening.'

'Ever tasted that Scottish stuff?' I enquired. '*Usquebaugh* they call it. The water of life. More like liquid fire, if you ask me. Disgusting taste! Distilled from grain, so they say. No civilized person would touch it.' I drank another mouthful of wine before handing back the bottle, starting to wipe my mouth on the back of my sleeve and then remembering that I was wearing Master Taylor's handsome yellow tunic, which eventually had to be returned to him. (Timothy would not be pleased if he had to pay extra costs for damages incurred.) 'So!' I leaned forward, clasping my hands loosely between my knees. 'What do you think I ought to do?'

John Bradshaw stoppered the bottle and restored it to his pocket. 'Nothing you can do, is there? Not as far as confessing the error of your ways, I mean.' I opened my mouth to speak, but he waved me to silence. 'You don't have to go over all the reasons for your silence again, lad. I understand perfectly well. I know what Timothy can be like when he gets on his high horse. He's a good friend of mine and an equally good man at his job, but conceited ain't the word for him. Not to mince matters, he's an arrogant little sod. I don't know much about the duke, mind. Don't often come face to face with him, not like you. But I wouldn't care to get in his bad books. There's a forbidding look about him on occasions that makes me think he could be the wrong man to cross. I reckon he could be unforgiving if he took against you. Like the Woodvilles, for instance. It's a well-known fact that at one time or another the whole Woodville clan have done their best to win his friendship, knowing how much the king loves and esteems him, but even after all this while, he remains their enemy. Especially these past four, nearly five years since the Duke of Clarence's death, which people who are close to him say he blames them for. Anyway,' he continued, 'we're straying from the point. I'm just saying that I understand why you didn't tell Timothy and His Grace everything. So! Let's consider what we know.' He slid off the bale of hay, opened the door of the stall, peered up and down in the blackness, then shut us both in again and resumed his seat. 'No one about,' he announced. 'Lamprey's gone for his drink in the ale room. I told him not to hurry. We have the stable to ourselves. Now—'

'There's one thing I want to ask you,' I interrupted. He raised his eyebrows. 'Something that's only recently occurred to me. Last Wednesday evening, the evening I saw William Lackpenny in Edward Woodville's train–' he nodded – 'why wasn't it the king who gave the banquet to honour Earl Rivers and his brother? Or why wasn't he at least present at the banquet given by His Grace of Gloucester? The only answer that suggests itself to me is that King Edward was too ill to do either. Do you think I'm right?'

My companion prised a bit of his supper loose from between his front teeth before replying. 'Your solution could well be the correct one,' he admitted. 'The rumours circulating around Westminster all say that His Highness is a sick man. Sicker than he or anyone close to him will let on. Gossip infers that the queen is very worried, that there have been certain secret meetings between her and her brothers, that messengers between Westminster and the Prince of Wales's court at Ludlow have doubled in the past few weeks, that during his stay in London, between the end of the Scottish invasion and his return to Ludlow, Earl Rivers has been in daily contact with Her Grace.' John Bradshaw turned his head and regarded me curiously through the gloom. 'Why are you interested? Might this have any bearing on...?' He broke off abruptly. 'No! Say nought! I don't wish to be told anything. It's better that way.' He offered me another drink from his bottle, but I refused it. The stuff was potent and I needed to keep a clear head. He nodded understandingly, putting it away again. 'Now, as I was about to say before this digression, let's reckon up exactly what is known and what is surmise.

'First, two men have been killed by having their throats cut. That is fact. Their deaths might be linked to whatever it is you're up to in Paris for Duke Richard. Maybe, maybe not. Probable but not certain. You saw William Lackpenny in Stinking Lane at the time of the first murder, but other than that – which could well be pure chance – there seems to be nothing to connect him with anyone else except, you think, Mistress Armiger.'

'I'm sure she was the woman I saw with him on the water-steps at Baynard's Castle,' I insisted. 'And we know she and her husband have been staying there.'

'True,' John agreed. 'But she's young and pretty, Lackpenny is young and handsome, and Master Armiger is elderly and dull. On the face of it, nothing puzzling about that. Somehow or another, the two young people have met and been attracted to one another, leading to secret meetings. On the other hand, we also know that Lackpenny is a member of Edward Woodville's household, which might be significant. And we haven't yet discovered why Master Blue Feather is going to France. I'll leave that to you, Roger.

I can't ask him. I'm only the servant.'

'I'll set Eloise on to do it,' I said. 'She likes to exert her charms. In which case, I must tell her all that I've told you.'

John Bradshaw shifted his position on the hay. 'I think it would be as well,' he agreed. 'But not all of it. Just about Lackpenny and the Armigers. As for the rest, I can only reiterate: trust nobody, be suspicious of everyone, including Mistress Gray, and watch your back at all times. Even the Armigers may not be as innocent as they seem. But regarding this man you thought you saw being landed at the castle in the early hours of Wednesday morning, are you sure about this? You might have imagined it.'

'No.' I was definite. 'I did see someone. And I've told you what followed. There was the murder of the boatman Jeremiah Tucker and then, the same evening, the fellow in the common hall who went to great lengths not to be seen by me. Too much of a coincidence, you must agree.'

My companion pursed his lips but didn't contradict me. Instead, he sighed and stared in front of him for a moment or two before finally saying, 'There's a great deal going on here, Roger, that either makes perfect sense or none at all, depending how you view things.' He gave vent to a fat chuckle that started somewhere deep in his throat and emerged as a sort of chortle. He slapped me on the thigh. 'Which,' he went on, 'is about as unhelpful a remark as you could ever wish to

188

hear. I'm sorry, lad! You did right to tell me. Two of us on our guard is better than one. I might even instruct Lamprey to report if he notices anything he thinks vaguely suspicious. I shan't say why, of course.'

'How is he? He won't let me near him, not even to express my regrets.'

John Bradshaw snorted. 'He says barely anything. I'm beginning to think he's enjoying his grief, wallowing in it. Oh, all right!' This as I made a gesture of protest. 'Maybe I'm wrong. If I remember aright, he was always a bit of a surly beggar when we were young, soldiering together in France. He certainly seems to have thought the world of this young woman he married. Her death must have been a great blow to him.' He slid from the bale of hay as he spoke and I followed suit.

'I'd better get back,' I said. 'Eloise will be suspicious of my protracted absence. There will be questions.'

Again came that throaty chuckle and another slap, this time on the shoulder. 'My, my! You and she are really entering into the spirit of the thing. You're beginning to sound like an old married couple. You'll have to be careful, Roger.'

I realized with a shock of dismay that John Bradshaw was right: I should have to be careful. I waited while he checked on the horses: then we walked together the length of the stables. It was as we were passing the last stall, which also appeared to be empty, that I stopped suddenly, causing John to bump into me and tread hard on my heels.

'What's the matter?' he hissed.

'I thought I heard someone moving in there. Don't worry! I'm just jumpy. If it's anything at all, it's most likely to be rats.'

'We'll see about that,' he whispered. 'Just take your leave as loudly as you can and bang the outer door.'

I did as he bade me, adding a yawn for good measure as I called, 'Goodnight!' He grunted in reply, then placing a finger to his lips, pounced forward, pushing the stall door wide and entering, his candle held aloft, the flame illuminating the narrow interior and flickering in some unidentified draught. I peered over his shoulder, but his bulk filled the doorway and all I could see were the shadows dipping and curtseying across the walls.

'There's no one here,' he said at last. 'It must have been a rat, like you said.' He snuffed the candle-flame between thumb and forefinger, grimacing at me as he did so. 'Calm yourself, lad.' We emerged into the cold night air. 'If you start jumping at every sound, you'll put yourself in danger. You won't hear the ones you ought to be listening for.'

With which parting shot, he went off to the kitchens, where he and Philip were sleeping, and I made my way back to the inn parlour to find a noisy game of three men's morris in progress.

★ ★ ★

'You were a long time in the stables, talking to John Bradshaw.' Eloise accused me as we undressed for bed.

It was an embarrassing situation. Last night, we had been too tired to be conscious of anything but the need to tumble between the sheets and fall into an exhausted slumber. Tonight, however, we were uncomfortably aware of each other's every move. Eloise had drawn the bed-curtains and vanished behind them, occasionally asking me to pass her things, like her night-rail, that she had forgotten to take with her. I was careful to thrust my arm between the drapes no further than just above the wrist, and retired to the furthest, darkest corner of the room to shed my own clothes, except of course for my shirt. I was quite glad, therefore, to divert my thoughts of spending a night by her side with a little conversation.

'There were things we had to discuss,' I said.

'Such as?'

'I'll tell you in a moment or two, when I've cleaned my teeth.'

I found the piece of willow bark I always carry with me and rubbed it around the inside of my mouth, by which time Eloise had drawn back one of the curtains and was revealed sitting propped against the pillows, her fair hair curling attractively over her neat, shapely little head. She wrinkled her nose when she saw me. 'Don't you ever change your shirt to go to bed? Don't you have a night-shift?'

'I usually sleep naked,' I answered shortly and not altogether truthfully, but it had the desired effect of quietening her. 'Besides,' I went on, 'you've grown very nice all of a sudden, haven't you? What about all those sweaty soldiers you slept amongst while you were masquerading as a boy? I'll wager they didn't bother with night-shifts.'

'Oh, get into bed,' she retorted irritably, 'and stop evading my question. What were you and Master Bradshaw talking about all that time?'

I did as she said, ostentatiously keeping to my side of the mattress as far as possible without actually falling out again, and sitting bolt upright. Since leaving John at the kitchen door, I had had time to consider the advisability of following his instruction not to tell Eloise everything, only what I had seen concerning William Lackpenny and Jane Armiger. Indeed, I couldn't think how I had been foolish enough to suggest otherwise. I still knew nothing more about her and where her true sympathies lay than I had done five days ago. I realized with a shock that, in spite of the past, I was beginning to like and trust her, and that both emotions could be fatal to my safety and to the mission I was employed on for Duke Richard. I was going to have to watch myself and guard against the strange fascination she was starting to have for me. I reminded myself that sorcery was one of the charges against her dead master, the Scottish

Earl of Mar.

'Well?' she demanded when I continued to be mute.

'If you must know,' I told her at last, 'we were talking about Master Lackpenny and Mistress Armiger, both of whom I've seen before.' I proceeded to tell her about their meeting on the water-steps of Baynard's Castle and how I had noticed the former landing on Wednesday evening from Edward Woodville's barge.

She was immediately intrigued, as I had known she would be, by the implied romance, but she was quicker-witted than that. 'And you said nothing to Master Plummer?' she queried with raised eyebrows and a little accusatory smile hovering on her lips.

'It didn't seem important at the time,' I excused myself, saying nothing of having seen my smart young gent in Stinking Lane.

'Not even when you found him to be a Woodville adherent?' She regarded me quizzically for a second or two, then burst out laughing. 'Confess it, Roger! You were afraid of a tongue-lashing because you'd omitted to mention him earlier.' She adopted Timothy's scathing, pompous tone when he was riding his high horse. '"Nothing is ever too small or too insignificant to be kept to oneself in this business. Your safety and the safety of others may well depend on sharing every single scrap of information. Do I make myself clear?"'

I had intended strenuously to deny being

afraid of Timothy, but her impersonation was so vivid and so accurate that I could only join in her mirth and smile ruefully. 'Perhaps,' I admitted.

She reached over and patted my hand where it lay on the coverlet. 'I shouldn't let it worry you,' she advised. 'I feel certain that you've merely stumbled on a secret love affair that has nothing to do with anyone or anything else but themselves. The fact Will is a member of Sir Edward Woodville's household is probably just a coincidence.'

Like the fact that he was on his way to France? Like the fact that he had been lying in wait for us – for that was how it was beginning to seem to me now – at Rochester? Like the fact that he had arranged to meet the Armigers, also making their way across the Channel, at Canterbury? I said none of this to Eloise, but as I have remarked before, she was nobody's fool.

'If the Armigers are going to France,' she pointed out, reading my thoughts, 'to visit her kinfolk, then don't you think her lover – if that's really what he is – would find some excuse to go, too? Will and the lady would have arranged this rendezvous here, in Canterbury. I doubt if Master Armiger had anything to say in the matter. A wily woman – and I can tell you that Jane Armiger is neither so silly nor so ingenuous as she looks: I know the sort – could easily persuade a doting husband of almost anything. She may seem afraid of him, and doubtless, in some respects, she has reason to be, but she can twist him round her little finger when she wants. You saw tonight how she coaxed him to play at three men's morris when all he wanted was to sit by the fire and read.' Eloise gave my hand another pat. 'No, no! I don't think there's any mystery about those three, not now you've told me about that meeting on the water-stairs. When he saw us at Rochester, Will must have considered how much more innocent his and Jane Armiger's meeting here would appear if he were attached to another party.'

'Yes, you're right,' I agreed.

But my relief was limited. Her reasoning, as far as it went, was good, except that I knew she was only in partial possession of the facts. Once again, I was tempted to take her fully into my confidence: she looked so pretty, sitting there a few inches away from me, those violet-blue eyes regarding me so limpidly, her mouth so soft and tender. Although I even had my own mouth open to speak, common sense reasserted itself at the crucial moment. I forced myself to think of the last time I had seen her before our recent meetings in London. There had been nothing vulnerable or yielding about her then, and however much she protested the opposite, I still could not bring myself to believe in her innocence.

She abruptly withdrew her hand from mine. She had sensed my change of mood and was not a woman to waste time trying to recover lost ground. She probably told herself that

195

there would be other opportunities. She could wait.

'I'm tired,' she said, lying down with her back to me and nestling into the pillows. 'Goodnight. God be with you. Sleep well.'

I grunted something ungracious in reply, feeling conscience-stricken and yet annoyed with myself because I had no cause to be. I blew out the solitary candle I had left burning on the table on my side of the bed, pulled the curtain to shut out the draughts and the glow from the dying embers of the fire, and settled down myself, my back also turned towards her.

It must have been an hour or so later when I felt her hand on my shoulder, shaking me awake. My first thought was that this was an approach I could well do without, but there was something about the urgency of her voice as she whispered, 'Wake up!' that made me revise my opinion.

'What is it?' I mumbled, heaving myself into a sitting position.

'There's someone in the room,' she hissed.

I listened but could hear nothing. 'Nonsense!' I said loudly.

'Quiet, you fool,' she breathed in my ear, but then cursed. 'There! You've frightened them away. Didn't you hear the door being opened and closed? Whoever it was has gone.'

I got out of bed, pulling back the curtains and lighting the candle. Long shadows leaped up the walls, but nothing else stirred. 'You must have been mistaken,' I said.

She also had got out of bed and now came to stand beside me. 'No. I distinctly heard someone moving.'

I went to the door and, opening it, peered into the blackness of the passageway outside. I held the candle aloft, but within its flickering radiance nothing moved. The only sound was the rhythmic snoring from behind one of the other closed doors. Master Armiger, or perhaps William Lackpenny, was sleeping off a too-large supper, partaken of too greedily and speedily for good digestion.

I withdrew into our bedchamber, closing, and this time not only latching but also bolting the door.

'There's no one there,' I said. 'You're imagining things. If someone had entered, I should have heard them. I'm a light sleeper.'

'You sleep like the dead,' Eloise retorted angrily. 'Even when you're tossing and turning and mumbling to yourself in your sleep, it's impossible to rouse you. You're like a log.'

The criticism stung me. I had always prided myself that I slept with one ear open, ready for any trouble that might be brewing – a man on the alert for any danger menacing himself or his family. I was on the verge of an indignant protest when I noticed that she was shivering, whether from cold or fear I had no means of knowing. But I did the instinctive thing and put an arm about her, drawing her close. She responded by returning the embrace.

'It's all right,' I comforted her. 'You saw me bolt the door. Nobody can get in.'

I was suddenly very aware of the warmth and shape of her body beneath the thin night-rail. I was also horrifyingly conscious of my own reaction, a reaction that must come to her attention at any moment. I hastily releas-ed her.

'Get back to bed,' I ordered harshly. 'The sheets will be like ice and we'll never get to sleep again.'

She made no move to obey, but did step away from me so that she was no longer sheltering within my arm.

'I can smell something,' she complained, sniffing delicately.

'What?' If I sounded irritable, it was be-cause I was not only furious with myself for the way in which I had responded to her closeness, but also because I was beginning to suspect her motives. Was this whole episode simply an attempt to seduce me? Had she really heard anything, or was it all a fabrica-tion?

'What can you smell?' I repeated, walking round to the opposite side of the bed. The fire was now quite out, the remains of the logs bearded with flaking ash.

'Dung, horses, the stables,' she answered. Her tone was as cold as the dead fire on the hearth.

I was about to tell her not to be stupid when I noticed the smell myself. There was defi-nitely a whiff of something equine. Then I recollected and, by the light of the candle-flame examined my boots, which I had discarded, along with my other clothes, in a heap at the end of the bed. The soles were still caked with mud and straw and manure from my visit to John Bradshaw. Silently, and a little defiantly, I held them out for Eloise's inspection.

Her strictures on my grosser habits, such as not wiping my feet before coming indoors, were delivered with all the venom of a woman whose schemes had again been thwarted. At least, that was how it appeared to me.

But as she got back into the cold bed, she reiterated, 'Someone was in this room, Roger, whatever you may think. And I know exactly what you think! But try not to be misled by your own conceited wishes.'

Without giving me time to catch my breath in order to phrase a suitable reply to this wicked calumny, she pulled the pillows down around her ears and the bedclothes up to meet them, leaving me standing at the foot of the bed feeling, and probably looking, re-markably foolish.

The remainder of our journey to Dover, the following day, was accomplished in almost complete silence between Eloise and myself, but the fact passed almost unnoticed in the general chatter of our enlarged party. Eloise and Mistress Armiger suddenly became great friends, their light-hearted chatter relieving them of the necessity of paying too much attention to their menfolk. Any animosity the former might have originally experienced towards the latter was submerged in the greater need to ignore my existence. As for myself, Will Lackpenny devoted himself to me and Master Armiger in equal measure, entertaining us and passing the weary miles with the sort of aimless conversation that needed little more than a polite smile or an infrequent nod of the head to give the impression that I was listening. The older man didn't even offer this much, seemingly sunk in his own all-absorbing reflections, but the fact that he made no interruption was enough encouragement for Will to continue with his artless prattle. John Bradshaw and Philip brought up the rear of our little cavalcade, exchanging nothing but the briefest and most necessary words concerning the journey.

To begin with, it was a day of sunshine and showers, the late-October sun occasionally emerging to stain fields and woodland pathways gold, but later on, towards midday, the sky grew overcast and the wind increased, blowing the clouds into an ever-changing panorama of shapes, the light that filtered between them becoming murky and unwholesome. A day for agues and the shivers. Each time I glanced back at John Bradshaw, his expression had grown a little more worried. The weather appeared to be worsening the nearer we got to the coast.

We faced the prospect of being stranded at

Dover for several days, perhaps much longer. My hopes rose. Maybe the crossing, everything, would have to be abandoned and we – Eloise, myself, John and Philip, that is – could return home.

Twelve

It was a hopeless dream, of course.

The weather had certainly worsened by the time we reached Dover, great squalls of wind and rain blowing in from the Channel, but no one was going home. John Bradshaw had been adamant about that, and there was no reason for the Armigers to abandon their journey to see Jane's French relations. Their time was their own and they could wait indefinitely for the weather to improve, but I did consider that William Lackpenny's might be limited, forcing him to return to his duties elsewhere.

Eloise was able to disabuse my mind of such a notion. 'He is, indeed, employed in the household of Sir Edward Woodville,' she told me, as we unpacked our saddlebags once again in the front bedchamber of the little quayside inn where we had all found accommodation for the night, and for however many more nights proved to be necessary.

'He is a gentleman-in-waiting, but has been granted an extended leave of absence by the steward to visit his sick mother.'

'In France?'

She laughed. 'No, stupid! In Salisbury. At least, that's what Master Steward believes. So you see, it would appear to be an afair of the heart, after all. In fact, he told me so and swore me to secrecy.'

'You seem to have wormed yourself well into his confidence,' I said, shaking out my yellow tunic, now looking somewhat crumpled from its frequent packing and unpacking. 'When did you discover all this?'

She gave a provocative smile, and for a moment I thought she was going to play silly, coquettish games with me, but then she said, 'Yesterday evening, after Mistress Armiger and I returned from our walk. We didn't stay out long, it was too cold, and Jane went upstairs to put away her cloak. During our absence, Master Armiger had also gone up to their bedchamber and it was a little while before they both came down again. A circumstance that I fancy didn't please our young friend overmuch, so he decided to flirt with me as a sort of revenge. I was able to extract quite a lot of information from him. I virtually accused him of being in the throes of an affair with her and he's so set up in his own conceit that he couldn't resist admitting it. They met, apparently, when he was sent to Baynard's Castle to arrange some of the details of the banquet with the Duchess of

York's high steward – like how many attendants Sir Edward would be bringing with him, their order of precedence at the table and so forth. He says it was love at first sight. He could tell right away that she was unhappy, and once he had clapped eyes on Robert Armiger, he could see why. Their friendship blossomed from there, and on the next occasion he visited the castle, she met him, by prior arrangement, at the top of the water-stairs. That must have been last Monday, when you saw them. The following day, Tuesday, Master Armiger was from home all morning, so Will went to call on Jane at her house near Aldersgate ... Now, why are you looking like that? As though you'd laid an egg?'

'Am I?' I queried, attempting to sound offhand and thanking heaven most devoutly for the interruption of a chambermaid arriving at that precise moment with a jug of hot water and the information that supper would be served in the inn parlour in half an hour's time. 'No reason. No reason in the world. I was just wondering if I wouldn't simply change my hose and wear this green tunic I have on with the blue. What do you think?'

She regarded me straitly, her head tilted to one side. 'I think you're trying to change the subject as well as your hose. But if you are going to continue wearing green, I shall put on my red dress. We don't want to look like twins.'

With which tart remark, she unfolded the

red gown from her saddlebag, along with a clean undershift, pulled the bed-curtains, as was becoming her habit, and vanished behind them.

'And don't use all the hot water shaving,' she admonished me.

I sat down on the window seat, listening with only half an ear to the drumming of the rain against the closed and bolted shutters, and to the wind whistling eerily between them and the oiled-parchment window panes. My mind was busy going over what Eloise had just told me.

If my smart young gent had spoken truly, then my sighting of him in Stinking Lane was explained. He had been on his way to Aldersgate to take advantage of Robert Armiger's absence and had had nothing to do with Humphrey Culpepper's death. But of course the question was, *had* he been telling the truth? He might well have been. On the other hand, if he was a Woodville spy and had been despatched to follow me and discover the reason for this journey to Paris on the Duke of Gloucester's behalf, he must have worked out by now that whatever Eloise learned she would pass on. Telling her was as good as telling me, and it was an explanation that fitted the facts as I must have grasped them over the past two days.

I sighed and got up to change my brown hose for the blue, then poured some of the hot water into an earthenware bowl in order to shave and wash my face. I felt travel-stained and weary and none too clean. To-morrow morning, whatever the weather, I should have to brave the pump in the inn yard, although stripping naked in this wind and rain held little appeal. (But I'd known worse. If you've never washed in the snow-broth of a Scottish burn or pump, you don't really understand what cold is.) I dragged a comb through my hair and rubbed my teeth with the willow bark, then sat and waited for Eloise to emerge from behind the bed-curtains, marvelling as she did so at how she always appeared sweet and fresh however many miles we had covered, and however tired she must be.

A particularly vicious gust of wind seized the shutters and rattled them like the teeth in an old man's head.

'How long do you think we shall be strand-ed here?' I asked miserably. Every day's delay added another seemingly interminable stretch to the time between me and my final arrival back in Bristol, where my family were eagerly awaiting my return. (Awaiting my return, anyway.)

Eloise glanced up from drying her face and hands, and smiled at me with a surprising amount of sympathy. 'Roger, I don't know,' she answered gently. 'Until this wind drops is all I can say. I did overhear the landlord tell-ing Master Armiger that there is a ship at anchor in the harbour, ready to sail to France once the weather breaks. *The Sea Nymph*, I think he said she was called. And once we're aboard, the crossing to Calais doesn't take long. A few hours. Now, if you're ready, shall we go downstairs? I don't know about you, but I could do with my supper.'

The Armigers and William Lackpenny were already in the inn parlour when Eloise and I entered. Jane Armiger was looking pale and slightly tearful, while her husband's face was blotched with angry red patches, as though they had been having a quarrel. Will Lackpenny, on the other hand, was his usual bumptious self, setting out to jolly everyone along and restore harmony to the evening ahead. He did cast an anxious glance at Jane Armiger once or twice, as though solicitous for her welfare, but he could hardly call Robert Armiger to account, as he would no doubt have dearly liked to do.

The inn had grown noisier since our arrival as those locals who had left the shelter of their own firesides and braved the weather were joined in the ale room by sailors from *The Sea Nymph* and another ship lying at anchor in the harbour. Only a narrow passageway, leading to the front door, separated the parlour from the ale room, and it seemed at times as though the general rowdiness – the guffaws, the shouting, the singing of bawdy songs – would drown out our own conversation. Robert Armiger, I could tell, was growing more incensed by the minute, and only the arrival of supper prevented his storming into the other room and presenting its occupants with a piece of his mind. A most ill-advised action had he done so, but fortunately a truly appetizing pigeon pie, followed by equally delicious apricot tartlets, the whole washed down with a light, amber, slightly musky-tasting wine, put him in a better humour. At any rate, he restricted himself to demanding, somewhat peremptorily it's true, but perfectly politely for all that, that the landlord bolted the outer door to discourage further incursions into the inn.

The landlord, a sensible fellow who plainly had no intention of carrying out this order, said nothing, merely muttering something under his breath that could have been mistaken for acquiescence. He was removing the last of the empty supper dishes, and had just instructed one of his assistants to make up the fire from the pile of logs at one side of the hearth, when a sudden lull in the noise from across the passage enabled us to distinguish the drum of hoof-beats on the slippery quayside cobbles. Immediately afterwards, a man's voice was raised, cursing and shouting for the stable boy, before being lost again in the howl of the wind and a crescendo of singing from the room opposite.

In spite of this, however, Jane Armiger's head jerked round, her whole body rigidly at attention, one forefinger slightly raised. 'That was Oliver's voice,' she said.

Her husband looked up from his book – a handsome folio bound in pale blue silk with silver tassels – and answered scathingly,

'Nonsense!'

For once, she felt strong enough to argue with him. 'It was, I tell you!' She had risen to her feet and was listening intently, but the uproar from the ale room made it impossible to hear anything else.

'Sit down, you silly child!' Robert Armiger snapped irritably. 'What on earth would your brother be doing here? He's snug somewhere inside Baynard's Castle, playing at dice, if I know him.'

He spoke, I thought, rather scathingly of his brother-in-law, decidedly at variance with his tone when he had first mentioned that worthy, the inference then having been that the young man held a position of some consequence in the Duchess of York's household.

'It is Oliver, I tell you,' Jane Armiger persisted, braving her husband's displeasure.

'Oh well! We shall soon find out,' William Lackpenny said peaceably, stepping nobly into the breach to protect his lady from another scolding.

Even as he spoke, the sound of the inn door being flung open, to be sent crashing back against the passage wall by the force of the wind, made further speculation useless for the moment. The landlord hurried from the room to greet the newcomer as someone possibly of importance and certainly from a distance. No local or sailor would be arriving on horseback.

Eloise turned her head. 'You are expecting your brother to join you, Mistress Armiger?'

she enquired.

It was Robert who replied. 'No! She is not!'

It struck me that he was very put out by the notion and I wondered why.

Eloise ignored this outburst. 'Jane?' she queried.

Jane fluttered a nervous glance in her husband's direction. 'As–as a matter of f–fact,' she stammered, 'Oliver d–did say he ... he might try to ... obtain leave of absence from Master Steward to ... to come with us to Paris.' She drew a deep breath and plunged on, 'He hasn't seen our aunt and cousins for several years now. He thought it would be a good opportunity for us to travel together. But when we left London, he still wasn't certain that he would be granted permission. He said if he were, he would ride hard and try to catch us up.'

It was obvious from Robert Armiger's face that this was the first he had heard of any such arrangement between the brother and sister. Throughout his wife's hesitant recital, his expression had been growing steadily more thunderous. There was alarm there, too, and unease. It occurred to me that he was ashamed of this Oliver, who was possibly of a more lowly status in the duchess's household than pleased the high and mighty Master Armiger.

This explanation had barely crossed my mind when the landlord came bustling back into the parlour, rubbing his hands in the manner of someone who has pleasant news to impart. He addressed Jane.

'Mistress Armiger!' He was smiling broadly. 'A happy surprise for you.' I saw Robert Armiger's expression stiffen with dismay. The landlord continued, flinging out his hands in what he was sure must be a shared delight, 'Your brother is here. He has caught you up.' He stood aside, beckoning to someone behind him to come in.

The doorway seemed suddenly blocked, all light from the passageway shut out, filled with an enormous specimen of humanity. Then the man stepped forward into the parlour, his arms held out to Mistress Armiger, dwarfing her. Dwarfing all of us, if it came to that, with his girth and height.

I recognized him at once.

It was the Duchess of York's master cook.

It was Goliath.

My first thought was that he would recognize me, and I stepped back into the corner shadows of the room.

Eloise had recognized him as well, from her brief glimpse of him as he had manhandled me into the common hall last Wednesday evening, but I was confident Goliath would not remember her: he had not, to the best of my recollection, even seen her. At the moment of my humiliation, she had been sitting some way away from the kitchen door. He had disappeared by the time she came to my rescue.

Second thoughts persuaded me that he was

unlikely to recognize me, either. Looking back on our unfortunate encounter, I realized that he had scarcely accorded me much real attention. He had been too anxious to be rid of me. He had simply picked me up and propelled me through the door, rather like swatting an irritating fly. It was unlikely that he would associate the poorly dressed menial with my present seeming affluence. I was worrying unnecessarily. I stepped forward again, full into the light. He turned towards me as Jane Armiger began to introduce us all. Now was the moment of truth.

'And this is Master Chapman,' she was saying, 'whose party Robert and I have joined. He is a haberdasher, travelling to Paris on business. And this is Mistress Chapman, his wife. Please allow me to present to you both my brother, Master Oliver Cook.'

My hand was crushed in the giant's until I could hear the bones crack, but there was no hint of recognition.

'I'm obliged to you, sir, for providing my sister with congenial company.' He shot a snide sidelong glance at his brother-in-law as he spoke, then turned to William Lackpenny. 'And you, sir! You are...?'

Jane Armiger introduced our travelling companion in a slightly breathless way that betrayed a sudden nervousness. Her brother glanced at her sharply, his eyes narrowing with suspicion. He looked again, more openly this time, at Robert Armiger, but the latter was too wrapped up in his own complacency to imagine, even for a second, that his wife might prefer anyone else to him. In any case, I guessed he was bracing himself for the moment when Master Cook's true position in the Duchess of York's household would be revealed.

Meantime, Goliath was subjecting Will to close scrutiny. 'Haven't I seen you before somewhere, Master Lackpenny?' he asked brusquely.

'You may have,' was the laconic reply. 'At any rate, I've seen you. I'm a member of Sir Edward Woodville's household and I was at the banquet at Baynard's Castle the other night. I saw you when the Duke of Gloucester ordered you to be brought before him and his mother at the end of the meal in order to thank you personally for the magnificent feast you had provided. A gracious gesture, I thought, but certainly not undeserved. Every course was superb.'

His condescending manner was lost on Oliver Cook, who merely grinned and said with utter confidence, 'I'm the best you'll find anywhere. Although,' he added disconsolately, 'my remarkable talents are largely wasted in the duchess's employ. She's too penny-pinching since she embraced the religious life. One of these days, I shall be forced to accept one of the many offers I'm always receiving from other members of the nobility to cook for them.' He released Will's hand and nodded. 'That must have been where I saw you, then. Although I wouldn't have said I noticed anyone in particular. I mean on the lower tables, of course.'

My smart young gent coloured a little at having been so easily placed among the menials, but he said nothing. There was, after all, nothing he could say.

'Well, Robert,' Master Cook continued, throwing one huge arm about his brother-in-law's shoulders, just as the landlord re-entered the parlour with a tray laden with food and a stoup of wine. 'I can tell you're pleased to see me.' He shook with suppressed laughter. 'Your expression is a picture, believe me.' He turned to Eloise. 'Robert doesn't like admitting he married a cook's sister. A cook's daughter, if it comes to that. Our father was even better at his trade than I am, wasn't he, Jane? And that is to say he was the very best of his generation. But Robert regards it as a lowly occupation and is secretly ashamed of not being able to resist a pretty face.'

I expected Master Armiger to bluster and deny the charge, but he didn't. He just picked up his book again, hunched his shoulder towards the rest of us and went on reading. Goliath chuckled, pulled up a stool to the table and attacked the cold pigeon pie.

I took the opportunity to slip out of the parlour and cross the passage to the ale room, hoping to find John Bradshaw among its many occupants. It took me a few minutes to locate him, but I discovered him at last tucked into a discreet corner by the hearth, drinking steadily, but soberly, alongside Philip

213

Lamprey, who seemed as morose as ever. As he glanced up and saw me struggling through the crowd towards his corner, Philip gave me what could only be construed as a look of desperation. He nudged his companion and muttered something before standing up and emptying his still half-full beaker of ale into the floor rushes.

'Here, you c'n have my place, Roger,' he muttered. When I protested, he said something about having to attend to the horses and had vanished into the rowdy throng before I could stop him.

I sighed, sitting down beside John on the narrow bench. 'He's no different, then?' I groaned.

'Give him time,' John grunted. 'What are you doing here? Masters don't join their servants in the ale room. And by the way, while I think of it –' he lowered his voice, although no one could have overheard us in that din – 'don't forget to settle with the landlord about the lodging and maintenance of the horses while we're in France. Pay him half whatever he asks and promise the rest on our return.' I nodded, trying to look as though I had already worked it all out, when in fact I had given no thought whatsoever to the animals or what was to become of them during our absence. John went on, 'So? Why have you come to find me? What's happened now?'

I explained about the arrival of Oliver Cook and his relationship to Mistress Armiger and reminded him of the story of my own fraught encounter with the giant of the Baynard's Castle kitchens.

'Has he recognized you?' John demanded, but not too anxiously.

'Not yet.'

'Nor will he.' John spoke confidently and, slewing round, eyed me up and down. 'You look nothing like your normal self. Those clothes give you a different appearance altogether. You give the impression of a confident, prosperous merchant. A master tradesman.'

'And I don't normally?' I was indignant, and also perturbed. His words had shattered my self-deluded image.

He grinned and shook his head. 'Now go back to the parlour,' he advised. 'And don't come frequenting the ale room too often. It will occasion remark.'

'How long are we going to be stranded here?' I asked savagely.

'I don't know. I'm no King Cnut, trying to command the wind and waves.'

'He didn't,' I retorted. 'He was just trying to teach his sycophantic courtiers a lesson – that he wasn't God.' On which erudite note – a sop to my battered self-esteem – I stomped off to rejoin my fellow travellers in the parlour.

The next day, the weather had improved enough to make sailing a possibility, but the master of *The Sea Nymph* had scruples about putting to sea on a Sunday and hoped, apologetically, that we would share them.

We had no choice, which he well knew, so we all went to church and confessed our sins, then hung around the inn, praying that the weather would improve even more by the following morning.

It was a long and trying day, with a bunch of ill-assorted people, at least two of whom thoroughly disliked one another, cooped up in a small inn parlour, having too much time on their hands and too little to keep themselves occupied. Walking was limited because of the weather, which, as I have said, was less stormy, but still did not permit of much outdoor exercise. Mistress Armiger and William Lackpenny did, on one occasion, manage to disappear at the same time, but if the lady's husband seemed unaware of the fact, her brother did not, and went in search of her almost immediately. Within a very short space of time, Jane returned to the parlour in company with Goliath, an angry spot of colour in either cheek, to be followed sometime later by Will, sporting what was undoubtedly a black eye. His tale of having walked into an open door was, to say the least, unconvincing, but as Robert Armiger apparently failed to notice the injury, or accepted the explanation for it without question, there was only Eloise and myself to be amused by the black looks Will directed in Oliver Cook's direction for the rest of the day.

The excellent meals did, it was true, provide some respite from our collective boredom, but towards evening, just after supper, a bitter quarrel broke out between Robert Armiger and his brother-in-law. I was not present for the beginning of it, having gone to relieve myself in the outside privy, but recriminations were in full flow by the time I returned to the parlour. It didn't take me many moments to realize that Jane Armiger was the cause of the contention, with Oliver accusing Robert of not taking sufficient care of her, and Master Armiger bitterly regretting that he had allowed himself to be trapped in an unsuitable marriage. Words and phrases such as 'low connections', 'greasy scullions' and 'thick-headed yokels' escaped his lips in an insulting stream until Oliver, goaded beyond endurance, hit him, a good right-handed punch that sent Robert crashing to the floor.

Jane screamed and fell on her knees beside her husband, ineffectually patting his hand. 'You've killed him!' she accused her brother tearfully. 'You've killed him.'

'Poppycock!' Oliver exclaimed scornfully. 'It was the merest tap. He'll regain consciousness in a minute or so. I'm off to bed.' And, as good as his word, he left the room.

He was quite right. It might have seemed an age to those of us anxiously awaiting Master Armiger's recovery, but in fact I doubt that it was more than a couple of minutes before he stirred and asked dazedly, 'What happened?'

'Master Cook hit you,' Will Lackpenny informed him, and made no attempt to conceal a smile. He had an assault of his own to avenge, and I guessed he was deliberately trying to foster trouble between the two men.

Master Armiger struggled to his feet, spurning my proffered assistance, and turned venomously on his wife. 'Your brother will regret his actions, madam,' he barked, 'and when you see him, you may tell him I said so. Now, you may help me up to bed.'

Jane nodded, gulping a little, but once she and Robert had quit the parlour, Will expressed what I was thinking.

'I don't suppose any threat that Master Armiger can make will worry that great madman.' His lips thinned. 'He has the advantage of weight and height and knows it. I can't imagine that even someone as tall and well built as you are, Master Chapman, would be a match for him.'

Recalling my treatment at Goliath's hands, I could only agree. 'No, indeed,' I said. 'I'm afraid Master Armiger's words were as empty as that jug there.' I indicated the ewer that had held the supper wine. 'Nor can he prevent Master Cook from travelling to France with them.' I added maliciously, 'Mistress Armiger won't care very much for that, I fancy. Oliver appears to be a very strict and watchful brother.'

Will's face fell, then took on a strange expression that it was impossible to interpret. 'We'll see about that,' was his only answer.

Thirteen

By the following day, the wind had dropped and the rain clouds blown away to the west, revealing a morning of chilly sunlight. While we were all still at breakfast, the master of *The Sea Nymph* sent word that he would be sailing on the afternoon tide, adding a polite request for all passengers to be aboard by noon.

I think we were all relieved not to be spending more hours in one another's company within the narrow confines of the inn. The hostility between Robert Armiger and his brother-in-law was no better for a night's sleep and sober reflection and although Oliver Cook had apologized handsomely for knocking the older man down, pleading a hasty temper and having, from boyhood, always been too handy with his fists, Robert's bruised and swollen jaw prevented him from accepting the apology. Will Lackpenny, too, regarded the cook with resentment from a blackened eye. He was offered no expression of regret, nor could he fail to notice the grin of satisfaction that split Oliver's features whenever he looked at him. In consequence, breakfast had been a meal of sullen faces and strained conversation until the master of *The*

Sea Nymph's message was relayed to us by the landlord.

The succeeding bustle to pack our saddlebags, to get them carried aboard ship, to settle our accounts and to make all necessary arrangements for the stabling and feeding of the horses until our return gave us each something to occupy our minds and keep us busy.

'It will be very cold mid-Channel,' Eloise warned, 'so wrap up warmly. And remember to put your hat on the right way round.'

This had been one of her running jokes ever since that first morning when I had accidentally put it on back to front. At first, it had irritated me, but it had now ceased to do so to the extent that I jogged her memory whenever she forgot to mention it, so I grinned in acknowledgement. She was standing very close to me, smiling up into my face, her lips slightly parted, her eyes half closed in amusement. I felt my breath catch in my throat and, almost involuntarily, had encircled her with one arm when one of the inn servants rapped on our bedchamber door and asked for the baggage he was to convey to the quayside.

'A close call, Roger,' she mocked, following the servant out of the room.

We were the last down and found the other six already aboard *The Sea Nymph* and waiting impatiently for our arrival. But even when we and our saddlebags were safely conveyed across the gangplank, and though the sails were set and the tide on the turn, there was a delay.

'What are you waiting for, master?' Robert Armiger demanded angrily. He had a hand clamped to his swollen jaw, which was obviously causing him some trouble. 'What's keeping us?'

For answer, the master went forward to greet a middle-aged man whom I had seen in conversation with the landlord in the courtyard of the inn just before Eloise and I came away.

'Monsewer Harcourt,' he said, and when the man smiled familiarly, added, 'welcome aboard.' He signalled to one of the hands to fetch the newcomer's baggage, still standing on the quay. 'This French gen'leman's sailing with us,' he informed the rest of us, before striding away to resume command of his ship.

'Raoul d'Harcourt,' the Frenchman said, introducing himself to the rest of us, but offering no further information.

Attempts by William Lackpenny to draw him out encountering only the briefest of responses, the rest of us eventually lost interest and left the monsieur to his own devices. As we had now left the shelter of the harbour and were embarking on the choppier waters of the Channel, I went below with the two women.

It's no good expecting me to write in detail about the voyage. I know as much about ships as I do about horses: that they are useful for getting you from place to place, but very little else.

It was a rough crossing, I can tell you that – far rougher than we had been led to expect by the ship's master when we left Dover. A nasty squall blew up when we were halfway across. Black clouds appeared on the horizon, trailing rain and sleet in their wake, and accompanied by the bleak, ominous light that presages an easterly wind.

I had been up on deck for a while by then, with the other three men I thought of as belonging to our party. I had no idea where John Bradshaw and Philip were sheltering, and the Frenchman had disappeared. When the weather suddenly worsened, it was borne in upon me that it was going to be a game of bravado, a competition as to who could prove himself a man by remaining on deck and impressing us all later with stories about the size of the waves and the gusts of wind that had nearly blown him off his feet. Will Lackpenny was particularly anxious to prove himself a better man than the rest of us. (He was, of course, hoping to command Jane Armiger's respect and admiration.) As for Robert Armiger and Oliver Cook, their natural antipathy forced them into contention. They were behaving like children, although the latter was better equipped to play the game without coming to serious harm.

I wasn't such a fool. I retreated below deck again to join the two women in the master's cabin, which had been put at their disposal. I tried to persuade Robert Armiger to join me, but he refused, with the assurance that he found the fresh air bracing after being cooped up in the inn at Dover. Eloise was at first inclined to taunt me with cowardice, but the continued lurching and plunging of the ship soon changed her mind and even made Jane Armiger begin to fear for her husband's safety.

Somewhere around mid-afternoon, he descended to the cabin, looking distinctly green about the gills and cursing Will Lackpenny for a pig-headed fool. 'He's letting Oliver goad him into braving the elements and into proving that he's as good a man as that behemoth. He's an idiot. I told him so. "You'll be forced to take shelter below in the end," I said.'

He had just finished speaking when the cabin door opened on a blast of wind and rain to admit my smart young gent looking decidedly the worse for wear. Even his thick cloak was drenched, while the blue feather in his hat hung down sadly, no longer bravely upstanding but bedraggled past recognition, tickling his cheek. Both ladies exclaimed in horror, urging him to sit down while they chafed his hands (one each) and scolded his imprudence in remaining aloft.

'Pooh! I've crossed in worse gales than this,' he boasted. 'This little squall will soon blow itself out, believe you me!'

However, he was in no hurry to quit the shelter of the cabin again, and remained until well after an improvement in the weather had sent Robert Armiger up on deck to see if land were anywhere in sight. My and Eloise's presence prevented anything more than a tender look or two passing between the lovers, and frustration finally decided Will Lackpenny to follow suit.

I was just debating whether or not to go, as well, when the cry of 'Land ahoy!' made the decision for me. Both Eloise and I hurried up on deck, she because she was feeling a little sick after hours of confinement in the stuffy cabin, I because this was my first view of Calais and I was anxious to get a glimpse of so famous a town.

It was by now late afternoon, almost twilight, but the weather had moderated and visibility improved. I could see the two great fortresses of Hammes and Guisnes, which protect Calais, quite plainly through the gathering gloom, and as *The Sea Nymph* edged its slow way into the splendid harbour, I was amazed at the quantity of shipping anchored there.

'It's one of the busiest times of the year,' Eloise told me, slipping one small hand into the crook of my elbow and looking every inch the doting wife. 'All the shipments of wool for Burgundy and Flanders come through Calais. It's our most important staple town and the only English port where we keep a standing garrison.' She tilted her head and looked up at me. 'Can you smell that smell?'

'Fish? Salt water, do you mean?' I asked, puzzled. 'There's nothing odd in that. Every port I've ever visited has the same stench.'

'No! The smell of money,' she answered, laughing. 'Calais is the home of very many very rich men. You'll see some magnificent houses belonging to the owners of those vast warehouses you can just make out lining the quayside, where the wool is stored.' She gave an excited little laugh. 'There isn't much you can't get in Calais. Horses, hawks ... whores! All of them every bit as good as you'll find in London, and a dozen times better, I'm sure, than in Bristol. And if you want dancing lessons, singing lessons or to learn how to play a musical instrument, there's no problem.'

I glanced down at her, refusing to be impressed. 'I don't think I've time to learn a musical instrument,' I muttered sourly. 'I hope the inhabitants all speak English.'

'Nearly all of them.' She withdrew her hand from my arm, knowing the game I was playing. 'Don't worry! You won't hear much French until after we've crossed the Calais Pale.' Then she marched off to join the Armigers, who, like us, were watching *The Sea Nymph* ease her way into an empty berth between two great ships of war, riding at anchor, high and proud, in the water.

It must have been the better part of an hour later by the time we had all disembarked and were standing on the quayside, waiting for our baggage to be brought ashore. It was dark by now, the October days growing ever shorter as November approached and was very nearly upon us, but the myriad lights from the houses and ships made it seem almost as bright as day.

John Bradshaw, muffled in his good frieze cloak, tapped me on the shoulder. 'Sir,' he said respectfully, 'with your permission, Philip and I will go on into the town and bespeak lodgings. Also, we need to search out a good livery stable to hire horses for tomorrow. If you and the mistress will be good enough to stay here until our return, I hope not to keep you waiting too long.'

As I nodded and he turned away, Robert Armiger raised a restraining arm. 'Master Chapman,' he said, 'if your man could find an inn able to accommodate Mistress Armiger and myself as well, I'd be obliged.'

'Of course,' I answered stiffly, and looked at John.

He nodded curtly, probably thinking the same as I was: that it would be safer to keep everyone under our eye until the time arrived for a natural parting of the ways, or it became necessary to give our companions the slip.

'Oh, don't forget Master Lackpenny and Oliver!' Jane Armiger exclaimed. 'They also need lodgings.' She smiled timidly at John and darted an uneasy glance at her husband, afraid she might have said too much.

'Yes, indeed!' confirmed my smart young gent, whose appearance had not yet recovered from the battering it had suffered. (The blue feather still hung forlornly down over one shoulder.) 'I'd be very grateful, Master Chapman, if your fellow there could do the

226

same for me.'

'Do your best, John,' I instructed, trying to sound as if I was used to giving orders, rather than receiving them.

'Sir!' He called to Philip and the two of them disappeared through a gap between the houses, an alleyway, presumably, leading further into the heart of the town.

I turned back to discover that the baggage had by now been dumped on the quayside by a couple of hefty sailors, and that Robert Armiger was testily putting some question to his wife.

'Well, where is he?' he was demanding in a low, angry voice. 'The rest of us are here. The baggage is here. So where, in Jesu's name, is your brother?'

Until that moment, I hadn't realized that Goliath wasn't amongst us, and neither, I think, had the others. A strange absence, considering his height and bulk, to overlook, but so it was.

'And where's the Frenchman?' I asked, glancing around me. 'Master Harcourt.' I gave the name its full brutal, aspirated pronunciation, just to prove, in my aggressive English way when dealing with foreigners, that I was starting as I meant to go on.

'Monsieur d'Harcourt,' Eloise reproved me, as Gallic as I was being Anglo-Saxon, 'took his baggage roll and left while you were speaking to John. Presumably he is well acquainted with Calais and can find his own lodgings without our help.'

'Never mind the Frenchie,' Robert Armiger interrupted angrily. 'Where's Oliver? That's what I want to know. Why hasn't he come ashore like the rest of us?'

I caught a little of his uneasiness. To the best of my knowledge, Oliver Cook had stayed up on deck throughout the voyage. Why he should now have gone below was a mystery. And why he was remaining there, when he must be aware that *The Sea Nymph* had docked, was an even greater one.

I called to one of the sailors and asked him to fetch the ship's master. When he came, Robert Armiger explained the situation. 'His baggage is here,' he added, kicking a somewhat worn and scuffed leather saddlebag with one foot.

'I'll have the vessel searched for him, Your Honour,' the master said, irritation mingling with a note of concern that he could not quite keep out of his voice. 'You're certain he hasn't come ashore already and wandered off on his own?'

'No,' Jane Armiger answered firmly. 'I've been watching for him ever since I got ashore. He ... Well, he isn't exactly the sort of person you can miss.'

'I suppose he couldn't have left the ship before the rest of us?' Eloise suggested.

Jane shook her head. 'We were all standing in a group as *The Sea Nymph* was berthed. I even noticed Monsieur Harcourt. But I don't remember seeing Oliver.' Her little, flower-like face puckered anxiously and she wrung

228

her delicate hands. (I recall thinking that I'd never actually seen anyone do that before.) 'Wherever can he be?'

William Lackpenny took a hasty step forward, as though about to comfort her, before recollecting that it was not his place to do so. Instead, he looked reproachfully at Robert Armiger.

That worthy, however, was unmoved by his wife's distress. 'The fellow's a damned nuisance,' he burst out. 'What does he mean by keeping us all waiting like this? I warn you, Jane, I'm not prepared to hang around here until he's ready to appear! As soon as Master Chapman's man returns, we're off to whatever lodgings he's found for us.'

It struck me that his bluster hid a growing anxiety.

'Your brother-in-law must be still aboard somewhere,' I said, trying to sound positive. 'Maybe he went below deck towards the end of the journey and fell asleep. Facing into all that wind and rain crossing the Channel, as he insisted on doing, must have tired him out in the end.'

'The conceited fool has the constitution of an ox,' Robert Armiger snorted. 'This is probably his stupid idea of a joke, just to get us worried.' He turned furiously on his wife. 'Your brother is an ignorant dolt!' he spat at her. 'This is your doing, I suppose, persuading him to ask for leave of absence and come with us to France. If I'd only known what you were plotting, my girl, we'd have stayed at home. You're as big an idiot as he is!'

Jane burst into tears. Eloise, glaring at Robert Armiger, went forward and put a consoling arm about the other woman's shoulders, forestalling William Lackpenny's attempt to do the same.

'You speak out of turn, sir!' she said coldly. 'Can't you see that your wife is frightened?' She went on, turning to me and putting into words what none of us had so far dared to mention, 'Is it possible, do you think, Roger, that Master Cook might have fallen overboard?'

I frowned at her, but this bald statement of her worst fears seemed rather to calm Mistress Armiger than otherwise.

'That's what I've been wondering,' she murmured tremulously.

Before anyone else could say anything, *The Sea Nymph*'s master returned to report that no trace of the missing passenger could be found. 'We've searched the ship from prow to stern, sirs. We've looked in every place where even the smallest man might stow away, but without result. The gentleman's not on board, and you can take my word for that.' He chewed a broken fingernail. 'You're sure he didn't precede you off the ship?'

'No,' Jane assured him, her voice breaking. 'He didn't. He ... he's fallen overboard and drowned. Oh, Oliver! Oliver!'

She seemed likely to have hysterics. Her husband pushed Eloise unceremoniously aside and shook his wife violently. 'Be quiet,

230

you silly child! Be quiet! Of course he hasn't fallen overboard, not a great lump like him. It would take more than a few squalls of wind and rain to dislodge that enormous brute. The master's right. He slipped ashore ahead of us and is now wandering around the town. Probably looking for the nearest whorehouse, if I know him. Ah!' He glanced at someone over my shoulder. 'Here's your man back, Master Chapman. Now, my good fellow, have you seen my brother-in-law Master Cook anywhere in the town?'

I turned round to encounter John Bradshaw's look of enquiry. Briefly, I explained the situation and our fears for Oliver Cook's safety. I saw at once, by his sudden unguarded expression, that he put the worst interpretation on events, but he had his features under control in a moment, and addressed Jane Armiger with his customary placid common sense.

'No, we haven't seen him, mistress—' he indicated Philip's shadowy figure behind him – 'but we've had too much to do, arranging stables and lodgings, to take note of everyone who's passed us. The town's that full of people! I don't doubt your husband's right and your brother disembarked before the rest of us. He was on deck for the whole of the voyage. I saw him several times whenever I ventured out of the lee of the fo'c'sle, where Philip and I were sheltering. And the light's bad. You might well have missed noticing him.'

Nobody could have missed noticing the cook, and I could tell by the quizzical look in John's eyes that he knew it as well as anyone. But his words seemed to have a calming effect on Jane Armiger and her sobs diminished. Her husband released her, and Eloise again took over as comforter, wrapping Jane's cloak more warmly about her and murmuring gently in her ear.

'I think it would be as well,' she said, addressing the rest of us, 'if we went at once to the inn John has found. Food and drink and rest will make us all feel better, and maybe, in an hour or so, we might have some news of Master Cook. John, will you lead the way? And afterwards, when you've seen us settled, perhaps you and Philip will come back for the baggage.'

The Blue Cat was a small inn in a side street not too far from the quay, wedged between an apothecary's shop and a baker's – not as grand as those we had stayed in previously on this journey, but clean and comfortable for all that. Three bedchambers had been put at our disposal – one for the Armigers, another for Eloise and myself, and a third, not much bigger than a cupboard, for Oliver and Will – and I discovered later that they comprised the Blue Cat's total sleeping accommodation. When I asked John how this miracle had been worked in a town already teeming with visitors, he grinned and said it was better I didn't know, which left me to draw the conclusion that a goodly sum of money had changed hands. (I feared Timothy Plummer was likely to have an apoplexy when we finally returned to London, to discover how much of his money had been spent. Or squandered, as he would no doubt call it.)

Eloise and I were favoured with the largest of the three chambers (again, John's doing), and once we were alone, we were able to express our growing concern as to Oliver Cook's probable fate.

'He's gone overboard,' she said, sitting down on the edge of the bed. 'I feel it in my bones.'

'I'm very much afraid you're right,' I agreed gloomily, opening the window shutters a little, in spite of the weather, and staring down into the bustling street below.

It was by now quite dark, but the busy scene was illumined with wall torches, flaring and tearing sideways in the wind, the scent of the pitch-soaked rags adding to the other smells of sea water, fish, rotting refuse and unwashed bodies that make up the stench of most big ports. It reminded me of Bristol. I felt a nostalgic pang for home, and it was with an effort that I made myself attend to what Eloise was saying.

'Was it an accident, or was it...?' She raised her eyes to mine, willing me to finish the sentence for her.

'Or was it murder?' I obliged.

'Yes.'

I thought about it, and was still thinking

233

about it when one of the inn servants brought up our saddlebags and deposited them, with a sigh and a thump, on the bedchamber floor. I took the hint and handed him a coin, which he eyed with suspicion and tested between his teeth, before finally taking himself off again. Eloise gave a little giggle, but sobered almost immediately.

'Well?' she asked.

'But if it's murder,' I answered, 'what's the motive? That's the problem.'

She thought about this for a moment or two, nibbling an elegant forefinger. 'Well,' she said at last, 'don't let us forget that Oliver quarrelled violently with Master Armiger, nor that we believe him to have been responsible for Master Lackpenny's black eye. I never for one second credited the story that Will walked into a door. And then again, Jane herself must have realized that Oliver was going to be a stricter chaperone than her husband, who's far too set up in his own conceit to conceive of a rival to his manly charms. She and Will would find it difficult, with Master Cook around, to carry on their secret meetings.'

I shook my head over this last suggestion. 'No. Not Jane Armiger. If Oliver Cook was murdered – and I'm not entirely convinced of that – he was thrown overboard. Taken unawares and heaved over the side. But only consider his size and weight. His sister could not possibly have done it. Besides,' I added, a thought striking me, 'wasn't she below with you all the time she was aboard?'

'I think you're right.' Eloise began to loosen the silver net that bound her still boyishly short hair. 'Now you mention it, I don't recall her going up on deck on her own.'

'No, but Robert Armiger joined you both in the cabin a short while after I did. Don't you remember him cursing Lackpenny for a fool for trying to prove himself as good a man as his brother-in-law?'

She ran her fingers through her fair curls and nodded. 'Will came in shortly afterwards. He was soaked to the skin.'

'That proves nothing. The weather had worsened considerably by then.'

'But it means he was alone for a while with Master Cook.'

'But so was Robert Armiger,' I pointed out. 'He went up on deck before the rest of us to see if land was anywhere in sight. He could have tipped Oliver over the side then. And if it's a choice between him and Will Lackpenny, I'd choose him. He's by far the stronger of the two. Moreover, if it wasn't him, surely he'd have noticed that Oliver wasn't where he'd left him.'

Eloise shrugged. 'Not necessarily. Or if he did, he could just have presumed that Master Cook had taken himself off to another part of the deck. And if we're assuming murder, what about the mysterious Frenchman, Monsieur d'Harcourt?'

I grunted. 'I keep forgetting him. On the other hand, if we start casting him in the role of murderer, what does it make him? Certainly not the innocent traveller taking his way home aboard an English ship. No, no! Forget Master Harcourt. It complicates matters beyond all reason. We're not even sure that Oliver's disappearance is murder. It could easily have been an accident – an extra large wave, a buffet of wind that even he couldn't withstand – or he might not be dead at all. Perhaps he did disembark before the rest of us without being noticed and will turn up presently, asking in that lovable way of his why, in Beelzebub's name, we're all making such a bloody fuss, and curse us for a pack of womanish fools.'

That made Eloise laugh, and sliding off the bed, she began to unpack her saddlebags prior to pulling the bed-curtains and performing her vanishing trick behind them. At the same time, one of the inn servants came upstairs with a ewer of hot water. The familiar evening ritual of the past five days had begun. I experienced an uneasy qualm: it occurred to me that, except in one vital respect, we were falling into the habits and routine of a married couple. With a great effort, I conjured up the faces of Adela and the children, but realized that it was becoming daily more difficult, that, very often, Eloise's features would superimpose themselves on my wife's, while the children's were growing increasingly hazy.

The sooner this adventure were played out and finished, the better.

Unfortunately, it seemed to be getting ever more confusing and, probably, dangerous.

Fourteen

My sleep that night was disturbed by dreams – nothing of any significance or much that I remembered clearly the following morning, except one sequence when I was standing in the cloisters at St Paul's and the skeletons from *The Dance of Death* all left the walls and cavorted round me, nodding and grinning. I could hear the clicking of their bones as they gradually drew closer, a circle tightening like the noose about a felon's neck. The sweat was pouring from my body and I could barely breathe. I gasped for air, great rasping sounds forcing themselves from my chest and throat. One of the skeletons reached out a hand and took me by the shoulder.

'Wake up, Roger!' Eloise's voice, full of alarm, sounded in my ear as she shook me violently. 'What is it? Are you ill?'

I struggled to sit up, shivering suddenly as the chill of the bedchamber – the fire had long ago dwindled away to ashes – stroked my clammy skin. 'No, no!' I assured her. 'Just riding the night mare, that's all. Thank you for rousing me. I'm well enough.'

'Praise heaven for that,' she said, snuggling down under the bedclothes again. 'You had me worried for a moment. Mind you,' she added, 'I'm not surprised you're having bad dreams. I've had a few myself. What do we do tomorrow? Or today as I suppose it is by now. Do we start for Paris, or remain here with the Armigers, to see if Oliver Cook turns up?'

'Ride on,' I answered. 'John has had word that your kinsman, this Olivier le Daim, will be in Paris no later than the end of the week, and, according to him, it will entail some hard riding on our part to reach the capital in time. Besides, John is convinced that Oliver Cook is drowned, whether accidentally or on purpose it doesn't matter as far as he's concerned. What is important is that you should see and speak to your cousin and try to discover what King Louis's intentions are regarding the Burgundian alliance and the marriage of Princess Elizabeth to the dauphin. We must leave the Armigers here to make their own enquiries.'

'I hate abandoning Jane in these circumstances,' Eloise murmured as I lay down again, pulling the bedclothes up around me. 'Particularly as I sense she'll get very little sympathy from that brute of a husband, who seems to be almost pleased by the notion that his brother-in-law might be gone for good. He showed no signs of distress this evening, while the rest of us were waiting for news. The only moment of anxiety he displayed was when we thought that Master Cook might, after all, have shown up. But, instead, it was only Monsieur d'Harcourt to say he'd picked up one of Robert Armiger's saddlebags by mistake and was returning it.'

The Frenchman had indeed appeared half-way through the evening, having, according to him, searched for our party in half the inns of Calais before finding us, a mere two streets away, at the Blue Cat. On quitting the harbourside, he had, or so he said, walked off with a saddlebag belonging to Master Armiger and had brought it back. He had been thanked, but absentmindedly, by Robert, who admitted that he had not, so far, even noticed it was missing, and had then been apprised of our unhappy situation. The Frenchman had been all polite sympathy, but unable to help us, and had taken his leave as soon as he could decently do so without seeming to be too callous or unconcerned.

He gave the impression of a man chary of becoming entangled in other people's problems – for which I could not blame him – but nevertheless, I felt uneasy. I did not understand how he could have picked up one of the Armigers' saddlebags by mistake when he was possessed of only a baggage roll himself, and could not help wondering if it had been taken on purpose, the mistake, if there was one, being that it was not mine. Was he the innocent traveller that he seemed, or did his joining us at Dover have more sinister connotations?

Eloise's sleepy voice cut across my teeming thoughts. 'How can John be so certain that Monsieur le Daim is to be in Paris by the end

239

of the week?'

'Oh, he got word somehow,' I answered in a voice as apparently sleepy as her own, followed by a very good imitation of a snore.

She seemed satisfied with this, turned her back to me and, a few minutes later, was breathing sweetly and deeply, fast asleep. I, on the other hand, remained awake a little while longer, reflecting that deception seemed to be an integral part of this mission; no one, including myself, was quite what he or she appeared to be.

During the course of a long, miserable evening of useless speculation and deepening fears, I had gone outside to get a breath of air and shake off the oppressive gloom of the inn parlour. Turning down a narrow alleyway that ran alongside the building, I had seen, at the end, standing beneath a wall-cresset that supported a flaming torch, John Bradshaw's solidly upright figure in conversation with a little whippet of a man, who was talking earnestly in a low tone and fidgeting with the buckle of his belt. Neither man saw me nor heard my approach until I was close enough to realize that both men were speaking French. Admittedly, John's was heavily overlaid with an English south-coast accent – Hampshire at a guess – but his language was fluent and rapid, and I could not help but remember how he had played down his ability to speak French to Eloise when they first met.

When the little man – who turned out to be

one of Timothy's agents, bringing the news about Olivier le Daim – had departed, I taxed John with his deception.

He laughed. 'If you think back, I did say that I could parlez vous as well as you two, but when young madam took exception to my remark – her mother having been French – I didn't bother arguing the point. I let her think what she liked. And, of course, up to a point, she's right. No Frenchman in his right mind would mistake me for a native, but he'd understand me, I don't doubt. The truth is, one of my grandmothers was a French-woman. Can't recollect which one, but she came from somewhere called Clervaux. Any-way,' he continued, sobering and slapping me on the back, 'we must be off first thing in the morning. Dawn if possible. We've a lot of ground to cover and not much time to do it in. This business of Oliver Cook is a bugger, but we daren't let it hold us up.'

I had asked him what his thoughts were on the subject, but his reply had been cagey. It was fairly obvious that he considered foul play to be the answer and it was making him edgy, anxious to get on and to get our mission over and done with. Whether or not the cook's murder – if that was what it really was – had anything to do with our reason for being in France, he refused to speculate.

'All I know,' he had said quietly, as we walked indoors together, 'is that here is as good a chance as we're likely to get to shake off the Armigers and Master Lackpenny. And

I tell you straight, Roger, I shan't be sorry to see the back of them, especially Master Blue Feather.'

And lying there in bed, staring into the darkness, listening to Eloise's gentle breathing, I could not doubt his sincerity, any more than I could deny my own relief at seeing the last of our unwanted companions. With a sigh, I turned over on to my side and tried to get back to sleep, but it refused to come. Recalling John's words about his grandmother had reminded me of something I had half forgotten: that Jane Armiger also claimed a French grandmother, who had been one of the Dowager Duchess of York's seamstresses. I had intended to quiz Jane on the matter, but somehow, what with one thing and another, it had slipped my mind.

I rolled on to my back and shut my eyes tightly, willing myself to sleep, but still unable to command it. Instead, all I could see inside my closed lids were the grinning skeletons of my earlier dream, bearing away their harvest of dead bodies. There had been too many bodies since my return from Scotland and being charged with this new mission for Duke Richard: Humphrey Culpepper, the boatman Jeremiah Tucker and now, seemingly, Oliver Cook. As an accompaniment, there had been the news of more personal deaths: Jeanne Lamprey and Reynold Makepeace.

Abruptly I got out of bed, slipped silently between the bed-curtains and went across to the window, softly opening one of the shutters. A shaft of light from a nearby sputtering wall torch illuminated a wet and windy world. In the distance, a watchman cried the hour, and a mangy cat slipped by across the gleaming cobbles, in search of its unfortunate prey. A dog barked and then fell silent. In a doorway on the opposite side of the street, a shadow moved. A beggar, perhaps, seeking shelter for the night? But then it resolved itself into the figure of a man whom I thought I recognized, the same one surely that I had seen that other night landing at the water-stairs of Baynard's Castle. The features were hidden by a hood drawn well forward over the face, but the movements, light and quick as he slipped along in the shadow of the houses, were surely the same. I leaned further out of the window, but he was gone, melting into another doorway further along the street.

Frustrated, and increasingly uneasy, I went back to my cold half of the bed and awaited the coming of morning, convinced that I should never sleep. Eloise stirred, muttering unintelligibly to herself, turned over and flung an arm across my body, at the same time snuggling into my side, but without awakening. The human contact was unutterably comforting and I held my breath, afraid to move and disturb her. Cautiously, I freed my right arm from the bedclothes and eased it around her head, my hand coming to rest on her shoulder. And so, finally, I slept.

During the night, she must have moved again, for when I awoke to the crowing of some distant cock and the faint light of dawn seeping through the slats of the shutters, she was lying on her back on her own side of the mattress, the tip of her cold nose just showing above the blankets, scenting the early morning air, like the snout of some small animal emerging from its burrow. As I sat up, the great violet-blue eyes turned in my direction, with a slightly puzzled expression as though she was struggling to remember something.

The bed by now was icy cold and I resigned myself to the prospect of getting up. I pushed aside the bedclothes and reluctantly put my feet to the floor.

'We didn't...?' she murmured. 'Did we...?'

'If we had,' I answered roughly, 'you'd remember it. So you can rest easy on that score. You've been muttering and snoring all night.'

The softness, almost tenderness, drained from her face and she bounced up in bed, spitting venom. 'Conceited pig! If it comes to snoring,' she retorted, 'you take the prize. And you can add farting to that, as well.'

'Oh, just get dressed! John wants us on the road as soon as possible.' I dumped both her saddlebags on the bed, closed the curtains again and began pulling on my breeches.

It was obvious that the journey ahead of us would not be easy. I wondered what was wrong with the pair of us that made us so scratchy and unfriendly all the time.

But I suppose, really, in my heart of hearts I knew the cause.

Our travelling companions were not yet out of bed when, after gobbling our breakfast, the four of us – John Bradshaw, Philip, Eloise and myself – left the Blue Cat and made our way towards one of the great gates.

A quick word with the landlord of the inn had ascertained the fact that no Oliver Cook had turned up during the night. But then, nobody had really expected him to. The lady, his sister, had insisted on sitting up until midnight had been called, when her husband had more or less carried her bodily upstairs.

'In floods of tears, poor soul,' the landlord had added. 'There's no doubt her brother's drowned. The Channel can be a treacherous beast in the autumn gales, that's for certain.'

He had then assured us that he would make our farewells to the rest of the party, giving it as his opinion that they were all so worn out by their trouble that none of them was likely to put in an appearance until dinnertime.

Here, however, he was wrong. I happened to be alone, while John and Philip went to the nearby livery stable to fetch the horses they had hired the previous day, and while Eloise was upstairs doing whatever it is women find to do before setting out on even the shortest of journeys, when Jane Armiger entered the parlour. She had looked dishevelled and distraught, her uncombed hair tumbling down her back, a cloak flung anyhow over her night-rail, two dark rings, like bruises, under eyes, which were wild and staring.

'Oh!' she said, pulling up short when she saw me. 'I ... I heard a noise. Voices. I thought ... perhaps...' She broke off, her lips quivering, tears welling up and running down her cheeks.

'No. I'm sorry. It was only my–my wife and me. We're leaving early.' I went forward and led her to a chair. 'Sit down, my dear child. Have some ale.' I reached for the jug of small beer, still standing on the table among the remains of our breakfast, poured some into a beaker and pushed it towards her.

She gave me a watery smile and took a few sips. 'Robert's asleep,' she explained. 'Of course,' she added quickly, 'he's just as worried as I am, but ... but...'

'He needs more rest,' I finished for her. 'I understand.' I pulled up a stool and sat down beside her. I was more than a little ashamed of what I was about to do, but it was too good an opportunity to miss. 'Try not to think about your brother for a minute or two. It will give your mind a rest and make your trouble seem less.' Oh, the lies we tell when self-interest is at stake! 'Do you remember saying that your grandmother was one of the Duchess of York's seamstresses, forty years or so ago, in Rouen, when the duke was governor of France and Normandy?' She looked at me dazedly, as though I were talking a foreign language, but then, after a second or two, nodded. 'Did your grandmother,' I went on hurriedly, aware that I probably had very little time before one of the others put in an appearance, 'ever mention any scandal concerning Duchess Cicely? In connection, maybe, with one of her bodyguard? With one of her archers?'

There was no reply. Jane Armiger simply sat there, twisting a lock of hair round and round one finger. I wondered if she had even heard me, or comprehended what I was asking. I wanted to shake her and demand an answer. I could hear voices and the clop of horses' hooves in the inn yard and hurried footsteps overhead, making for the stairs. But at the same moment, I was seized by the conviction that I had made another of my unthinking blunders. I was not supposed to ask this question of anyone but the unknown Robin Gaunt and his wife. Supposing either Robert Armiger or William Lackpenny should really be a Woodville spy and already suspicious of me – if Jane told them of my interest, it would at once alert whichever one of them it was to the reality of my mission in France.

The parlour door burst open and John Bradshaw came in, an irritated frown wrinkling his brow. 'I thought I told you—' he was beginning, then broke off abruptly as he became aware of Mistress Armiger's presence. 'I apologize for disturbing you, sir,' he continued smoothly, 'but I was under the impression you wanted an early start. We're ready and waiting for you. The mistress, too.' He glanced at Jane, who still sat at the table, staring, empty-eyed, in front of her. He raised his eyebrows. 'There's no news of Master Cook,

247

I take it?'

'No, none.' I got up and raised one of Jane's limp hands to my lips. 'I must be going, mistress. Please give my adieus to your husband and Master Lackpenny.'

She made no response. John jerked his head imperatively towards the door, while standing deferentially to one side for me to precede him from the room. I was halfway through the doorway when Jane Armiger turned her head in my direction and said clearly, 'Yes.'

I paused, looking back at her. 'Yes?' I queried.

She had stopped playing with her hair and was looking straight at me. 'The answer to your question,' she said, 'is "Yes."'

That was all, after which she seemed to lose interest in me, hunching further into her chair, her knuckles white as she clenched its arms, looking deep into the heart of the fire that had been kindled on the hearth. I waited a moment to see if she would say anything else, but when it became obvious that she was not going to, I went out into the frosty morning and mounted, not without a great deal of misgiving, the mettlesome-looking grey that John had hired for me.

And so we set off through the Calais streets, heading for the Pale and the beginning of our journey into France.

We were a silent bunch as we put the weary miles between ourselves and Calais, first as we crossed the Pale and then as we headed south into France itself.

Philip, of course, was always silent nowadays, resisting all my efforts to draw him out or involve him in any sort of conversation, efforts that had grown more half-hearted with every passing day as he failed to respond. My exasperation had increased as my sympathy ebbed until I found myself content to ignore him and treat him like the servant he was pretending to be.

John Bradshaw also seemed wrapped in his own thoughts during that first day's ride, only raising his voice to urge us all to greater efforts and to chivvy us into moving again each time we stopped – which wasn't often – for refreshment. Paris was now his goal and he would only be happy when we got there. In a burst of confidence during one of these rests, he did repeat how glad he was to be freed from the company of the Armigers and Master Lackpenny, and even went so far as to consider the disappearance of Oliver Cook as a blessing in disguise.

'I wouldn't wish death by drowning on any man – a nasty, protracted business, I should imagine – but I have to say that I found the fellow extremely offensive. I had known of his reputation in Baynard's Castle, although we had never actually met face to face, and his removal has meant the freedom to be ourselves for at least that part of each day when we are not in the company of fellow travellers.'

I understood this. For a man used to

directing others, playing the role of a servant must have been irksome in the extreme, especially when it meant deferring to someone as new to, and as ignorant of, the spying game as myself.

Eloise's silences, answering only when I addressed her directly, and then with the minimum of words, I had no difficulty in interpreting. She was still angry about my treatment of her that morning, and was beginning to experience the frustration of playing a part most hours of the day and night. At first it had probably seemed like a game to her, a chance to goad and needle me with impunity. She had known that I didn't trust her, and with good reason, but as the days, and then a week passed, the game palled. I liked to think that she felt my attraction as I felt hers, and that being thrust into the most intimate of situations with me without being able to relieve the emotional strain was making her short-tempered. To make matters worse, she was at liberty to give full rein to her natural instincts: I was the stumbling block with my marriage and my children and my much vaunted determination to remain faithful (or at least not to stray again, as I had done with Juliette Gerrish in Gloucester – not that Eloise knew about that).

As for myself, I was preoccupied with my own stupidity in having spoken to Jane Armiger about the Dowager Duchess of York in that unguarded fashion without first thinking of the possible consequences. At least I derived some comfort from the knowledge that I would never make a good spy. I was too impetuous, too careless of orders, too unthinking for the devious, double-dealing world of Timothy Plummer and his ilk. I was glad of that.

But what exactly had that 'Yes' of Jane Armiger's been intended to convey? Yes, her grandmother had once mentioned rumours of a love affair between Cicely Neville – as so many people, even now, still thought of her – and one of the archers of her Rouen bodyguard? Or had Jane, in her dazed and bereft state, merely been answering some question of her own poor, exhausted mind and which had nothing to do with what I had been saying to her? Yet she had looked at me as she spoke, a direct, steady gaze that seemed to indicate she had heard me and was offering a response. But how could I be certain in the state that she was in, grieving for her brother, even if no one else considered him much of a loss? And perhaps grieving even more because others appeared so indifferent to his fate.

John Bradshaw had of course been curious to know the meaning of that 'Yes', but had accepted, without much persuasion, the explanation that Mistress Armiger was distraught and that it had been nothing more than an expression of her own distress of mind.

And so the first day passed more or less in

silence, with three of us, at least – Eloise, Philip and myself – oblivious for much of the time to anything but our own glum thoughts, and saying as little as possible to one another. John Bradshaw was apparently content to have it so until we racked up for the night at some wayside inn – *auberge*, as I suppose I should call them from now on – when, as we dismounted in the yard, he snapped at us in English, and without bothering to lower his voice, that he was tired of our childish behaviour. This, of course, was meant for Eloise and me. Philip he continued to ignore except to ply him with orders about stabling the horses and making sure they were rubbed down and properly fed before he turned in for the night.

Someone came out through the doorway of the inn and gave a discreet cough. 'Do you always allow your servants to speak to you in that insolent fashion, Master Chapman?' asked a voice that was vaguely familiar, but that I could not immediately place. It was only when its owner moved out of the shadows and into a pool of light made by a wall torch that I recognized, much to my astonishment, the Frenchman, Master Harcourt, who had made the Channel crossing with us.

'You–you've made good time, sir,' was all I was able to stutter. I didn't dare look at John, who was no doubt cursing himself roundly for not being more careful in a public place.

It was Eloise who stepped into the breach

while he and I were still gathering our wits. 'Monsieur d'Harcourt,' she purred, offering him a hand, which he gallantly kissed. She then proceeded to burble away to him in French, which he answered in his accented but perfectly intelligible English.

'Yes, indeed, madame. I was up before dawn and waiting at the porter's lodge of the town gate for it to open. But you, yourselves, have not been tardy. I could not have been much more than an hour or so in front of you anywhere on the road. I regret infinitely that I gave you no chance to catch up with me. I would not willingly have foregone such attractive company.'

Eloise simpered. Raoul d'Harcourt might be middle-aged, but he was a good-looking man for all that, and he had what I supposed women meant by 'Gallic charm'. Frankly, it made me want to spit.

'Are you staying at this inn?' I asked abruptly.

He smiled. 'But of course. It is the only inn for some miles.' He glanced curiously between John and me, once again kissed Eloise's hand and turned to re-enter the inn. 'I shall look forward to your company at supper,' he said.

I grunted and received an understanding smile for my pains. Eloise said something gracious in French, and John stomped off to the stables to vent his anger with himself on Philip and any unfortunate stable hand who happened to be present. I could hear him roaring away in both English and his own broad-vowelled version of the French tongue as I followed my 'wife' indoors.

At that time of year, there were fewer travellers than usual on the roads, and, apart from Master Harcourt, Eloise and I were the only people sitting down to supper in the comfortable room at the back of the inn.

To begin with, I was too preoccupied poking around the contents of my plate in order to find out exactly what it was that I was eating to pay much heed to the conversation of the other two, even though it was conducted in English for my benefit. It was the name of Oliver Cook that finally caught and held my attention.

'You heard about his disappearance, then?' I asked, raising my head from the contemplation of a suspect piece of something or other swimming around in my spoon.

Raoul d'Harcourt inclined his head. 'But naturally. If you remember, I called on you to return Master Armiger's saddlebag. In any case, Calais is a veritable hotbed of gossip. Nothing happens that isn't known throughout the town in a matter of hours, and the presumed drowning of one of my fellow passengers aboard *The Sea Nymph* was of more than just a passing interest to me.'

'"Presumed drowning"?' I asked, returning the suspect something to my bowl of broth and absentmindedly watching it sink to the bottom. I raised my head and looked our

254

companion in the eye. 'Why do you say "presumed"?'

'Because,' was the answer, slowly and deliberately given, 'I am certain Master Cook's death was no accident. I feel sure in my own mind that he was murdered.'

Fifteen

'Why do you say that?' I asked sharply, while Eloise, forgetting to look soulful and beguiling, turned to stare at our supper companion.

Raoul d'Harcourt smiled a little and then pulled from his belt a serviceable-looking knife. 'This was found on the deck of *The Sea Nymph* by one of the crew.'

'And how did you come by it?' My tone was accusatory.

The smile deepened. 'He, of course, handed it to the ship's master, who brought it to me at my inn late last night—'

'Why did he bring it to you?' I interrupted fiercely.

Eloise made a little sign to me to calm down.

Raoul d'Harcourt saw and his grey eyes twinkled appreciatively. 'It's all right, madame,' he said. 'Your husband is naturally curious. The master of *The Sea Nymph* is an old friend of mine. I have crossed the Channel many times aboard his vessel. You may have noticed that he obligingly delayed the ship's departure from Dover in order that I might come aboard. So I was naturally the person he thought of when the discovery of the knife was made. The missing gentleman's brother-in-law (as I understand him to be), the other gentleman of the blue feather and your husband were all strangers to him.'

I leaned back in my chair, pushing my bowl of broth to one side. Eloise frowned at me, indicating that I should drink it up, but I ignored her and concentrated my attention, instead, on the Frenchman.

'Why did the ship's master consider this knife of any significance?' I demanded. 'It's an ordinary meat knife, the sort most of us carry. Was there something particular about it that excited his suspicion?'

Monsieur d'Harcourt shrugged slightly. 'He was uneasy concerning it. That was all he could say.'

'Why? Anyone could have dropped it. Did it have blood on it? Was that it?'

'In that weather? With rain lashing the deck?' The tone was mocking. 'It would have been washed clean in a moment. No. It was rather that at one point during the voyage he thought some sort of altercation was going on between Master ... er ... the man who has disappeared—'

'Cook,' Eloise supplied. 'Master Oliver Cook.'

256

'Thank you, madame.' Raoul d'Harcourt bestowed a smile on her that had the unfortunate result of making her simper again. 'Master Cook – Maître Cuisinier – I shall remember. As I was saying, my friend the ship's master thought he saw some argument going on between Master Cook and two other men, standing alongside him. At the time, he merely presumed that this pair were trying, very sensibly, to persuade their companion below deck and thought no more about it.'

'Did he see who these men were?' I asked eagerly, but received only a shake of the head.

'No. Unfortunately the visibility at that moment was too poor. Moreover, he knew none of the passengers sufficiently well to be able to distinguish one from the other at a distance. Master Cook, of course, he could not help but recognize because of his great size.'

'And this incident made him suspicious when the knife was discovered ... when?'

'After you were all ashore and members of the crew were searching the ship for the missing man.'

'And he thought that Oliver Cook might have been knifed and pushed overboard?'

The Frenchman pursed his lips. 'I'm not sure that my friend had formed that conclusion. He simply felt a trifle uneasy in his mind and so came to me for my advice.'

'And what was that?'

Here, we were interrupted by the entrance

of the landlord and his assistant, bringing the main dish of two plump fowls, stewed in butter, with mushrooms and shallots. My spirits insensibly rose. This was better fare for an Englishman. I was pleased to be rid of a broth whose contents I found extremely dubious and more than a little foreign. (I noticed that Eloise had disposed of hers with relish.)

When the fowls had been carved and served, and the landlord and his assistant had withdrawn, amidst a flurry of what I took to be good wishes for the enjoyment of our meal, I returned to the subject in hand.

'So what advice did you give your friend, monsieur?'

'I told him to think no more about it. I offered to take the knife and restore it to its owner if that was possible. I said I was sure it had nothing to do with the missing man's disappearance.'

'And he was satisfied with that?'

Raoul d'Harcourt smiled again. He smiled rather a lot, too much in my opinion. 'Let us say that he wanted to be satisfied,' was the cautious answer. 'I'll say no more than that.'

'But you are not. Satisfied, I mean. You think this knife has some significance. Why?'

The Frenchman emptied his mouth of food, wiped his lips on the back of his hand and grimaced. 'If you wish me to be honest, I have no real reason. It is just that when I called on you all yesterday evening, to return the saddlebag I had taken from the quayside by mistake and learned that Master Cook was missing and assumed to be drowned, I was surprised – no, rather let us say astonished – by the lack of any great concern except on the part of his sister. Master Armiger, who should by rights have been as distressed as his wife, seemed, if anything, indifferent to the news that his brother-in-law had probably been washed overboard and drowned. And so, when, later, my friend the ship's master sought me out at my inn and told me about the discovery of the knife and the argument he thought he had seen, I began to wonder if perhaps Master Cook's death had not been an accident at all, but murder.'

There was silence for a moment or two except for the crackling of the fire on the hearth. Finally, I asked, 'And this is your sole reason for believing there might have been foul play?'

'You think it insufficient?'

'I do.' I tried to speak positively, at the same time surreptitiously kicking Eloise under the table.

'You believe it to have been an accident, then?'

'Without doubt.' I spoke with a confidence I was far from feeling. Indeed, I had been growing hourly more convinced that the cook had been done away with like Humphrey Culpepper and Jeremiah Tucker before him. The Frenchman's story had reinforced this belief, and I had a clear vision of someone sneaking up behind Oliver Cook, either slitting his throat like the other two or simply stabbing him in the back and heaving him overboard. Yet what the motive behind such a killing could possibly be I had no idea. For some unknown reason, I did not wish to share my doubts and uncertainties about Oliver Cook's disappearance with this stranger. I distrusted him, although why I was unable to say, except that he was a foreigner. A good enough reason, you might think, for an Englishman, and you'd probably be right. We're an insular, suspicious lot. The highest compliment we can pay anyone from abroad is to say that he is like one of us.

Apart from that, however, there was something about the Frenchman that I could not warm to.

I returned to the attack. 'You seem very certain that Master Cook was murdered and not simply washed overboard in the storm. Why is that?'

Our companion shrugged. 'I am sorry. I spoke a little too positively. I cannot, of course, be certain. But as I said just now, I have crossed La Manche many times, and the weather was not nearly so bad as I have known it on other occasions. What you term a storm was, to me, nothing but a bad mid-Channel squall, insufficient to wash a man over the side – especially a man of Master Cook's impressive build. You must admit he was – is – a very large gentleman.'

'That doesn't mean to say it couldn't happen,' I argued stubbornly, and addressed myself to my supper with a determination that signalled the end of the discussion. To make doubly sure, however, I turned the conversation by asking through a mouthful of mushrooms and gravy, 'And what brings you so often across the Channel and back, monsieur? Do you have so much business in England?'

Eloise scowled at my discourteous tone, but Raoul d'Harcourt merely smiled. 'I am a goldsmith by trade, Master Chapman, and since our two countries are at present at peace, and have been for the past seven years since the meeting of our sovereigns at Picquigny, I travel to London several times a year to both buy and sell among the goldsmiths of Cheapside. I have a shop on the Quai des Orfèvres in the Île de la Cité.' He turned to Eloise as he spoke, deducing correctly from her almost perfect French that she probably knew Paris as well as he did.

She smiled and nodded. 'I am acquainted with it, monsieur, although,' she added with a throaty chuckle, 'not as a customer.' At the same time, she sent me a significant look, which I entirely failed to interpret until about ten minutes later, when I recollected that the object of Olivier le Daim's visit to the capital was to consult with the Parisian goldsmiths. (About what we had no idea, but knowing the ways of kings and princes, King Louis was most likely trying to raise a pledge of money from them.) I kicked myself mentally. I really was getting absentminded.

Until he jogged my memory, I had completely forgotten the Frenchman's calling on us at our inn in Calais yesterday evening to return the Armigers' saddlebag and now the reason for Eloise's cousin being in Paris had all but slipped my mind. Why this sudden lack of concentration? What was wrong with me? One glance at Eloise's flower-like countenance, her large eyes fixed with interest on the Frenchman's face, her lips slightly parted as though breathless for his next few words, was enough to tell me that I was suffering from the pangs of frustrated passion. Not love: not for a moment did I delude myself that it was that. I had been in love twice in my life, once with Rowena Honeyman and a second time with Adela, and I knew gold from dross. But I was most certainly in lust with Eloise and it was distracting me from the job in hand. And that could prove very dangerous.

After supper, when the covers had been drawn, I excused myself, saying that I needed to speak to John Bradshaw about the following day's itinerary, which was the truth as far as it went. But there were other matters I needed to consult him about, as Eloise, by the slight flicker of her eyelids, obviously guessed.

'Don't be too long, then, sweetheart,' she said, playing her wifely role to perfection. 'And don't stay drinking with him. Really,' she added, turning towards Raoul d'Harcourt with a small, resigned shrug, 'John is more like a friend than a servant to my husband. You must have wondered at the way he was speaking to Roger out in the courtyard, but too much familiarity always breeds contempt, as I have pointed out time and again, but to no avail.' She rose from her chair and kissed my cheek, also playfully patting my rump. 'Now, remember! Not too long!'

Truly, the girl had all her wits about her. She had effortlessly explained away that unfortunate scene in the courtyard when John was berating the pair of us whereas my only way of dealing with it had been to ignore the episode entirely and hope the Frenchman read nothing of significance into it.

'I won't linger,' I promised, returning her kiss with a chaste salute on her lips. They tasted of the wine we had been drinking. 'Do you travel with us tomorrow, monsieur?' I asked politely, but without enthusiasm.

'Since you ask, thank you, I should be grateful for the company,' he answered, his eyes mocking me.

'Splendid,' I said in a flat voice. This time, he gave an involuntary grin, but disguised it as best he could by honouring both of us with a little bow. 'And allow me to congratualate you on your excellent English.'

He repeated the bow. 'Thank you, monsieur. I have a flair for languages. I can also speak Spanish and Portuguese with reasonable fluency. There is nothing very clever about it. It is just a knack.'

'A very useful one.' I summoned up a smile.

'I shan't be gone long. My wife will entertain you while I'm away.'

'Enchanted,' he said, turning to Eloise with his most engaging smile.

She returned it, dewy-eyed.

I left them to it.

For once, John Bradshaw and Philip were not bedding down in the stables, which were empty apart from the horses. I eventually ran them to earth in the kitchens, Philip already asleep, lulled by the unaccustomed warmth, curled into a corner on a pile of old sacks. Two young lads were taking the spit apart, ready for cleaning, jabbering to one another, and for one short moment I thought how clever they were to be speaking a foreign tongue at their age. Then reality took hold and I gave myself another mental shake. I must sharpen up, I thought disgustedly.

I looked around for John and found him seated on a stool by the slowly dying embers of the fire, knife in hand, whittling a piece of wood into a cruciform shape, one arm of which he had already embellished with delicately carved leaves and flowers. There being no other seat available, I dropped on my haunches beside him and admired his handiwork.

'That's beautiful,' I said.

'It's a talent I've had from boyhood.' He sounded faintly surprised. I was surprised myself. With his big hands it seemed unlikely that he could be capable of such fine work.

'Did you want me?' he added.

'I've come to warn you that we shall have company again tomorrow, on the road.'

'The Frenchman?'

'Who else?'

John bit his lip. 'I didn't see him lurking there in the courtyard this evening. He must have wondered when he overheard me addressing you and Mistress Gr— Mistress Chapman as I did.' He shook his head sadly. 'I'm growing careless. A sure sign that I'm beginning to get rattled.'

'Don't worry,' I reassured him. 'Eloise has explained the incident to his satisfaction.' And I told him what she had said.

'An intelligent woman,' he confirmed. 'Is that all you wanted to tell me?'

'No, there's more.' I glanced around to make certain that no one else had entered the kitchen without us noticing, but there were still only the two scullions and a slatternly girl washing the dirty dishes. 'Monsieur d'Harcourt thinks that Oliver Cook was murdered.'

John Bradshaw stopped his whittling and turned his head in my direction. 'Tell me,' he murmured.

I related the story of the knife found on the deck by one of *The Sea Nymph*'s crew and how it came to be in the Frenchman's possession. When I had finished, John said nothing for a moment or two, then asked, 'Do you believe him?'

'Why would he make up such a story?'

'To divert suspicion from himself, perhaps.

After all, what do we know of him? He appears out of the blue at Dover. No one seems at all sure where he was throughout the voyage; he picks up one of the Armigers' saddlebags, apparently by mistake, at Calais, in spite of the fact that he has no saddlebag of his own, merely a baggage roll; and we only have his word for it that this knife was discovered by a member of the crew and brought to him at his inn.'

'You think he might be a Woodville agent?'

'Or a French agent. On the other hand, he could be exactly what he says he is, a goldsmith travelling home to Paris, and his story a true one. But it must have occurred to you that Oliver Cook might well have been murdered.'

'Well, yes,' I admitted. 'Except that I can see no reason for it. We know he's not the agent of anyone. He's the head cook at Baynard's Castle.'

John Bradshaw laughed softly. 'And you think that means he couldn't have been recruited or suborned by someone? Offer enough money and you can buy almost anything or anybody. Not everyone makes spying their only profession.'

'Like you and Timothy.'

'Exactly.'

I sighed and straightened up. 'I suppose all we can do is to keep an eye on Master Harcourt. And if he's to travel with us tomorrow, we can do that easily enough.' I held out my hand for the half-finished cross and he laid it

266

carefully in my left palm. I examined it closely in the remaining light from the fire. 'It truly is beautiful,' I said with the admiration of one who couldn't carve a leg of mutton without making a botched job of it. I grinned as I got in a little dig at him in return for his dressing-down of Eloise and myself earlier in the evening. 'Not bad for a Hampshire hog.'

He raised his eyebrows. 'What makes you think I'm a Hampshire hog?'

'I thought I recognized the accent.'

He laughed. 'Well, you're out there, my Bristol bumpkin. I'm a Suffolk swine. My home town is Ipswich. Most of my kith and kin live there, or roundabout.' He took back the cross from me. 'As a matter of fact, I'm making this for one of my young cousins, Tom Wolsey. His father, a relation of my mother in the third or fourth degree, is a butcher, and a good one, too. As skilful a carver in his own way as I am in mine and a pleasure to watch. Young Tom's handy with a knife, as well. A big, well-set-up young chap. Only ten years old, but already as strong as an ox. Looks a bit like me,' he added proudly.

'A good thing in a butcher,' I said.

John Bradshaw gave a shout of laughter that made the scullions and the girl turn to stare at him. He lowered his voice again. 'The good Lord love you! Thomas ain't destined for the shop. He has brains as well as brawn and his father has ambitions for him. It's Oxford for Master Tom and then probably the Church. Or a secretaryship to some great churchman.

That's why I'm making him this.' He touched the half-finished cross with a beefy forefinger and then resumed his carving.

'I'll see you in the morning,' I said.

He nodded. 'Sun-up. We need an early start.'

'Don't we always?' I grumbled.

Thomas Wolsey. That was the first time I ever heard a name that now, in this, my seventy-sixth year, is as familiar to me as my own and a great deal more familiar than the majority of others. Young Master Tom from Ipswich has certainly risen further than most of his generation, and his talents would just as certainly have been wasted in a butcher's shop.

Eloise and Master Harcourt were still seated where I had left them, one on either side of the inn parlour fire, talking away together in rapid French, which slid politely and effortlessly into English as I made my reappearance. It seemed, upon enquiry, that they had been exchanging horror stories about Paris. Or so they claimed.

'Monsieur d'Harcourt,' Eloise said, 'has been telling me of a terrible winter, at the beginning of this century, when icebergs floated down the Seine and even the ink froze solid on the quill. And less than fifty years ago, wolves got into the city and killed and ate more than a dozen people in the market gardens and scavenged the dead bodies from the great gibbet at Montfaucon.' She gave a crow of laughter at my look of disgust and added triumphantly, 'And the Seine has over-flowed its banks more then twenty-seven times. Once, it brought the entire city to a standstill for more than six weeks.'

'Dear God!' I murmured, crossing myself.

The Frenchman's eyes twinkled. 'Ah, madame,' he said, 'you have forgotten the outbreaks of mumps and scarlet fever and smallpox, and the thirty-six outbreaks of plague during the past thirty-two years.'

'Enough!' I exclaimed, flinging up a hand. 'I didn't think there could be an unhealthier spot on earth than London, but it seems I was wrong. We shall be starting at sun-up, as usual, my dear,' I added, addressing Eloise, then bowed stiffly to Raoul d'Harcourt. 'If you still wish to join us, monsieur, you are welcome, as I told you earlier.' He inclined his head graciously and murmured some-thing in French, which I ignored. 'And now I'm for my bed.'

I stalked to the door, but unfortunately trip-ped over one of my own feet as I made what should have been a dignified exit. I heard Eloise's gurgle of mirth and shut the door with unnecessary force behind me.

When she followed me up to our bed-chamber some time later – how much later I wasn't sure – I pretended to be sleeping.

Once again, I had a restless night, but I was growing used to it. My slumbers were broken by dreams without any rhyme or reason; farragos of nonsense that had no shape and melted away like dew in the sun almost as soon as I regained full consciousness. Awake, staring up at the bed-tester, moving aside the curtains a little to stare into the shadowy depths of one strange bedchamber after another, I was always acutely aware of Eloise beside me, of the soft murmurs she made while she slept, of the curve of her body and the scent of her hair. That particular night, she had once again curled into my side, one hand resting lightly on my right thigh, and it took every ounce of my moral strength not to rouse her and make love to her there and then. I was thoroughly roused myself, and was sweating with desire, lust, whatever you like to call it, cursing Duke Richard and Timothy Plummer for sending me on this mission to Paris with a woman who was not my wife. I don't know how long I lay struggling with my emotions, listening to the sounds of the night from beyond the closed shutters – the hooting of an owl, the neigh of a horse, the barking of a dog – until my better self gained the upper hand and I fell at last into a sleep of exhaustion.

It was hardly surprising, therefore, that Eloise was up, washed, dressed and had descended to the inn parlour for breakfast before I was even out of bed. As it was, I cut myself shaving, scrambled into the first clothes that came to hand (blue hose, green jerkin, a dirty shirt and my old patched boots), failed to comb my hair or brush my teeth and, judging by Eloise's glare of disapproval, arrived at table looking the wreck I felt. But it was with relief that I saw Raoul d'Harcourt was not yet present. Perhaps he, too, had suffered a disturbed night.

As I sipped my beaker of small beer and swallowed a basinful of gruel – at least, I think that's what it was meant to be – I remarked smugly on his absence. 'He heard me say sun-up,' I said.

The innkeeper entering the parlour at that moment, Eloise turned and addressed him in rapid French. There was a good deal of Gallic shrugging of shoulders and spreading of hands – the usual waste of time – before mine host trundled off to look into the matter. He returned, after a wait of some minutes, to say that the gentleman had gone. He was not in his bedchamber or anywhere else in the inn. Even I could understand that much.

There was yet another rapid exchange between Eloise and the landlord – it sounded like an explosion of hailstones on a tiled roof – before she told me, looking nonplussed, 'It seems that although Monsieur d'Harcourt is nowhere to be found, his baggage is still in his room.'

'Gone for a walk?' I suggested. The French were so excitable!

Eloise regarded me scornfully. 'Hardly! With his boots and his cloak still in his room? It's raining like the Great Flood out there, or are you still so drugged with sleep you haven't noticed?'

As a matter of fact, I hadn't, but now she

mentioned it, I was suddenly aware of the sound of heavy rain spattering on the roof and the street cobbles.

'Maybe he likes walking in the rain,' I argued. 'Maybe he has a spare pair of boots and another cloak. He looks rich enough to have two of everything. What about his horse?' I added with a flash of inspiration. 'Is it still in the stables?'

Investigation proved that it was.

'There you are, then! He's gone for a stroll. Some people enjoy walking in the wet. But I think it's the end of his riding with us. John won't wait on his fits and starts. He wants us on the road now, if not sooner. He's determined we'll be in Paris by Thursday.'

And so it proved. John Bradshaw was indifferent as to what had become of the Frenchman. Perhaps relieved, really, that it would be just the four of us without any need for play-acting.

'It's his own fault if he's not ready to go with us,' he said flatly. 'I'll tell Philip to bring round the horses.' He noticed Eloise's troubled expression and frowned. 'Don't worry about him, mistress,' he said curtly. 'I doubt he's come to any harm. And now we're nearly at our journey's end, we've worries enough of our own.'

Sixteen

Thanks to one of the horses throwing a shoe (or whatever it is that horses do with shoes) and also to John Bradshaw being laid up for the best part of a day with stomach cramps – owing, he reckoned, to a bad piece of fish he had eaten – it was late on Friday afternoon before our somewhat bedraggled party of four entered Paris by the Porte Saint-Denis.

November had come in with its usual melancholy weather, and a thin rain had settled, mist-like, over our cloaks and assorted headgear, lowering our spirits even further. Conversation had been minimal for the past two days, decreasing until it was little more than absolute necessity dictated. John, naturally enough, was still suffering from the after-effects of his colic, but he had been sour before that. Something had irritated him and seriously ruffled his temper, but he did not confide in me and I could only guess at the cause. We were at last nearing our destination, and there were so many things that might go wrong. He seemed intent on shouldering the entire responsibility for the success or failure of the mission, in spite of my pointing out to him that he could hardly be blamed, at least in my particular case, for something he knew nothing about.

'Timothy won't see it like that,' he grunted.

'Don't pretend you're afraid of Timothy Plummer!' I scoffed, but he merely shrugged and terminated the exchange by turning to upbraid Philip for some imagined misdemeanour.

I hadn't failed to notice his growing exasperation with Philip, demonstrated almost hourly by an angry shout or even, at times, a blow, all of which Philip took with a kind of surly acceptance far more irritating than an angry response would have been. I think there were moments when John would have welcomed a bout of fisticuffs just to relieve the tension between them. I know that I often longed to take my old friend by the scruff of the neck and shake some life into him. My earlier sympathy, indeed my own grief for Jeanne, had been eroded by his behaviour.

As for Eloise, her continuing concern over the missing Raoul d'Harcourt was beginning to stretch my tolerance in another direction. For the first day after our leaving the inn, she had talked of nothing else, wondering, speculating as to his present whereabouts and whether or not some harm had befallen him. A particularly sharp exchange of views the following bedtime had resulted in my dragging pillows and one of the covers off the bed and spending the night on the floor. Since then, we had adhered rigidly to the most commonplace remarks and, on occasion, had even resorted to addressing one another through the medium of a third party. This childish behaviour had naturally enough added to John Bradshaw's worries and contributed to his increasing bad temper.

By the time the walls of Paris came in view through the murky November twilight, we were all exhibiting the strains and tensions of an ill-assorted party thrown together for days on end and unable to escape one another.

Paris, like London, could be heard and smelled from several miles away, the noise and stench increasing the nearer one got. By the time we passed through the Porte Saint-Denis and proceeded down the Rue Saint-Denis, my senses were reeling, and it was all I could do to remain upright in the saddle.

Eloise, on the other hand, seemed suddenly to revive like someone given a refreshing draught of wine. Her hitherto drooping form straightened up, and her head began to turn this way and that as she looked eagerly about her. This part of the city, she informed me, was known as La Ville. The Town. We were riding south, she went on, towards the Île de la Cité and beyond that, on the far bank of the Seine, was the suburb of the Université, so called for the simple and obvious reason that it was where the various colleges were situated, amidst the surrounding sprawl of houses, fields and churches. As far as she was concerned, she had come home.

I, in contrast, was feeling more and more

275

like a stranger in a strange land – which, of course, I was. But up until then, in the towns and countryside we had passed through, I had not felt too alienated. There had been many similarities to England. Paris, however, was altogether different. The Rue Saint-Denis was packed with people and traffic – ten or eleven carts, I'd swear, to every furlong of road – and everyone jabbering away, nineteen to the dozen, in an incomprehensible language. And not only talking, but also gesticulating wildly. (Why, oh, why do our French neighbours find it so necessary to discourse with their arms as well as their tongues?) And the smell was almost overwhelming.

'That's the market,' Eloise explained, waving a hand vaguely to her right. 'Les Halles.' She turned her head. 'How much further, John?'

'Keep going,' he answered roughly, but in a voice weakened by exhaustion. 'Cross by the Pont aux Meuniers into the Rue de la Barillerie, then wait. Someone should be meeting us there. A house has been rented for us. At least, I hope to God it has and nothing's gone wrong.' He crossed himself devoutly. His face looked grey with fatigue, a man at the end of his tether.

The bridge by which we eventually crossed, leading from the quayside to the Île de la Cité seemed to be one of three – two of stone and the third, ours, built of wood. I did rouse myself sufficiently to enquire of Eloise why all the houses on them had green roofs, to which she replied that they had turned that colour from mould and water vapour off the river. This was not reassuring and almost immediately I started to cough.

My companion laughed unfeelingly. 'Don't tell me you're falling into a consumption,' she protested, a petty jibe I chose to ignore.

The Rue de la Barillerie was almost a continuation of the Pont aux Meuniers, one of the warren of narrow streets that covered the island and surrounded the great cathedral of Notre-Dame. As we left the quayside – where, in spite of the advanced hour of the afternoon, washerwomen were still down on the strand, pummelling and soaking their washing, calling to one another and shrieking with laughter at the latest ribald joke – and plunged into the gloom between the overhanging houses, a man detached himself from the shadows of a doorway halfway along the street and walked towards us. I recognized him at once as the person I had seen talking to John Bradshaw outside the inn at Calais.

He said something in French and jerked a thumb back across his shoulder, indicating a tall, narrow house, wedged between two similar neighbours, its frontage originally stained red and green, but whose paint had now peeled away, leaving only traces of the colours as a memento of past glory.

'Journey's end,' John Bradshaw said, and never did words fall more kindly on my ears.

'This house will be our lodging while we are in Paris, and a woman has been hired to wait on us and attend to our needs. Her name's Marthe; that's all you need to know. She speaks a little English, but not much, so, Roger, you'll have to rely on Mistress Eloise and myself to translate for you. Philip!' He spoke sharply to Philip Lamprey, who was slumped forward in his saddle, the usual picture of dejection. 'There's stabling for the horses in the next street. Jules here will lead two of the animals and show you the way.' John eased himself to the ground with the sigh of a man weary unto death. 'See them fed and watered and bedded down properly for the night, then return here. Do you understand?' A brief nod was the only indication that he had been heard. John sighed and turned back, giving his hand to Eloise to help her dismount. 'You'll be in need of your supper, my dear,' he said in the gentler tone he reserved for women, as being delicate creatures in constant need of male strength and reassurance. (It was this attitude that convinced me he had probably never been married and had most certainly never had daughters of his own.)

My memory of that first night in Paris is lost in a haze of lassitude similar to that of our very first night on the road after quitting London. Marthe, contrary to my expectations, turned out to be a jolly, red-faced woman and an excellent cook, who seemed to find it excessively amusing each time I addressed her by the English version of her name. To begin with, I did it simply to annoy Eloise (who was convinced, rightly, of my laziness where trying to speak a foreign language was concerned), but I continued doing so just for the pleasure of watching Marthe shake all over like a jelly whenever I slipped an arm round her ample waist and called her 'Martha, my lover' in the best West Country tradition.

Our housekeeper apart, however, nothing remains in my memory except eating and then climbing the stairs to the first-floor bedchamber I was to share with Eloise during our stay in Paris. I don't recall that she even went through the nightly ritual of undressing behind the bed-curtains, so accustomed had we grown to one another's company. But I do remember waking in the middle of the night, in a sweat, conscious of a strange city all around me with its odd nocturnal noises, and uncomfortably aware that I must shortly begin my quest to find Robin Gaunt and his wife, a task of impossible proportions with which I should never have been burdened. With which no man should have been burdened, I thought resentfully. But even fear and resentment failed to keep me awake for long, and almost before I knew it, a faint, misty sunlight was rimming the shutters and Marthe was knocking at our bedchamber door with a pitcher of hot water for our morning needs, while the tantalizing smells of hot oatcakes and bacon collops wafted up

279

the stairs.

Shaved, washed, hair combed, teeth cleaned, dressed in brown hose and yellow jerkin, I descended to the small parlour overlooking the street, where John Bradshaw, no longer forced to play the servant, except when we went abroad, joined Eloise and myself at table.

'Where's Philip?' I asked.

John shrugged. 'Prefers to eat in the kitchen with Marthe. He seems to have taken a fancy to her. Leastways, he appears in a slightly happier mood than he's been in since we left London, although that ain't saying much. He's managed a couple of smiles for her, and she grins and nods at him even though neither can understand a word the other's saying.' He took a swig of ale and continued, 'Now! We're in luck. Jules tells me that your cousin–' he nodded at Eloise – 'won't be in Paris until Monday at the earliest. King Louis has delayed sending him until next week. Indeed, there was a rumour that Maître le Daim might not be coming after all. But now the king has changed his mind again, and if all's well, he'll be here on Monday, like I said.'

'Do we know where Cousin Olivier will be lodging?' Eloise enquired, delicately wiping her lips on the edge of a green, squirrel-trimmed sleeve.

John Bradshaw shook his head. 'Not yet. Jules will let us know as soon as he finds out. Meantime, I suggest you two get acquainted with the city, and you, Roger, try and look like a haberdasher and hawk around a few of those samples of cloth and other goods you brought with you.'

'I don't need to get acquainted,' Eloise retorted indignantly. 'I know this city like the back of my hand.'

I grinned nastily. 'You forget, John, she was here with my lord of Albany earlier this year and last.'

'We were with the court at Plessis-les-Tours,' she snapped. 'I know Paris because it is my mother's city and I spent part of my childhood here.'

'Then you'll be able to show Roger around like the native you are,' John Bradshaw said, rising to his feet, at the same time indicating to me that I should remain behind when Eloise left the parlour.

I duly lingered over my last oatcake. As she disappeared upstairs to fetch her cloak and gloves, I raised my eyebrows. 'You wanted to see me?'

He swallowed the dregs of his ale. 'I just wanted to say, let Mistress Eloise show you the city today, but after that, if you need to wander Paris on your own, give me the wink and I'll try to find some excuse to detain her indoors or elsewhere.' Before I could interrupt to thank him, he went on, 'But as to going on your own, I'm not so sure that's wise. There are as many footpads and robbers and pickpockets here as in London, and an obvious Englishman like yourself is going to be fair game. Take someone with you. Take

Philip.'

'Philip? What good will he be? He has the same amount of French as me – which is to say none at all – and in his present depressed state far less sense.'

'Two are more unlikely to be set upon than one man on his own.' John grinned suddenly. He was looking better this morning: a night's sleep had refreshed him and his old vigour had returned. 'And of course three would be even safer, especially if the third's a Frenchman. Take Jules as well. You needn't worry about his discretion. He's a taciturn devil at the best of times, and I shan't interrogate him as to what you're up to. I've told you already, if the duke don't want me to know, then I don't, either. And Jules ain't interested in the affairs of an English prince.'

'Then what's he doing in your pay?' I demanded sceptically.

'A personal grudge against the French authorities.' John laughed. 'Two of his brothers were counterfeit coiners and had the bad luck to be caught. They were both boiled alive in the great cauldron in the pig market, out beyond the Louvre, towards the Porte Saint-Honoré. A very unpleasant and agonizingly slow form of execution. Malcontents like Jules are always useful, if you can find 'em.'

'All right,' I agreed, after a moment or two's consideration. To have someone who could speak the language and knew the city would make my almost impossible task immeasurably easier. 'But in that case, I shan't need

Philip.'

John rose from the table as Marthe came in, ready to clear away the breakfast things. 'Oh, for the Virgin's sweet sake, take him with you, man! Give him something to do. I'm sick to death of his long, mournful face and his refusal to say more than half a dozen words together. I wish to heaven I'd never brought him with us. There were others I could have employed. I just felt sorry for him, that's all. An old comrade-in-arms who'd fallen on rough times.' He straightened his jerkin and said a few words of greeting to Marthe before slapping me on the back. 'You'd best go. Mistress Eloise will be growing impatient as well as curious by now. Just familiarize yourself today with as much of the city as you can, and if you can give the impression of a prosperous haberdasher with an interest in buying French goods, as well as trying to sell a few of your own, all the better.'

He left the room, exchanging a cheery word with Eloise as she entered, none too pleased at being kept waiting.

'What on earth have you two been talking about all this time?' she demanded, throwing my cloak and hat down on the table as she spoke. Without waiting for an answer, she continued, 'Before we go anywhere else, I want to visit the Quai des Orfèvres.'

The Goldsmiths' Quay was only a short walk away, along the Rue Barthélemy and turning right at the Pont Saint-Michel, one of the two

283

bridges that crossed to the Université district.

'What are we doing here?' I grumbled. 'Do you have money to spend?'

'Fool!' she retorted angrily. 'I'm hoping to locate Monsieur d'Harcourt's shop. If there's someone there – and he surely must leave an assistant in charge when he goes away – we might glean some information.'

'Such as?'

'Such as whether they've heard anything from him, or whether they think he's still on his travels. I'm worried about him, Roger. First, Oliver Cook goes missing and now Raoul. I don't like it. I feel in my bones that something's amiss.'

'And since when have you been calling him by his Christian name?' I demanded with some heat.

'Since he asked me to,' she snapped back. 'And in any case, I don't see it's any business of yours. Once we've accomplished what we came to Paris to do and returned to England, there's no reason why we should ever willingly see one another again.'

'Good! That's something to look forward to,' I said, seizing her elbow and guiding her around a puddle in the road. (Although there were surprisingly few of these, as the Paris roads were in very much better condition than London's. Eloise told me later that the capital's streets had been paved centuries earlier on the orders of Philip Augustus, the grandfather of St Louis.)

She made no reply to my ill-natured

remark, only shaking off my arm and quickening her pace a little until we came to the goldsmiths' workshops lining the quayside. But here we drew a blank. A Raoul d'Harcourt certainly owned a shop on the Quai des Orfèvres, but the smiling, portly gentleman who admitted to that name, and who gallantly bowed over Eloise's extended hand, was certainly not the man we had met for the first time on board *The Sea Nymph*, or later in Calais, or later again somewhere in the vicinity of Amiens.

We left the shop in some confusion, our previous dispute forgotten.

'You're sure he understood who you were enquiring for?' I asked, once the situation had been explained to me.

'Oh, don't be stupider than you really are, Roger!' Eloise exclaimed angrily. 'You must have heard me say the name Raoul d'Harcourt yourself. Even you must have understood that much! And that was him, the man I was speaking to. He is Raoul d'Harcourt. And he swears there is no other man of that name on the quay.'

I dragged her out of the way as two carts, one loaded with fish, the other with bales of hay, went past neck and neck, each driver determined to be first into the narrow opening that led to the Rue Barthélemy.

'Look,' I said, pulling her round to face me, 'our man is an impostor, that's clear. For what reason, and what his game is, there's no saying. When we get back to the house, I'll tell

285

John, though I doubt he'll be able to offer any explanation. The masquerade could well mean his disappearance is voluntary, which, in turn, might mean no harm's come to him. And that might set your mind at rest, you being so anxious about his welfare.'

Her expression lightened somewhat. 'That's true,' she said, and tucked a hand in my arm. 'In that case, I'd better do as Master Bradshaw instructed me and show you the city.' She thought for a minute, then nodded. 'Of course!' She smiled mischievously. 'I promised you, didn't I, that you should see the original of *The Dance of Death*?'

So we returned through the rabbit warren of streets that make up most of the Île de la Cité, to recross the Pont aux Meuniers and make our way again up the Rue Saint-Denis.

The Cemetery of the Innocents was to the left some few hundred yards along the street, and its cloister walls were indeed decorated with the same grinning skeletons as adorned the north cloister of St Paul's. I felt a shiver go down my spine, and I thought of the Frenchman Jules's two brothers, boiled alive in the pig market in front of a jeering crowd. Of course I knew that criminals had to be punished, and the more horrible the death, the more it deterred others from doing the same, but I had never been one for public executions or made of them the sort of holiday that others did, with regular eating and drinking and neighbourly gossip through the victims' screams. Had I been less well able to defend myself, I suspect that I should often have been accused of an effeminate squeamishness by more robust friends and acquaintances who enjoyed watching a felon dancing on air at the end of a rope, or being sliced open while still alive and his entrails burned before his eyes.

Eloise's voice rescued me from my grim thoughts. *'La Danse Macabre,'* she said slowly and, like me, suddenly shivered, clutching at my arm again for comfort. 'I don't know why it is,' she went on, 'but until now I've always thought it slightly humorous, all those dancing bones and grinning skulls. Yet today they strike me as sinister. What's the reason, do you think, Roger?'

I covered the little hand tucked into the crook of my elbow with one of my own. 'You're overtired and nervous,' I said, 'and strange things have been happening during the past week.' I grinned weakly. 'And I don't suppose having to pretend to be my wife has made matters any easier.'

'Oh, that,' she said, and gave a half-laugh, half-sob. Turning to look at her, I was amazed to see what could have been tears sparkling on the ends of her lashes, but before I could say anything more, she swung on her heel, taking me with her. 'Enough of this dismal conversation!' She squeezed my arm. 'You wanted to see Paris, and Paris you shall see.'

I can't remember how far we walked, but I

know that by dinnertime my legs were aching as they had never ached before. Eloise was an indefatigable and informative guide to a city she plainly loved with all her heart, and dragged me from place to place with an enthusiasm that seemed completely to have supplanted her earlier malaise, so much so that I could not help suspecting that it was a little spurious. But I said nothing, applying myself instead to taking note of my surroundings so that I could, if necessary, find my way around on my own. Relieved as I was to follow John Bradshaw's advice and take Philip and the Frenchman, Jules, with me, I could foresee times when it might be essential to be alone.

One of the things that puzzled me were the fragments of old, ivy-covered wall and broken gateways that stood sentinel among the crowding houses and gardens, until Eloise explained that these were the remains of the original city wall erected at the command of Philip Augustus in the thirteenth century. It had never properly been demolished when, over a hundred and fifty years later, Charles V had ordered a new wall to be built, the one that now surrounded La Ville. The old wall still did for La Université on the south bank of the Seine, but the great palaces and churches of La Ville had to be afforded better protection.

By the time we eventually paused for refreshment in the Rue Saint-Antoine, close to a group of menacing black towers, enclosed by a circular moat, drawbridge raised, port-cullis lowered, which Eloise named as La Bastille, I was more than ready to leave any further knowledge of Paris to my own wanderings.

'Weakling!' Eloise scoffed. 'We haven't seen a quarter of even La Ville.'

'I'll take your word for it,' I said, tucking in to an eel pie, washed down with a rough red wine that made my head spin after only one or two gulps. (I noticed it had no such similar effect on my companion.) But it generated a warm glow against the chill of the November morning. I began to feel more relaxed.

A man entering by the nearby Porte Saint-Antoine reminded me of John Bradshaw: middle-aged, well-fleshed, square of face with a thatch of brown hair, English-looking.

'Did you know,' I asked Eloise, suddenly recalling a surprising fact, 'that John had a French grandmother?' She shook her head. 'So he told me,' I went on. 'You wouldn't think it, would you, to look at him?'

She wiped her mouth daintily on the back of her hand. 'Poor man,' she murmured ironically. 'A French grandmother! What a cross for him to bear!'

'I didn't mean it like that,' I answered stiffly.

'Didn't you? You English think you're only one step down from God.'

I could see that we were on the brink of another of our pointless disputes. I said, 'She came from Clervaux. John's grandmother, that is.'

Eloise raised her eyebrows. 'From Clair-vaux or Clervaux?' she asked.

'What sort of question is that?' I barked irritably. 'I warn you, I'm in no mood for playing games.'

'You're so ignorant,' she replied coldly. 'I'm not playing games. Did John Bradshaw's grandmother come from C-L-A-I-R-vaux or from C-L-E-R-vaux? The first is in Champagne, where St Bernard founded his great monastery. The second is in the Grand Duchy.'

'Grand Duchy?'

She sighed wearily, a well-travelled woman dealing with an ignorant stay-at-home. 'Luxembourg.'

I had to admit that I didn't know the answer, nor had I realized that there was any question to be asked in the first place. I suggested austerely that we go back to the Île de la Cité and the Rue de la Barillerie. Eloise agreed with a rather superior smile, which annoyed me even further.

We returned by the Pont Notre-Dame, eventually emerging into the square in front of the cathedral, where three streets converged on a space that was overhung on one side by the frontage of what my companion informed me was the Hôtel Dieu, a strange building whose roof looked as though it had suffered a very nasty rash of pustules and warts. I was just about to ask Eloise the reason for this architectural aberration when a fist smote my shoulder and a familiar voice addressed us in English.

'Master Chapman! Mistress Chapman! What a pleasure to see you both again!'

It was William Lackpenny.

Seventeen

'M–Master Lackpenny!' I stuttered. 'Will! Y–you're in Paris, then!'

'We arrived this morning.' He beamed.

'We?' Eloise queried. 'Are the Armigers with you, as well?'

'Indeed. They are at this moment settling into Mistress Armiger's cousin's house in the Rue de la Tissanderie, off the Rue Saint-Martin. Perhaps you know it? For myself, I've found a very comfortable lodging not far from the Hôtel de Ville in the Place de Grève.'

'But what has happened about Master Cook?' I asked. 'We imagined you still in Calais, waiting for news.'

Will Lackpenny shrugged. 'There was no news, that was the trouble, and we couldn't wait for ever.' He added hastily, realizing how callous he must sound, 'At least, Master Armiger felt that to remain there any longer was a waste of time. He was certain that his brother-in-law had been washed overboard and drowned mid-Channel. No hope of the body ever being found, so he persuaded Jane – Mistress Armiger I should say – that they might as well continue their journey. Naturally, she, poor girl, didn't wish to leave Calais until something definite had been heard. But even I, far more sympathetic, I assure you, than that cold fish of a husband of hers, could see that to remain was useless. Oliver's dead: I don't think there can be any doubt about it. So we left a day and a half after your good selves. We made excellent time on the roads and here we are. And who should I encounter almost as soon as I set foot out of doors but the two of you!'

He seemed so genuinely pleased at the meeting that I began to feel churlish at our lack of response. But I knew John Bradshaw would feel the same. If Will Lackpenny and the Armigers were to plague us with their attentions, we should have to be constantly alert, ready to slip into our respective roles as master and servant at a moment's notice. I found myself wondering about Robert Armiger's insistence on following us to Paris so soon, and whether or not there was something sinister to be read into it. Or had my smart young gent of the blue feather – now dried out and perked up again after its salt-water baptism – persuaded the older man that no good could be achieved by loitering in Calais? Was he a Woodville agent, or were they, all three, exactly what they seemed to be?

I became conscious of Eloise nudging me in the ribs.

'Sweetheart, Master Lackpenny is speaking to you.' She gave a tinkling little laugh. 'I'm always having to scold him, Will,' she apologized, 'about this bad habit he has of going off into a fit of abstraction when he's talking to people. Isn't that so, dearest?'

I smiled weakly and nodded.

'Oh, I can see you're a busy man, Master Chapman.' He indicated the satchel slung over my left shoulder. 'You've been hawking your wares around some of the Paris shops and appraising their goods in return with a view to buying. You're preoccupied and I mustn't keep you.'

I started guiltily. Of course, it was exactly what I should have been doing, establishing my presence in the French capital as a prosperous haberdasher, but which, in my usual slipshod fashion, I had forgotten all about. I was never going to make one of Timothy's little band of spies and foreign agents, not if I lived to be a hundred (which seemed highly unlikely in my present state of jangled nerves and stomach-churning apprehension). I made up my mind there and then that as soon as this jaunt was over, I was going back to my family and to being an ordinary pedlar again, no matter what inducements were offered or what commands were laid upon me, not even if they came from the king himself.

Will Lackpenny finally took his leave of us

with a flourish of his blue-feathered hat, and we watched him vanish into the crowds as he made his way back to the Pont Notre-Dame and the Place de Grève. Or would he go straight to the Rue de la Tissanderie to report our meeting? And if so, from what motive? Innocent? Or with a more sinister intention behind it?

As I had anticipated, John Bradshaw was not best pleased with the information that Will Lackpenny and Robert and Jane Armiger were already in Paris.

'I was hoping we'd seen the last o' them,' he grumbled. 'I trusted we'd have been on the road home by the time they arrived.' He heaved a sigh. 'Ah, well! It can't be helped. If they come calling, as I don't doubt they will, I'll have time to make myself scarce for a chinwag with Mother Marthe in the kitchen. So, Roger,' he went on, 'do you think you can find your way around Paris on your own now?'

'Why should he want to go on his own?' Eloise asked, shedding her cloak and draping it elegantly over one arm. 'I'm supposed to be his wife, and he's here to escort me. At least, that's what I understood from Master Plummer.' She regarded us both with sudden suspicion.

I hurriedly recounted the details of our meeting with the real Raoul d'Harcourt on the Quai des Orfèvres, and if I failed to divert Eloise's attention completely, I certainly grabbed and held John Bradshaw's.

'I always knew there was something smoky about that fellow,' he muttered. 'I felt it in my bones.'

He continued to brood about it for several minutes, and even when he finally appeared to shrug the news aside, I could see that it still worried him. When he finally left the room on some pretext or another, I made an excuse to follow him out to the kitchen, where, surprisingly, we found Philip turning two capons on a spit, while Marthe made pastry and smiled approvingly at him and crooned a little tune under her breath.

'A miracle,' John grunted, although I got the impression that he was none too pleased by the sudden and apparently ripening friendship between this oddly assorted couple.

He opened the back door and went outside, where there was a tiny yard, surrounded on three sides by a rough stone wall, above which crowded the jumble of sloping roofs and conical towers of the neighbouring houses.

'What do you want, Roger?' he snapped, plainly irritated to discover that I had followed him.

I shrugged. 'I thought maybe there was something you wanted to discuss with me.'

'Such as?'

'Master Harcourt. Or the man posing as him, whoever he might be. Because whatever uncertainties we harbour about the Armigers and Master Lackpenny, we now know for sure that Raoul d'Harcourt is not who he claims to be. So what do you think has happened to him?'

John leaned his shoulders against the wall of the house and sighed wearily. 'I don't know,' he admitted. 'I wish by all the saints that I did, but I don't. I tell you, Roger, that I shall be thankful when this mission is accomplished and we're safely back in London. Nothing is going according to plan, and from almost the very beginning we've been beset by too many other unexpected players in the game: the Armigers, Master Lackpenny and now this Frenchman – if he is a Frenchman at all, which I'm starting to doubt.'

'Mistress Gray seems to believe he is, and I should consider her judgement sound in such a matter.'

John snorted. 'Don't be taken in by her,' he advised, adding spitefully, 'She's not anywhere near as clever as she thinks she is. And, for the sweet Virgin's sake, remember she's your wife!' He heaved himself away from the back wall of the house and thumped it. 'Just recollect, these things have ears. Her name is Mistress Chapman until we set foot on English soil again.'

'And how long will that be?' It was my turn to sound morose and despondent.

John Bradshaw straightened his shoulders. 'Well,' he said, 'if Maître le Daim does arrive in Paris on Monday, then it's up to Mistress Eloise to make herself known to him as soon as possible after that. Necessary, too, because we don't know how long he'll be remaining in the capital. Jules will alert us as soon as he finds out where he's staying.'

'And if he won't see Eloise, or won't satisfy her curiosity concerning the Burgundian alliance? What then?'

'Then we return home.' He shrugged philosophically. 'We've done our best. But I'm willing to wager a considerable sum that she'll get the information from him. She has a wheedling way with her has Mistress Eloise. She ain't going to ask him outright, of course, but I reckon she'll find out what we want to know.' He took a deep breath and faced me squarely. 'No, it's you, Roger, and this secret mission you're on for Duke Richard that bothers me. Somehow or another you've got to get out and about without the lady accompanying you, and without arousing her curiosity any more than it's aroused already. So what I suggest is this: tomorrow's Sunday, so just play the good husband and take your "wife" to church and wherever else she wants to go—'

'In other words, allay her suspicions,' I interrupted.

John nodded. 'Exactly. But come Monday, she'll have to stay at home waiting for word of her cousin's arrival, and maybe the next day, and even the day after that. Meantime, you take Philip and get on with whatever it is you have to do.'

'What about Jules?'

My companion shook his head. 'He won't be available until Olivier le Daim is safely inside the city. I'm sorry, but I was a bit premature there in offering his services.' He gave another sigh. 'I'm afraid I'm getting too old for this job. I'm growing addle-pated.'

'You've too much on your mind,' I comforted him. 'But how do we explain my absences to Eloise?'

'Do I have to think of everything?' he demanded peevishly. But a moment's thought gave him the answer. 'You're playing your part, of course! The haberdasher buying and selling your goods, trying to establish an overseas market in these peaceful times. You're merely lulling any suspicion that you might not be what you seem to be. That should satisfy Mistress Eloise.'

'And if – when – she goes to visit Mâitre le Daim, do I accompany her?'

'We shall do what seems best at the time.' The spy flexed his arm joints. 'Now go away, Roger, and leave me in peace and quiet for a few minutes. Indeed, it was for that reason I came out here, only to find you at my heels. I need to collect my thoughts. Go and make your peace with your "wife". I don't doubt but what she's fretting at your absence.'

'You think she's fond of me?' I asked, surprised.

John grinned. 'Not for a moment,' was the honest reply. 'But she's a woman, ain't she? Never met one o' that breed that wasn't born with the curiosity of a cat. And that one's got a damn long nose on her – like you! In that respect, you're well suited to one another.' He emitted one of his deep-throated chuckles. 'P'r'aps it's a good job you ain't really married or the sparks would fly.'

Eloise was nowhere in the house.

I returned to the kitchen and, by dint of much miming and nodding and smiling, together with interrogative shouts of 'Madame?' Marthe and I managed at last to establish that Eloise had gone out while I had been talking to John in the yard. It was only when we were both exhausted by our efforts at understanding that I remembered Philip.

'Why didn't you tell me, you great lump?' I shouted at him.

'You didn't ask me,' was the surly response. 'Besides,' he went on before I could give full vent to my wrath, 'I couldn't absolutely swear to what they were saying.'

'Lying bastard,' I said, but with less heat. 'I'll wager Eloise told you in plain English that she was going out, didn't she?' He grinned and I suddenly saw something of the old Philip who had been absent for so long. 'Didn't she?' I repeated.

'Perhaps,' he admitted. Then the grin broadened. 'To be honest, the pantomime between you and Mistress Marthe here was too good to interrupt.' He went on, 'Mistress Eloise came looking for you to bear her company to see the Armigers, wherever it is they're staying. Seems they've turned up again, along with that silly fellow with the blue feather in his hat. They must've made

299

pretty good time from Calais to be so hot on our heels.'

I regarded him affectionately. 'Do you know,' I asked, 'that you've just said more in the last minute than you've uttered in a whole week?' I dropped a hand on his shoulder and pressed it.

He let go of the handle of the spit, rose from his stool, shrugging off my hand as he did so, and turned towards me, his face suffused with anger. 'Don't you treat me to any of your patronizing airs and graces, Roger. Just leave me alone!'

This abrupt change of mood from the old Philip to the new was shocking. I felt as though he had dealt me a physical blow, and I heard Marthe making tut-tutting noises under her breath. She looked distressed, and although she had not understood what we were saying, Philip's sudden descent into fury was painfully apparent. She glanced questioningly at me, obviously wondering what I had said to bring about such a transformation.

When I had brought my breathing and my temper under control, I said coldly, 'I'm going out and I need you to accompany me. John Bradshaw's orders. Get your cloak on while I fetch mine.'

'No,' Philip answered truculently. 'I ain't coming. Bradshaw's given me no such order.'

The door into the yard opened and closed.

'Who's taking my name in vain?' John demanded.

I explained the situation and he raised his eyebrows.

'You're going out now? I thought we'd agreed...' He paused, grimacing. 'Oh well, if Mistress Eloise has gone a-visiting, perhaps you should take advantage of her absence.' He looked at Philip and his features hardened. 'You'll do as you're bid,' he instructed harshly. 'Get your cloak on and make no more bones about it.' He turned back to me as, to my amazement and without further demur, Philip shuffled over to where his cloak hung on a nail beside the kitchen door and put it on. 'Be careful, Roger,' John urged. 'Keep with Philip at all times. And Jules will be free today. If you decide you want his company, you'll most probably find him in Le Coq d'Or in the Rue de la Juiverie. That's the road that joins the Petit Pont on the south bank to the Pont Notre-Dame on t'other. It's his usual drinking den.'

I thanked him and returned to the parlour to collect my own cloak from where I had carelessly thrown it over the back of a chair, and to retrieve my hat from where I had dropped it, even more carelessly, on the floor. (Anyone could tell that I was unused to smart clothes.) By the time I was ready, having had to search around for the latter before spotting it under the table, Philip was waiting for me outside the street door, looking cold and disgruntled.

The November afternoon was well advanced, and, above us, the sky was dull and over-

301

cast. A chilly wind was blowing off the Seine, whistling between the canyons of the houses and bringing with it the smell of rotting fish and the faint tang of the sea that is reminiscent of all cities built on great rivers. It reminded me poignantly of my adopted town of Bristol and for a moment I was dumb with homesickness.

I took a deep breath. 'Which way?' I asked Philip.

He shrugged, indicating that he either didn't know or was bent on being obstructive. I gave him the benefit of the doubt and steered him in a westerly direction, having recollected that Eloise and I had returned to the Île de la Cité by the Pont Notre-Dame earlier in the day and must have crossed the Rue de la Juiverie to get to the square in front of the cathedral. The streets were still crowded, the noise still deafening, and I pulled Philip into the shelter of a doorway, where I could make myself heard. A couple of disease-ridden beggars reluctantly made way for us and rattled their tins, abusing us roundly when we ignored them. (I presume it was abuse. They certainly didn't sound as if they were giving us the time of day.)

'Now listen to me, Philip,' I said, 'and listen carefully. I'm going to have to trust you. And I do trust you. You may be behaving like a right little shit-house at the moment, but I've known you for years and we've been good friends in the past, so I'm going to tell you what I've even kept secret from John.'

'I don't want to know,' he shouted, and clapped both his hands over his ears.

'I don't care what you want,' I snarled back. 'You're damned well going to listen!' Seizing his wrists, I forced down his arms. He struggled to free himself.

The beggars, seeing only what they thought to be a servant defying his master, whooped and cheered and banged with their collecting cups against the wall of the house where we were all sheltering. I heard one of them mutter, *'Anglais! Anglais!'* followed by some imprecation, while the other fanned out his fingers behind his back in the semblance of a tail. (It crossed my mind, fleetingly, that for the English and French it would be almost impossible to live without one another. Who else would the denizens of both countries find to revile, despise and ridicule so virulently except the pestilential rapscallions on the opposite side of the Channel?)

Keeping Philip's arms pinioned to his sides, I said through clenched teeth, 'You're going to hear what I have to say whether you like it or not.'

The fight suddenly seemed to go out of him and his thin, emaciated body went limp, but I knew him for a cunning little rogue and kept a firm grip on him while I outlined, briefly, the gist of my mission for the Duke of Gloucester. When I had finished, he appeared genuinely shocked, releasing himself gently from my grasp but making no further effort to escape it.

He let out a long, low whistle and murmured, 'Hell's teeth!' For the first time since we renewed our acquaintance, someone else's predicament had caught his attention and evoked his sympathy. He lowered his voice, even though the two beggars, disappointed of the expected brawl, had now moved on. 'So that's the way the wind's blowing, is it? This is dangerous stuff, Roger.'

'You don't need to tell me that,' I responded feelingly. 'If the Woodvilles should get an inkling of it, I'd be a dead man long before I could report back to the duke. That's why it was thought best to keep it a secret even from John.'

'And now you've told me.' Philip sounded bitter and I realized guiltily that by doing so, I had possibly endangered his life as well as my own.

'I'm sorry,' I said. 'But you must see for yourself that I'm in desperate need of some help. Finding a former English soldier who, after forty years, most likely speaks French like a native, in a city the size of Paris is a near-impossible task. Added to which, there's no positive evidence that this Robin Gaunt lives here at all.'

'Oh, that sort of thing's only to be expected,' my companion snorted savagely. 'Our lords and masters issue their orders, no matter how impossible they may be, and we poor underlings are expected to carry them out. And woe betide us if we fail!'

'I don't think the duke would—' I was

beginning, but Philip interrupted me.

'Princes, nobles, officers, gentlemen, they're all the bloody same if you ask me! I never met one who was any different. But all this jabbering ain't going t' solve your problem.' He chewed a dirty fingernail. When I would have spoken, he raised an equally grimy finger and wagged it under my nose. 'Bide quiet a minute, can't you, and let me think. Mind you,' he went on, 'after what you just told me, I'm buggered if I can think proper. You're dabbling your fingers in treason here, Roger. And so's Prince Richard.'

'Depends if it is treason,' I argued. 'Depends on what I find out.' I glanced over my shoulder, then whispered, 'Maybe His Grace is already the rightful king. Maybe he has been since the execution of Clarence. And maybe Brother George was rightfully king before him, and that's why he had to be got rid of.'

Philip clapped one of his hands over my mouth; it smelled of smoke and garlic. 'Will you keep your great gob shut? Just to please me!' He started chewing his nail again, nodding his head up and down and staring vacantly into the distance before suddenly coming to a conclusion. 'Best thing you can do—'

'We can do,' I corrected him.

He ignored me. 'Best thing you can do,' he continued, 'is to enquire around the inns and taverns if anyone knows of an elderly Englishman married to a French wife. An old soldier,

305

someone who might once have been part of the occupying forces forty years ago.' He stopped, giving vent to a rusty, reluctant chuckle. 'O' course, you could just ask if anyone knows a man called – what was it? – Robin Gaunt.'

It was so good to hear him laugh again that, for a moment, I joined in his merriment, but other considerations soon had a sobering effect. 'It sounds like excellent sense, Philip, except that it overlooks one thing: I can't speak French. And neither can you.'

His face fell; then he rallied. 'It's surprising how much you can make yourself understood if you try hard enough. Just keep repeating the name Robin Gaunt and tell 'em he's English, *Anglais. Femme française.* Do you know them? If so – by some miracle – where do they live? Keep saying things long enough and loud enough and something'll get through to somebody. Provided, of course, there's someone somewhere who knows something. Which I very much doubt.'

'No, wait!' I said. 'We've forgotten Jules. John told us where to find him. Le Coq d'Or in the Rue de la Jui— something or other. Anyway, the street that runs from a bridge on the south bank to the Pont Notre-Dame. I know where that is. Eloise and I crossed it earlier today. We'll go and find him.'

Philip's mouth set in familiarly stubborn lines. 'No,' he said.

'What do you mean, no?'

'I'm not dragging Jules into this.'

'Why not? John told me—'

'I don't trust him. That's why not.'

I was astonished at Philip's vehemence. 'Why don't you trust him?'

He hesitated for a moment or two, searching for an answer. Finally, he came up with, 'He's a Frenchie, ain't he? That's reason enough.'

'Not in this case,' I argued. 'It was John's suggestion, and he said Jules wouldn't be interested in anything I might be up to. And, indeed, why should he be? All we need is for him to ask a few questions for us. If by any chance he should evince any curiosity, we're just trying to find an old friend who might have settled in Paris. Surely that should satisfy him.'

'No,' Philip repeated even more forcefully than before. 'If you want to ask Jules for help, you'll go on your own. Try and force me to go with you and I'll kick up such a rumpus that you'll have half of Paris crowding round. I mean it, Roger. We do this alone or not at all.'

I was puzzled as well as annoyed. 'You can hardly know Jules,' I said. 'He's obviously one of John's French agents, but you can have seen very little of him, I should have thought. Why do you mistrust him so?'

Philip avoided my gaze, or, at least, it seemed to me that he did. I convinced myself that I was mistaken.

'I've told you,' Philip muttered sulkily. 'He's a Frenchie and I wouldn't trust a single one of 'em with my name and direction, let alone a secret of this magnitude.'

'But he won't—'

Philip rounded on me furiously. 'Look, Roger,' he hissed, seizing my arm and digging his nails in so violently that I could feel them even through the material of my sleeve, 'I ain't coming with you if you confide in that there Jules and that's my last word. So it's him or me. Take your pick.'

I finally accepted that he was serious. There would be no changing his mind and I had to choose between one and the other. The sensible choice was Jules, who could speak a little English as well as fluent French, whereas Philip's knowledge of the latter was non-existent, like mine. So why was I hesitating? But I knew Philip of old; we had been friends for years, and some of his distrust of the Frenchman had begun to convey itself to me. I knew it was foolish to let myself be influenced, particularly when Philip's attitude seemed to have nothing to give it substance, but there might be some reason behind it that he wasn't telling me. In the end, the devil I knew was better than the one I didn't.

'All right,' I agreed. 'We won't bother Jules. We'll leave him to enjoy his ale in peace.'

Eighteen

Of course it was inevitable that, entering the Rue de la Juiverie from a side alley, we should find ourselves almost directly opposite Le Coq d'Or at the precise moment Jules was leaving the inn. Moreover, he was not alone. John Bradshaw was with him, glancing up and down the street as though expecting momentarily to see someone he knew.

Philip hauled me back into the shadows of the overhanging houses and the noisome filth of the little lane, where a dead dog was rotting alongside a sheep's head – both crawling with maggots – and piles of other decaying rubbish that did not bear too close an inspection.

'Jules,' he hissed.

'I know. I saw him,' I answered irritably. 'And John's with him. He'll have warned Jules to look out for us, so we might as well—'

Philip shook his head. 'I told you, I don't trust him. Just wait here a moment, quiet, like, until they're gone.'

I sighed. 'And if they decide to come this way? We shall look a right pair of fools skulking around in this cesspit.'

'Well, they ain't coming this way,' Philip said. 'Look!' The two men had indeed turned towards the south bank and the Petit Pont. Philip grabbed my arm. 'Quick!' he grunted and dragged me across the street, bumping into several irate citizens and narrowly missing being run down by a couple of carts, into Le Coq d'Or. 'Last place they'll think o' looking for us, for a while at least.'

And so we started on a long round of the Paris inns, ale houses and drinking dens, trudging from the Île de la Cité to La Ville and back again, then across to the Université, where we accidentally entered a whorehouse and were set upon by one of the ugliest madames I had ever seen, determined that her girls should avail themselves of our services on what was obviously a slack afternoon. The discovery that we were English added to our charms for once, the ladies being intrigued by the prospect of men with tails, and we only made our escape by the skin of our teeth and a swift backhander to the madame to call off her bevy of beauties.

'That's it,' I said to Philip, leaning against the wall and breathing heavily. 'That's enough for one day. And where has it got us? We've nearly been raped by a bunch of harpies and we're no nearer tracking down this Robin Gaunt than when we started. And I don't suppose we ever shall be.'

'Oh, I don't know,' Philip murmured, stroking his chin. In spite of himself, he had become interested in the quest and, despite his

310

total lack of French, had managed to make himself understood far better than I had. He had a way of ingratiating himself with people that gained their confidence, while years of coping and haggling with foreigners in Leadenhall Market had taught him a sign language that seemed to be universally recognized, interspersed as it was with certain mongrel words that bridged the gap between different tongues. He went on, 'That ale house out towards the Porte Saint-Honour, beyond the old Loover Palace, or whatever they call it – it ain't a Christian language, that's for sure: you can't get your bloody tongue around it – the landlord there mentioned a Robert of Ghent. Seemed to think he might be the man you're looking for.'

'Ghent's in the Low Countries,' I snapped.

My feet were hurting and I was feeling miserable and depressed. It occurred to me that, within the course of an afternoon, Philip and I had changed places. Now I was the one who was gloomy and pessimistic, while Philip appeared to have overcome his lingering grief, for the time being at least, in the interest of the chase. I recalled the inn he had mentioned, an uninviting place near the Porte Saint-Honoré, dark, dingy, lit only by rushlights and smelling of human sweat and ordure, where strangers were stared at with even more suspicion than was normal in such places. Hostility emanated from every corner and I had felt my scalp tingle with fear, warning me of danger. To my utter astonishment,

Philip had seemed thoroughly at ease, but then I remembered that he had grown up in the Southwark stews. This ale house, as he had rightly called it – it was impossible to dignify it with the name of tavern – was home from home to him. The regular customers accepted him instinctively as one of themselves, regardless of the fact that he was English, while I was tolerated simply because I was his companion.

An added bonus had been that the landlord, a hulking fellow with a broken nose and a fiery birthmark that covered practically the whole of one side of his face, spoke a little English, enough at any rate to make communication somewhat less of a hit-and-miss affair than it had been in previous taverns we had visited. Philip's enquiries, while we drank a rough red wine that depressed my spirits rather than elevated them, elicited the fact that this Robert of Ghent lived somewhere in the warren of streets near the pig market, with its infamous cauldron. But by that time, with the Université still to investigate, I had declined being drawn into a fool's errand and refused point-blank Philip's suggestion that we search him out and at least establish that he was not the man we were looking for.

'These fools wouldn't know the difference between an Englishman and a Fleming,' I grumbled, rubbing the aching backs of my legs with both hands. 'And the sooner we get out of this place, the happier I shall be.'

'Please yourself.' Philip had shrugged. 'You're probably right.'

But now, leaning against the wall of the brothel while we caught our breath, he seemed to think we might have made a mistake by not pursuing the matter. 'It is the only lead we've got,' he pointed out.

'So far,' I agreed. 'But not much of one. We'll have to start again on Monday.'

'We?'

'So John says, and he's in charge. Until this Olivier le Daim makes his appearance, Jules will be otherwise engaged. Now, remember, Philip, I haven't told you what it is I'm doing for Duke Richard here in Paris. John doesn't know and he doesn't want to know, but he'd be upset and more than a little angry if he thought I'd confided in you. And, for the sweet Virgin's sake, not a word to anyone else. You can imagine that if the queen's family got wind of this, they'd go straight to the king and heaven alone knows what would happen to us all, including the duke. I'm willing to wager my last groat that Clarence knew about the bastardy story, and look what happened to him.'

Philip regarded me malevolently, and when he spoke, his tone was bitter. 'You don't need to remind me to keep me bone-box shut, thank you very much. I know what sort of bloody risk we're running.'

'Good,' I said. 'Now let's go back to the Rue de la Barillerie. 'I've had enough for one day. And the episode in this place–' I jerked a thumb over my shoulder – 'was the final straw.'

The following day, Sunday, was quiet. Everyone seemed out of sorts and disinclined for conversation. We all seemed to be nursing a private grievance, not openly stated, but nonetheless potent for all that. From the few words he did let fall, it was obvious that John was angry I had flouted his suggestion that I take Jules with me while I could, particularly as he had taken the trouble to visit the Coq d'Or to apprise the latter of my imminent arrival.

'You and Philip were so long farting around before you left the house I was able to slip out ahead of you in order to warn Jules you were coming. And then you didn't show up.'

I apologized and made some feeble excuse, which he accepted grudgingly, but remained taciturn for the rest of the day.

Philip kept out of my way, whether deliberately or by chance I couldn't determine, but he remained in the kitchen with Marthe, doing odd jobs for her and easing the burden of looking after four people single-handed. Or, at least, so Eloise informed me, having had some conversation with the housekeeper when she visited the kitchen after breakfast.

As for Eloise herself, she was as generally uncommunicative as the others, and for this a blazing quarrel the previous night was responsible. She had been short with me all evening and, when we finally retired to our

314

bedchamber, had reproached me in no uncertain terms for not accompanying her to
the Rue de la Tissanderie.

'Jane and Master Armiger thought it most
strange that I should go alone, and so, I'm
sure, did Will Lackpenny.'

Tired, worried, depressed, I had rounded
on her with a viciousness I regretted almost at
once. Seizing her by the shoulders and shaking her violently, I hissed, 'For Jesu's sake, get
it into your stupid little head that I am not
really your husband, and stop treating me as
though you were my wife! This is a game
we're playing, and what's more, I'll tell you
this: if we were man and wife and you spoke
to me like that, I'd take my belt to you and
leather you senseless.' And with that, I had
flung her away from me so that she went
sprawling across the bed.

She lay perfectly still for a moment, and, to
my horror, I saw that she was crying silently,
the tears streaming down her face. I was immediately contrite, appalled by my behaviour, and had sat down beside her, trying to
soothe her, trying to explain that I hadn't
meant a word I'd said. I had expected recriminations, even a hail of blows, but had
been unprepared for the quiet dignity with
which she had repelled my efforts at recon-
ciliation and finished preparing for bed. It
had made me feel an even bigger bully boy
than I did already, and although I recognized
that this was her intention, I nevertheless
knew that the way I had behaved would take

315

a lot of forgiving.

So the morning's coldness was hardly a surprise and I made no attempt at atonement. I reasoned the less said, the better, and that her own sense of justice would eventually lead her to realize that, however badly I might have acted, she herself had not been blameless. Her tirade against me had been both undeserved and foolish.

We went to Mass, to Tierce, having risen far too late for Prime, and I left the choice of the Île de la Cité's twenty-one churches to her. She decided eventually upon Saint-Pierre aux Boeufs, with its lovely slender spire, and stood beside me, eyes downcast, like a sweet and dutiful wife. As we left, she tucked a hand into the crook of my elbow and gave my arm a squeeze. If not entirely forgiven, I was not the pariah I had been an hour or so before.

'Let's go for a walk,' she said, but still quiet and inclined to be sombre. In much the same spirit I agreed.

So we strolled around the Île, saying little but with a growing sense of harmony, from the groves of the Jardins Royals in the west, by way of the cloisters and galleries behind the cathedral of Notre-Dame and the Bishop's Palace to the tangle of wasteland in the east, with its view of the neighbouring islands of Notre-Dame and the Île aux Vaches. I remarked again on the splendid flagging of the streets with their furrows for the horses' hooves and was intrigued by the little twisting turret staircases and the conical roofs of the houses. From one of the tarred booths of the Palus Market, already open for Sunday trade, I bought Eloise a green ribbon to match her green dress. And finally, in the shadow of the nearby Sainte-Chapelle, we stopped and faced one another, holding hands.

'Tell me I'm forgiven,' I said. 'My behaviour was abominable.'

'No, I was the one to blame,' she answered gently. 'Mine was the original fault. I must have sounded like a shrew, and without reason. I'm sorry.'

I smiled at her. 'Then we'll forgive one another, and I'll go with you to see Jane and Robert Armiger after we've eaten.'

I didn't add that I had an ulterior motive in wanting to speak to Jane Armiger again. It seemed wiser not to.

And so, after dinner – a meal that Eloise and I ate together in the parlour, neither John Bradshaw nor Philip putting in an appearance – we crossed back to La Ville and made our way to the Rue de la Tissanderie, to a house only a few doors distant from the great main thoroughfare of the Rue Saint-Martin.

We were fortunate in finding the Armigers in sole possession, Jane's French kinfolk having, so we were told, gone to visit yet another relative who was ailing and had sent that morning, demanding their immediate assistance.

'Tante Louise is rather demanding,' Jane said, obviously feeling the need to excuse her

317

relations' absence.

'A miserable, exigent old harridan,' Robert snorted in his usual forthright fashion. 'But I don't suppose Master and Mistress Chapman are worried whether your cousins are here or not, my dear.'

He was right, of course, but his brutal way of expressing himself only upset his wife further. Her eyes were constantly full of unshed tears, which she surreptitiously wiped away before they could provoke another outburst from her husband. I saw Eloise compress her lips and guessed that she was, most unwisely, on the verge of giving Master Armiger a piece of her mind, but the arrival of Will Lackpenny averted what might have turned into an unpleasant situation.

It struck me that Robert was not as happy to see his fellow traveller as he had once been, and I wondered if his suspicions were at last aroused or if he had simply tired of Will's company. But the visit could not have served my purpose better because Eloise, in a spirit of sheer mischief, immediately set out to monopolize Will's attention, preventing him from getting close to Jane and bombarding him with a series of questions that he was too polite too ignore.

I seized my opportunity and drew my stool nearer to where Mistress Armiger was sitting, a little removed from the rest of us, by the window. After ascertaining that there was no more news of her brother, and sympathetically patting her hand when she showed signs of breaking down, I asked swiftly, 'What exactly did you mean, that morning in Calais, when you said, "Yes"?' She stared at me uncomprehendingly, and I went on, 'I'd asked you if your grandmother – the French one, the seamstress – had ever mentioned any scandal regarding the Duchess of York and one of her bodyguard of archers. You didn't answer at once, but just as I was leaving, you said, "Yes." Do you remember?' She gave me a watery smile and nodded. 'You haven't mentioned my enquiry to anyone else, have you? Your husband or ... or Master Lack-penny?'

'No.' She added apologetically, 'I haven't really thought about it since,' and gave a little sob. 'There ... there have been...'

'Other things on your mind. Of course. I understand that. And I don't want you to say anything to either of them. To anyone at all. I ought not to have asked you what I did. But ... well ... as I did, what made you say, "Yes"?'

'Because I did once overhear my grand-mother tell my mother that there had been some scandal concerning the duchess and an archer while she was in Rouen.'

I was glad to note that she had lowered her voice almost to a whisper and I couldn't resist glancing over my shoulder. Eloise still held Will Lackpenny in thrall, while Robert Armiger was looking at them both, distinctly bored.

'Did your grandmother happen to mention the name of the archer concerned?'

319

Jane Armiger shook her head. 'No. I think, from what I can recollect, that she didn't know much. There had been some talk among the women, but that was all. In fact, young as I was, I can clearly recall her saying that the duchess was far too proud a woman to take a common archer to her bed. She didn't believe it, she said.' Jane nodded again. 'Yes, I can remember her saying that.'

I sighed. I was no further forward. But there had been a rumour; that was something, I supposed. I still needed to find Robin Gaunt, however. I leaned a little closer to Jane. 'Will you promise to say nothing to anyone about this conversation? I ... I'm sorry. I can't explain, but it is important.'

'I shan't say anything.' She smiled sadly. 'I don't talk to my husband much anyway.'

'And ... Master Lackpenny?'

The smile deepened and grew tender. 'Oh,' she murmured shyly, 'we ... we have other things to talk about.'

We were interrupted by Eloise, who had grown tired of flirting with Will and now wanted to reclaim my attention.

'What are you two talking about so cosily over here?'

'I was asking Mistress Armiger if she had received any more news of her brother,' I answered, getting to my feet. 'And commiserating with her concerning his loss.'

'I keep telling her Oliver's dead,' Robert Armiger said bluntly. 'And she might as well make up her mind to it.'

There was an awkward silence; then, not surprisingly, Jane Armiger burst into noisy tears. 'Oh, Robin, how can you be s–so cruel?' she gasped and fled from the room.

Her husband had the grace to look uncomfortable, but he brazened it out. 'Women!' he exclaimed disdainfully. 'What unaccountable creatures they are! There's no reasoning with them.'

Eloise had her mouth open to refute this statement. I could see that she was fuming and caught her by the arm, giving it a little nip with my fingers.

'We must be going,' I said, and extended my hand to Robert Armiger. 'Please convey our farewells to your wife and say we perfectly understand how she feels. I don't know if we shall see one another again – it depends how long we stay in Paris – but if we do, I trust you may have happier news to give us.'

He snorted sceptically, making no effort to detain us, and we were barely clear of the house before Eloise, unable any longer to contain herself, forcibly and loudly expressed her opinion of Master Armiger's manners.

'Hush,' I reprimanded her. 'He might hear you.'

'I don't care if he does,' was the spirited retort. 'He's a great brute! An unfeeling bully! He ... he ... He's a man!'

'Oh, Mistress Chapman, you mustn't judge us all by Robert Armiger,' came a voice from behind, and we spun round to find William Lackpenny close on our heels. 'I just couldn't stay another instant in the same room with that man,' he added by way of explanation. 'If I had, I wouldn't have been responsible for my actions.' He fell into step beside us. 'Did I understand you to say that you would be leaving Paris soon? You've finished your business already, Roger? In so short a time?'

This interest in my affairs immediately re-animated my suspicions regarding my smart young gent. Why did he want to know?

'Oh, nothing's decided,' I replied airily. 'I shall see how things go. We may bump into one another again, I daresay, but for now, we'll say goodbye.'

He smiled slightly, but took what was virtually a dismissal very well. He was, in any case, close to the Place de Grève, where he was lodging.

'And God be with you, too,' he answered, bowing low over Eloise's hand. 'Mistress Chapman, your humble servant.'

'You weren't very polite to him,' Eloise chided me as we crossed back to the Île de la Cité by the Pont aux Meuniers and entered the Rue de la Barillerie, but it was a gentle reproach, not at all like her usual abrasive self. Indeed, she didn't pursue the subject, not even waiting for me to justify myself or think up an excuse to satisfy her. Instead, she gave my arm a squeeze. 'I'm beginning to like it,' she went on seriously, 'when people call me Mistress Chapman.' She glanced up at me. 'Do you feel the same way, Roger?'

I was struck dumb. What could I possibly

say? I was a married man. I had children. I loved my family, but at the moment, they seemed a very dim memory and very far away. I hadn't seen any of them for months, and in the meantime I had been to Scotland. Now I was in France. And I couldn't deny that, over the past two weeks, I had, against my will, grown fond of Eloise. No, more than that if I were honest. And it was this need to suppress my feelings that had led to many of the quarrels and most of the tension between us.

She was expecting an answer; I could see it in her face. She was not going to turn it into a joke, as she had done once or twice before. She had caught me on her hook and this time she was not going to free me.

I took a deep breath. 'I...' I began feebly.

Suddenly, her grip on my arm tightened. 'To your left, Roger,' she whispered excitedly. 'There!' She pointed with her other hand. 'He's just disappeared into one of those alleyways. Quick! We can catch him if we run!'

'Who?' I demanded distractedly. 'Who's just—'

'Raoul d'Harcourt! I only caught a glimpse, but I'm certain it was him.'

'Raoul d'Harcourt? But—'

'Oh, come on!' she cried impatiently, and, hitching up her skirts, began to run.

I followed her across the busy street and into the narrow opening between two houses, but here we came to a stop. Unlike most of the alleyways off the Rue de la Barillerie, it led nowhere, a six-foot-high wall at the end making it impossible to proceed any further, while the walls of the two enclosing houses rose solidly on either side. Of Raoul d'Harcourt – or whatever his real name was – there was no sign.

'There must be a door somewhere,' Eloise insisted. 'He can't just have vanished into thin air.'

But there was no trace of a door or window, and it was only as we were about to leave, defeated, and as my eyes grew more accustomed to the gloom, that I became aware of a number of stones in the end wall standing proud of the surface, enabling a fit man to gain a toehold and thus climb over it. Cursing, I clambered up, but our quarry had long gone, vanishing into the noise and bustle of the next street.

'Shit!' I said, brushing down the front of my green tunic and noticing a dark stain on one knee of my brown hose. They were already snagged in various places and it was only by the grace of God that I hadn't just ripped them on one of the projecting stones. It was not that I was growing particular in my dress, but I had no doubt at all that Timothy would subtract money for any damage done from whatever payment was due to me on our return to London.

I took back my cloak from Eloise, who had been holding it while I scaled the wall, and wrapped it round me. The November day had suddenly grown extremely cold, with a sharp wind blowing off the Seine, and as we re-entered the Rue de la Barillerie, a shaft of light from an upstairs window showed frost already glittering on the paving stones. It was going to be a bitter night. Moreover, I was suddenly conscious of the non-stop pealing of the church bells echoing and re-echoing in my ears, making my head ache.

I asked almost angrily, 'Are you sure it was Raoul d'Harcourt that you saw? The light is poor. You could easily have been mistaken.'

'No, I'm certain it was him.'

Her confidence riled me. 'I don't see how you could possibly tell. You admitted yourself a glimpse was all you had.'

'Then where did he go, if not over that wall? And why would he do that unless to avoid a meeting with us?'

'Perhaps you were wrong in thinking anyone entered the alleyway at all.'

We were still arguing when Marthe, who had seen us coming, opened the door of our lodgings and urged us, with many gestures, to come in out of the cold.

John Bradshaw was in the parlour, warming his hands at the fire and shivering slightly as if he, too, had just got in. Our raised voices must have preceded us because as we joined him, he said, in a voice that trembled with exasperation, 'For the love of God, can't you two make friends? Must you be forever squabbling like a pair of children?' But when he heard what the argument was about, he took the possible sighting of the Frenchman far more seriously than I had expected him to, opening the window and staring uneasily out into the street. 'I'll send Philip to go and look around,' he decided. 'He's done nothing all day but loaf around the kitchen.'

It struck me that he had never really liked Philip from the very beginning, but that his dislike had increased during our travels. I supposed – no, I knew – that Philip could be awkward and that the loss of Jeanne had made him more so. Indeed, there had been times during the past week when I had found it difficult to keep my hands off him. All the same, I could not help wondering why John had risked the displeasure of both Duke Richard and Timothy Plummer in order to bring Philip with us. There must have been other old soldiers he could have hired to help with the horses, old friends from those long-ago days when our armies had fought and rampaged their way across France.

Philip, when he finally answered John's summons, had reverted to his former surly mood, doing as he was bidden with a look of sullen defiance. As he let himself out into the street, I noticed that he had a great bruise covering almost the whole of one cheek. When he had gone, I looked an enquiry at John, who grimaced sheepishly, hunching his shoulders.

'*Mea culpa*,' he admitted. 'I shouldn't have done it, I know. It was wrong of me. But he makes me so angry.'

Before I could answer, there was a knock on

the street door, and when I opened it, Jules pushed past me, addressing himself immediately to John in a stream of rapid French. When he had finished, John swore.

'It seems,' he said to Eloise, 'that your cousin Maître le Daim has postponed his visit until the middle of the week. We shall be here for a few days more yet.'

Nineteen

Philip discovered no trace of Raoul d'Harcourt, nor had I expected him to. In fact, I doubted if he had even tried to find the man, and on his return half an hour later, his breath smelled suspiciously of wine. The information that Maître le Daim's visit to Paris had been delayed affected him less than the rest of us, but then he was already in an ugly mood. For my own part, the news came as a mixed blessing. On the one hand, it meant a longer stay in the city, but on the other, that was to my advantage. It gave me more time to search for Robin Gaunt, for I had made up my mind that when Eloise's part had been played, and the necessary facts obtained from her cousin Olivier (or not), that would be the end of our mission and we would all return to England. Quite when I

327

had reached this momentous decision I wasn't sure, but probably sometime during the previous day when the enormity and nigh impossibility of the task imposed upon me by the duke had struck home with even greater force than before.

Eloise and John Bradshaw both appeared disheartened by the check to our immediate plans, but again this worked in my favour. Eloise's amorous mood seemed to have been dissipated, and the remainder of Sunday was spent in desultory speculation between her and John as to the likelihood of the Fleming actually making the journey to Paris at all, King Louis' fickleness of purpose being notorious. We all went early to bed, and, loitering by the parlour fire, I gave Eloise time enough to fall asleep before going upstairs myself.

For the next three days, Philip and I scoured the city, all three parts of it, making ourselves understood with increasing success but to no avail. An elderly Englishman called Robin Gaunt remained as elusive as I had always supposed he would be. Eloise grew ever more indignant at my protracted absences and refused to accept my excuse that I was fulfilling my role as a wealthy haberdasher, buying and selling wares to my French counterparts.

'Nonsense!' she exclaimed. 'Why are you taking Philip with you?'

'As my servant. A prosperous merchant must have a servant. Besides, another man is added protection. Two are less likely to be set upon than one.'

'You'd do better with my company,' she snapped. 'What can you and Philip possibly achieve when neither of you speaks the language?'

'You know John says you must stay here, just in case your cousin arrives unexpectedly.'

The same reason kept Jules from accompanying us as he waited hour by hour for news from whoever his informant was that Olivier le Daim was at last approaching, or had entered, the city. But Philip and I returned, footsore and weary, to the house in the Rue de la Barillerie at sunset on Wednesday evening to learn that Jules's latest information suggested Olivier might not be setting out from Plessis-les-Tours until the following Monday.

'If he comes at all,' John muttered lugubriously. 'I'm inclined not to wait very much longer. I'm coming round to your way of thinking, Roger. This is a fool's errand. By the time Maître le Daim arrives – if he arrives – King Edward will have his answer anyway. The streets and taverns here are buzzing with talk that the dauphin's betrothal to the Princess Elizabeth is to be broken off and that he will be married to Maximilian's young daughter. That means Louis is bound to be negotiating a treaty with Burgundy very soon, probably in the next few weeks. Before Christmas. So I think our continued presence here is pointless. His Highness will probably have the news before we get home in any case.'

As he spoke, he raised an eyebrow at me, plainly wondering if my secret mission was anywhere near completion. I gave a barely perceptible shake of my head, but later, after Philip had disappeared into the kitchen and Eloise had taken herself off to bed, I told him of my decision.

'Well, it's up to you. I suppose you know what you're doing. The duke will no doubt be disappointed, but he can't expect miracles if, as you tell me, what he's asked you to do is almost impossible.' He thought for a moment, leaning forward, elbows on knees, staring into the heart of the fire burning on the hearth. Then he straightened his back, turning towards me. 'I tell you what, Roger. Let's make an agreement that if Maître le Daim hasn't arrived in Paris by this time next week, we pack up and leave.'

I nodded. 'Agreed.'

He seemed relieved and accompanied me upstairs, climbing to his tiny attic bed-chamber above ours in better spirits than he had been in for days. I even heard him whistling to himself as he proceeded on up the next flight of stairs.

But my own sleep was disturbed by odd dreams. Over and over again I was standing in the parlour of the house in the Rue de la Tissanderie and Jane Armiger was saying, 'Oh, Robin, how can you be so cruel?' Several times I awoke and dozed off, only to return to the same dream each time.

I awoke in the chill first light of dawn to the drumming of rain against the shutters. The only other sound in the room was Eloise's steady, rhythmic breathing as she lay beside me, her fair curls fanned out across the pillow. Cautiously, so as not to disturb her, I raised myself to a sitting position and drew back the bed-curtains a trifle to allow in a little more air before giving my full attention to my dream. It was telling me something, I knew that. But what?

'Oh, Robin, how can you be so cruel?'

Robin. In this case short for Robert, but also interchangeable with it, another version of the same name. The man, mentioned to us by the landlord of the seedy tavern near the Porte Saint-Honoré, was known as Robert of Ghent and seemed, from what we could gather, to be roughly the right age (the landlord had indicated grey hair). But he was a Fleming.

Or was he?

That, now I came to consider it dispassionately, was my own assumption. My heart began to beat a little faster and my palms to sweat with excitement. But why would he be called Robert of Ghent if he were not Flemish? I could understand the change from the Anglo-Saxon Robin to the more Gallicized Robert, but why choose de Ghent as a surname? Then, suddenly, enlightenment burst upon me like the sun breaking through clouds on an overcast day. John, that doughty

331

son of King Edward III and brother of the Black Prince, had, I was sure, been born in Ghent, but the name had been Anglicized to Gaunt.

I found I was holding my breath and let it out in a great gasping sigh. Was I on to something? Had Philip's instinct – that this man could be the one we were after – been right all along? I had always known him for a shrewd little monkey, so why had I not listened to him, respected his hunch more readily than I had? Because I was a conceited fool who thought he knew better, but in truth couldn't see beyond the end of his nose, that was why. And I had been blinded by the conviction that I had been given an impossible task that could never be fulfilled. I told myself severely not to get over-optimistic, that I could still be wrong, but I swung my legs out of bed and tiptoed down through the silent house to the kitchen, where Philip slept beside the dead embers of the fire.

He was alone, Marthe occupying the second attic bedchamber at the very top of the house. I knelt down and roused him, pouring my theory into his ears before he was even properly awake, so that he blinked stupidly at me and I had to repeat myself over again. And again. Finally, however, I made him understand, but to my surprise, he seemed more concerned with disproving my reasoning than applauding it.

'It was yourself,' I pointed out indignantly, 'who suggested from the start that this

Robert of Ghent might be the man we were looking for. Why the change of heart?'

He shrugged. 'I've changed my mind.'

'Obviously,' I snapped, getting to my feet. 'Nevertheless, it's a lead I intend to follow up.'

'Then you'll go alone,' he said, lying down and turning on his side, pulling the grey blanket up over his head to cover it. 'I've had enough of this nonsense. You're right when you say it's a bloody impossible task. Forget it, Roger. Go home and tell the duke it can't be done, tracing a man you've never seen – and nobody else knows anything about – after forty bloody years.'

I stared down in bewilderment at his rigid form, defiant beneath its covering. I couldn't work out what had happened to bring about this uncompromising attitude, a reversion to the man he had been until a few days ago, when the old friendship seemed to have been restored between us. What had I said? What had I done?

'John says you're to come with me.' I was horrified to hear the words come out as a sort of childish whine.

'Fuck John!'

I turned on my heel and left him.

I found the tavern again, not without some difficulty, but not nearly as much as I had expected. My sense of direction stood me in good stead, and I remembered a ruined, ivy-covered gateway in the old wall of Philip

Augustus not far from the Louvre Palace – no longer lived in by the kings of France and used mainly as a prison – which was only a street or two from the inn I was seeking. The anticipated hostile silence greeted my entrance, all the more disconcerting because of the previous noise and bustle, but fortunately the landlord recognized me and, if not actually brimming over with goodwill, at least greeted me with a certain courtesy and a warning glance at his regular customers that said he wanted no trouble. Nevertheless, I could still feel the threat of cold steel between my shoulder blades.

I managed at length to make myself under-stood by dint of repeating 'Robert de Ghent' a number of times and drawing a crude picture of a house in the dust and spilled wine on one of the table tops. With comprehension came a greater friendliness, and because I was unable to follow the instructions given to me, one of the men sitting nearby slid off his bench, grabbed me by the elbow and jerked his head as indication that I should go with him.

He led me to an alleyway about three streets distant and, with another jerk of his head, pointed to a house about halfway along on the left-hand side. Then he walked away with-out once looking back. I approached the door indicated and raised my hand to knock, then hesitated.

I had told no one where I was going. I had breakfasted more or less in silence with John and Eloise, then, in the little bustle that always succeeds a meal, had grabbed my cloak and hat and slipped away into the rainy early morning streets. Now, I wondered if it had been wise to be so secretive, even if it had meant avoiding Eloise's catechism as to where I was going and what I was doing. I reassured myself with the thought that should anything happen to delay my return, Philip, at least, would know my destination and be able to lead John to the inn.

I glanced up and down the narrow street, which was beginning to stir into after-breakfast life, with smoke issuing from chimneys, shutters being cautiously opened against the raw November air, a cart rumbling past and goodwives emerging here and there from their doorways to sweep yesterday's dust into the alleyway and dispose of their refuse in the central drain. All very much, I reflected, as it would have been in England. There was nothing to be afraid of.

I watched the cart out of sight around the bend at the top of the street, then knocked loudly and firmly on the door. As I waited for an answer to my summons, I was aware, out of the corner of one eye, of movement to the right of me. I turned my head to look, but the alleyway on that side was empty, no sign of life anywhere. As I stared, puzzled, I noticed a slightly darker shadow within a shadow thrown by the upper storey of one of the houses. Was I being followed? Had someone tailed me from the Rue de la Barillerie? It seemed unlikely. Who would have been watching our house so early in the morning? Nevertheless, I felt I should investigate. But at that moment, the door in front of me opened and a woman's voice spoke to me in French.

I turned quickly to see an elderly woman, a few untidy strands of grey hair escaping from her spotless coif, regarding me enquiringly. Her features were of the plump sort that keeps wrinkles at bay, even in the late fifties or early sixties, which I judged her to be – indeed, which I knew she must be if she were the wife of Robin Gaunt – and her figure was as rotund as her face. For a moment there was silence between us; then I decided that the direct approach was the only one to use.

'Mistress Gaunt?' I said in English.

She looked thoroughly startled, as if both the name and the language had awakened long-forgotten memories.

'Who are you?' she asked, perfectly correctly but with a heavy French accent. All the same, her words were as good as an admission that I had come to the right house.

'I should like to speak to your husband,' I said confidently. 'Your husband, Robin Gaunt.'

'My husband is Robert de Ghent,' she answered, the suspicion in her eyes deepening to fear, and made to shut the door.

I hastily put a foot in the gap to prevent it closing. 'There's nothing to be afraid of,' I assured her with my most winning smile. 'I've been sent by His Grace the Duke of Gloucester, who merely wants some information about ... about ... well, about what may or may not have happened in Rouen forty years or so ago.'

The faded blue eyes widened in astonishment. 'In Rouen? Forty years ago?'

'Look,' I said, 'may I come in and speak to Master Gaunt? There's nothing to fear.' I held my cloak wide. 'I'm not armed, as you can see.'

'My husband's not here. He's gone to visit a friend and won't be back until late tonight. You had better come again later.' Again she did not deny that Robin Gaunt and Robert de Ghent were one and the same person. And she continued to speak English.

I swore silently at this piece of ill luck. By coming so early in the day, I had made certain of finding the old man at home. It meant I had had a wasted trip and entailed a second visit tonight or tomorrow.

But I wondered suddenly if it need, after all, be a wasted visit. 'Can I talk to you, mistress?' I asked, bringing all the old persuasive charm to bear.

'Me?' The woman was plainly astounded. 'What would I know about men's affairs?'

'This is women's affairs, as well. You, I believe, were a member of the Duchess of York's household in Rouen. That's how you met your husband.'

She stared at me for a few moments longer before stepping back and holding the door open. 'Come in,' she invited.

Hardly believing my luck, I followed her into a room where a fire burned on the open hearth and a rich aroma of savoury pottage made my mouth water. The furniture was sparse, but well made and some of it, I suspected, hand-carved. Several brightly coloured cushions and a blue-and-yellow woven cloth on the table saved the place from complete austerity, but there was not a lot in the way of creature comforts. Time had evidently not dealt too kindly with an Englishman abroad.

Mistress Gaunt, as I named her to myself, waved me to a stool by the fire while she took another opposite, where she could stir the stew every now and again. She looked at me, raising her eyebrows. 'Now, then! What is this about? Who are you, and how did you find us?'

So I told her the whole story and my own reluctant part in it while she listened attentively, only stopping me when my English became too rapid for her to follow with ease. For the most part, she seemed to have little difficulty in understanding me, and when at last I had finished my tale, I congratulated her on her mastery of the language.

She laughed. 'You don't marry an Englishman,' she answered drily, 'and expect him to speak your tongue. It takes years before he'll even try.' She took a deep breath. 'Now, let me see if I have these facts correctly. This is about the rumour that one of the duchess's bodyguard of archers was her lover during the time that the Duke of York was away fighting around Pontoise.'

I nodded eagerly. She rose and fetched two wooden beakers from a cupboard and filled them from a jug of that rough red wine the natives seemed to thrive on. Personally, I found it too strong for my taste, but I made my usual pretence of enjoying it. When I had taken a couple of mouthfuls, I asked, 'How long was the Pontoise campaign?'

Mistress Gaunt pursed her lips and considered her answer carefully. 'Six or seven weeks, perhaps. I think it was late August by the time the duke and his troops returned to Rouen.'

I leaned forward, resting my arms on the table. 'And during that time, was there any talk of the Duchess Cicely taking a lover from amongst her guard of archers?'

My companion shrugged and answered much as Jane Armiger had done in response to the same query. 'There were always rumours. She was an extraordinarily beautiful woman.'

'Did she have a roving eye? Did she like men? Was she a faithful wife?'

'If she wasn't, she was very discreet.' There was a note of asperity in Mistress Gaunt's voice and she showed a heightened colour.

'This archer,' I pursued relentlessly, 'this Blackburn or Blaybourne or whatever he was called, was he handsome do you remember?'

There was a longish pause before Mistress

Gaunt said, somewhat reluctantly, 'Yes. Very handsome.' There was something in her tone that made me think that she had fancied this 'very handsome' man herself.

'What was he like to look at?' I asked quickly before the little spurt of jealousy (if it was that) had time to fade. 'Tall and fair? Short and stout?'

'Short and stout?' She laughed dismissively. 'I've told you, he was handsome. Over six feet in his stockinged feet and so blond his hair was flaxen in the sunlight.'

I drew a sharp breath. She might have been describing King Edward in his golden youth, 'the handsomest prince in Europe'.

'Not like the Duke of York, then,' I suggested. 'I've always heard that he was short and dark, rather like the Duke of Gloucester.'

She eyed me narrowly. 'What are you saying? Do you think...?'

'What do you think?' I countered. 'King Edward's birthday is at the end of April. If he was not born prematurely and you count back nine months, that would mean conception was the end of July, when, according to you, the Duke of York was away fighting at Pontoise.'

Mistress Gaunt sat staring at me without speaking for at least half a minute while she bit at a rough piece of skin around her left thumbnail. Finally, with a shake of her head, she said, 'You might be right, but then again, you might not. If your king Edward had been late arriving, then who is to say that he was not conceived before his father left on campaign? I agree that his likeness to Archer Blaybourne is a point in favour of whatever it is you and your duke are trying to prove–' she was an intelligent woman: she knew exactly what we were trying to prove – 'but many children do not necessarily resemble their parents. In some cases that I know of, there is a great disparity of feature. King Edward may well look like his mother.'

I sighed. She was right, of course. There was nothing here to declare positively that Edward of Rouen was the son of a common archer and not the proud Plantagenet he claimed to be. And if Duchess Cicely still refused to confirm that long-gone accusation...

Mistress Gaunt broke in on my thoughts with the self-same query. 'What does my lady of York herself say? She is the only one who knows the truth.'

I finished the last mouthful of wine and rose to my feet. 'She says nothing, nor will she, I think, however much she secretly believes Duke Richard to be the rightful king.'

My companion gave a little cry. 'You think she really thinks that?'

It was my turn to shrug. 'Frankly, mistress, I don't know what anyone's thoughts on the subject really are. The only thing I'm sure of is that this was an abortive errand from the beginning, and unlikely to produce any positive evidence one way or another. The duchess...'

Mistress Gaunt was not listening. She had gone over to the window and pushed wide the shutters, letting in the cold November air as she leaned out over the sill, glancing up and down the alleyway outside.

'What is it?' I asked sharply.

She withdrew her head, looking sheepish. 'It's nothing. I was convinced I heard somebody outside, that is all, but there's no one there.'

'The street's full of people and wagons and animals,' I said, impatience colouring my tone. 'If you don't mind, I'll come back again this evening, mistress, and speak to your husband. At what hour do you expect him home?'

'Probably to supper,' she replied, but absentmindedly, as if she had suddenly remembered something. 'Of course,' she went on, 'there was that extremely odd business of the christenings. I don't think I've ever seriously considered it before, but now ... Yes, looking back, it does seem odd.'

'What business of the christenings?' I demanded eagerly.

She motioned me to sit down again and reseated herself on the stool opposite, where she appeared to drop into a reverie.

'Well?' The sound of my voice made her jump. 'What about the christening?'

'Christenings,' she corrected me. 'The lord Edward's and his brother's, the lord Edmund's, two years later.'

The lord Edmund? I cudgelled my brains,

then recollected vaguely that there had been another brother between King Edward and the Duke of Clarence: Edmund, later Earl of Rutland.

'Go on,' I urged.

Mistress Gaunt poured us both more wine and took several sips before continuing. 'Lord Edward's christening – remember he was the eldest son, the first-born male – was a very muted affair. No great fuss was made, no great throng of guests assembled, and it took place in a small, private chapel in Rouen Castle. But Lord Edmund's christening was magnificent. The ceremony was held in Rouen Cathedral – jewels, velvets, both English and French dignitaries present. Above all, the Duke and Duchess of York had managed to persuade the Rouen Cathedral Chapter to grant the supreme honour of allowing them to use the font in which Duke Rollo of Normandy had been baptized into Christianity, and which, ever since, had been kept covered as a mark of respect. It was an unheard-of concession. We were all amazed. You would have thought,' she added reflectively, 'that Edmund, not Edward, was his father's heir.' She shook her head ruefully. 'Why has that never struck me until now? And I was present, on both occasions.'

I was trembling with excitement. 'And it was Edmund of Rutland who was killed alongside the duke twenty-odd years ago, at Wakefield – which might mean nothing, or it might mean a preference by the Duke of York for his seemingly second son.'

My companion brought me down to earth. 'It's still not proof,' she pointed out.

'Not solid proof,' I admitted. 'But it means something, surely.'

'Perhaps. Yes, I think it is ... suggestive.'

'Oh, more than that,' I insisted.

She laughed and said in her astonishingly good English, 'I'm certain even the most inexperienced lawyer could find you a dozen good reasons why my lord of York preferred the company of his second son to that of his first-born. Fathers and eldest sons do not always see eye to eye.'

'Maybe not, when they're older. But I doubt discrimination starts in the cradle, as it seems to have done in this case.'

Nevertheless, as I made my way back to the Rue de la Barillerie through Paris's crowded streets, I reflected that Mistress Gaunt was right: her account of the two very different christenings, a pointer though it might be to the true state of affairs, was not the sort of solid proof that my lord of Gloucester could adduce to bolster his claim to the throne (if, of course, that was indeed his aim). I would return this evening, after supper, and talk to Robin Gaunt himself in the hope that he might be able to help me further, but I very much doubted his ability to do so. It was all too long ago. Duchess Cicely was the only one now who knew the truth, and she seemed reluctant to speak.

As I forged a path down the busy Rue

Saint-Denis, I got the oddest impression, every now and then, of the same figure weaving in and out of the throng of people and traffic just ahead of me – a faintly familiar figure but one that never paused long enough to be immediately identifiable. I quickened my pace, but the press was too great and I never managed to catch up with my elusive quarry. In the end, I decided I was imagining things.

I reached our lodgings in time for dinner and one of Marthe's delicious rabbit stews, but too late to accompany Eloise to the Hôtel Saint-Pol, where amidst royal splendour, Olivier le Daim was staying. According to John Bradshaw, word had been received from Jules, just after I had left that morning, of Monsieur le Daim's sudden arrival in Paris very late the previous evening, but with the additional information that his stay would be brief and that he would probably be quitting the city by tonight. It was therefore imperative that Eloise present herself at once, and upon discovering my absence, she had been forced to go alone. Whether or not she would get to see her cousin was another matter altogether, but she had to try.

'She's furious,' John warned me with a rueful grin. 'I suppose you've been out and about on business of your own, but of course I couldn't say so to the lady.' He grinned. 'I'd watch your back if I were you, or you may find yourself with a knife between the shoulder blades.'

I discovered that he wasn't exaggerating Eloise's anger. I was in our bedchamber when, sometime during the afternoon, she returned. I heard her run upstairs and she burst through the door like a small whirl-wind. Without even bothering to take off her cloak, she launched herself at me, fists hammering my chest, eyes flashing, feet kicking at my shins.

'Where have you been?' she shouted. 'Where were you? Sneaking off like that just when I needed you.'

I caught both her wrists and gripped them cruelly, making her gasp with pain. 'Be quiet, you termagant!' I yelled back. 'Can't you get it through your stupid little head that I am not your husband? That it's only a game we're playing! I'm sure you didn't need my help with your own cousin. You only had to flutter those eyelashes of yours and pout your lips to get past any number of his servants. So? Did you get to see him? Did you find out what the king wants to know?'

For answer, she wrenched her wrists free of my slackened grasp and clawed at my face. Or would have done, had I given her the chance. Instead, I caught her in a crushing embrace, savagely stopping her mouth with my own. I could smell the scent of her hair, feel the softness of her skin. My senses swam. For a moment or two, she fought me like a wild cat, but then, suddenly, surrendered. Her arms encircled my neck and she was returning my kisses with fervour.

346

I suppose what happened next was inevitable, and had been so for the past two weeks, ever since we were forced into playing this ridiculous charade of being man and wife. Well, at the time it seemed inevitable. That's my only defence.

I'm not proud of myself. I'm a married man. I knew I was laying up months, if not years, of regret and guilt, but at the time it seemed worth it.

But then, it always does. Doesn't it?

Twenty

Eloise and I descended to the parlour for dinner, both trying to appear composed and as innocent as if we had been discussing the weather, but I saw John Bradshaw glance at us and then glance again, a longer, more searching look that eventually produced a small, knowing, half-embarrassed smile. His eyes slid away from us as he turned to study the fire burning merrily on the hearth, and he stooped, holding out his hands to the blaze.

Marthe bustled in with the pot of stew, which she placed on the table, made certain we had everything we needed, then trotted out again. There was no sign of Philip, although I heard his voice upraised in the kitchen saying a few words in what even I could tell was execrable French, and which Marthe had evidently been teaching him. I was thankful to be spared his beady gaze. He was always more astute than people gave him credit for, and would have interpreted in a minute Eloise's suppressed air of triumph and my own faintly guilty look.

John took his seat and helped himself to a generous serving of stew before addressing the lady. 'So, mistress, you managed to see your cousin, or so you implied when you first came in. Since when, you seem to have been busy upstairs – as you ladies so often are.' He concentrated on the spoonful of pottage he was conveying to his mouth, refusing resolutely to look at either of us. He went on, 'Did you learn anything from Maître le Daim? Anything of what King Edward wants to know?'

'Oh, it wasn't difficult to gain access to him,' was the airy response. 'He recalled my mother and we talked a little of family matters. But after that, I asked him openly – simply as a woman who takes an intelligent interest in affairs of state – if the rumours that King Louis is to make peace with Burgundy and marry the dauphin to Maximilian's daughter are true.'

'And what was his reply?'

Eloise laughed. 'He seemed astonished that I didn't already know the answers, as I had so recently been in England. He thought it must be common knowledge there by now that a treaty is to be signed between France and Burgundy at Arras, at the end of next month. The marriage of the dauphin to Margaret of Burgundy will be arranged at the same time, and a part of her marriage portion will include the county of Artois.'

John Bradshaw drew a deep breath and laid down his spoon, staring before him, lost in thought. I could guess what those thoughts must be, but I waited for him to voice them. 'So that's the end of King Edward's pension from Louis,' he said at last. He added even more slowly and with conviction, 'It will kill him. That and the humiliation of his eldest daughter.'

'Oh, come!' I expostulated. 'It surely can't be as bad as that. It is humiliating, I agree, and the loss of the money is bound to be a blow to him, but as for killing him, that, surely, is overstating the matter.'

John raised his sombre eyes to mine and looked at me directly. 'I don't think you appreciate just how ill the king really is,' he said. 'He's lived life to the full and now his health is fragile. And he was relying on a marriage alliance between England and France to secure the money King Louis has paid him, ever since Picquigny, for the rest of his life. My guess is that we shall see King Edward the Fifth on the throne before a twelvemonth has passed.'

Was it my imagination or did his gaze intensify as he stared at me? Had he suspected, or even guessed, what my secret mission might be? I lowered my eyes quickly to my plate and concentrated on eating.

'But he's a child,' I heard Eloise say. 'A child ruler is never good for a country.'

'The Prince of Wales is twelve,' John Bradshaw reproved her. 'On the brink of manhood. And he has powerful uncles.'

So he did, but which uncles, I wondered, was John referring to? The prince had only one on the spear side of his family, but at least three on the distaff. And Anthony Woodville, Earl Rivers, had been head of the prince's household, at Ludlow, for many years now. His influence with young Edward must be predominant.

Eloise's voice interrupted my wandering thoughts. 'I told Olivier that I'm in Paris with my husband. He'd like to meet you, Roger, but as he must leave again not later than tonight, I promised I would take you to the Hôtel Saint-Pol after supper.'

I shook my head. 'I'm sorry,' I said abruptly. 'I can't come.'

I saw John look hard at me, and this time I met his gaze unflinchingly. He gave an almost imperceptible nod to show he understood.

Of course, that wasn't the end of it. Eloise tried her damndest to make me change my mind. She cajoled, she persuaded, she sulked, she even swore in a most unladylike fashion, and when I finally said that thank God I was not really her husband, she indulged in a minor bout of hysterics that only abated when she saw that I remained entirely unmoved by it. In fact, what had happened between us before dinner might never have been. Our former barbed relationship had been resumed, at least by me, and I think the realization that nothing had changed shocked her. I don't know what she had expected, and at that moment, I didn't care. I had other things to think about.

'Why not?' she demanded.

'Why not what?'

'Why won't you come with me to meet Cousin Olivier?'

'Because you have seen him and discovered what you came to Paris to find out. Why visit him again simply to perpetuate a lie? Besides, I have business of my own to attend to.'

She got up from the table, looking extremely white. 'I wish you were dead,' she said very slowly and clearly, then left the room.

John Bradshaw raised his eyebrows at me, but forbore to comment. Not that he needed to. His accusatory glance said all that was necessary, and in truth, I was beginning to feel guilty myself. I should have realized that Eloise's feelings had gone deeper than my own.

John's voice recalled me to myself. 'Do you go out this afternoon?' he asked.

I shook my head. 'This evening, after supper.'

'Then take Philip with you. It's dangerous abroad after dark.'

'He won't come,' I averred. 'For some reason or other, I seem to have offended him.

351

I shall be all right. I'm a big fellow and I'll carry my knife.'

The afternoon lagged past. John disappeared on business of his own – making arrangements for the return journey, he said – and there was no sign of Philip. I tried on three occasions to speak to Eloise, but she had locked our bedchamber door and refused to answer my knock. I ate supper alone, none of the other three putting in an appearance, much to Marthe's obvious distress, as she had prepared a mutton pie, which smelled and tasted delicious, except that, by this time, I was in no mood to appreciate it as it deserved. My feeling of guilt had assumed enormous proportions, and it was only by telling myself that no doubt this was precisely Eloise's intention, and that she had been as eager in promoting our lovemaking as I had been, that I was at last able to stop blaming myself alone for what had happened. A revue of my conduct persuaded me that I had never given her reason to believe I harboured any deeper feelings for her than that of a man thrown into close proximity with a pretty woman, nor that she felt differently about me. I consoled myself with the thought that a very few days more, a week at most, would see the parting of our ways.

In the meantime, I must make my way back across the city to speak to Robin Gaunt in one last effort to unearth another sliver of evidence that might give some credence to the Duchess of York's claim that her eldest son was a bastard. If I had had any doubt to begin with of what was really in Prince Richard's mind, of what he was hoping to prove, then John Bradshaw's words at dinner had dispelled them. If King Edward were really as ill as he had indicated – and I remembered his absence from the victory banquet at Baynard's Castle – then the thought of a child king, brought up in the shadow of his Woodville relations and necessarily influenced by them, could only spell trouble and possible danger for the Duke of Gloucester. If, therefore, he could prove the truth of his mother's erstwhile accusation, it would make him the rightful king, his brother Clarence's children being barred from the throne by their father's act of attainder. Oh, yes, I could see it all quite plainly, and I didn't know that I blamed him for what he was trying to do. I just wished he hadn't chosen me to assist him.

All these thoughts and more chased one another through my head as I crossed from the Île de la Cité to the Rue Saint-Denis and then made my way through a maze of back streets in the direction of the Porte Saint-Honoré. Twice I lost my bearings in the dark, once ending up close to the Porte Montmartre and having to make my stumbling way southwards, keeping close to the walls of the overhanging houses, the soles of my boots slithering on the slimy cobbles. It had turned even colder since the morning and I wrapped my cloak well around me. Beneath it, my right hand kept a fast grip on the haft of my knife.

But nobody challenged me. Several times I glanced over my shoulder, but no one seemed to be following me. I did think once that I saw a man wearing a hat with a feather in it, but he had disappeared by the next turn in the road. I reached the Gaunts' house without incident.

The shutters were fast closed, permitting no welcoming chink of candlelight to show. A sensible precaution, I supposed, in an area such as this, where even the rats scurried past as though afraid of their own shadows. I stepped forward and rapped on the door – only to find that it gave under my hand. It was already open. Cautiously, I pushed it wider and took a few steps inside.

'Master Gaunt!' I called.

There was no reply.

I tried again. 'Mistress Gaunt! It's me, Roger Chapman.'

The silence was deafening. Suddenly, my heart was beating faster and my palms were sweating. Every instinct screamed at me that something was wrong and to get out and away while the going was good. Then, unexpectedly, there was the scrape of a flint. Tinder flared and a candle was lit, the spurt of flame blinding me for an instant. Behind me, someone moved and slammed the door shut, imprisoning me. The candle was moved, but my eyes were still dazzled. I moved a step or two forward, stumbling over something lying on the floor. More than one thing ... As my vision cleared and adjusted to the gloom, I saw with mounting horror that they seemed to be bodies, and as two more candles were lit from the first, I yelled out in fear.

They were indeed bodies: those of Mistress Gaunt and, almost certainly, her husband. Both had had their throats cut.

'So here you are, Roger,' said a familiar voice, and John Bradshaw emerged into the pool of light in the centre of the room.

I stared at him, relief surging through me. 'John! Thank God,' I breathed. 'But ... but how did you get here? How did you know about the Gaunts? Where to come?' I seized him by the arm. 'Above all, do you know who committed this ... this outrage?'

For answer, he simply smiled and held out the bloody knife he was still clutching in one hand. 'If you don't struggle, it's very quick,' he said gently. 'My cousin Wolsey taught me how to butcher animals.'

'Butcher?' My brain refused to believe what he was saying. My thoughts were thick and stupid, refusing to accept the evidence of my ears and eyes.

John went on, 'I'm sorry, Roger, to have to do this. I like you. I really do. But I can't let you return home to my lord of Gloucester with that story of the christenings. I'm not a fool. I know it's not proof positive, but it's an indication that the duchess's story might be true. Enough, at any rate, to persuade the duke that he has some claim to the throne and to depose his nephew. I can't allow that. My loyalty is to the queen. Her mother, the old Duchess of Bedford, came from Luxembourg, and so did some of my forebears. I owe her and her sons my allegiance.'

Clervaux! Of course! I should have listened more closely to Eloise.

But my brain still wasn't functioning properly. 'Those–those other people,' I stammered, 'Culpepper, the–the boatman ... you killed them, too?' He smiled and nodded. 'But ... why?'

John shrugged. 'Culpepper simply on the off chance that he might know something that could put you on the track of whatever it was you were after. I didn't really know myself back then what it was all about, but Anthony Woodville himself informed me that there was something afoot. His spy in the Duke of Gloucester's household had alerted him.'

The man who had tried to steal my instructions and been thwarted because I had already learned them by heart. So much was beginning to fall into place.

'But why the boatman?'

John shrugged. 'That was simply a precaution,' he said. 'He had rowed my accomplice across from Southwark the previous night, and as it turned out, I was right to be cautious. For some reason or another, your suspicions had been aroused and you went after him.'

'Your accomplice?'

'He's standing behind you.'

I had forgotten the man who had closed the door. I whirled round and stared disbelievingly. 'Philip?'

'I didn't have any choice, Roger,' he muttered. 'It was do as Jack said or be hanged for murder. I'd killed a man the previous evening, in a tavern brawl. Jack recognized me as an old comrade from our soldiering days and got me away.'

'The murder at the Rattlebones,' I said, my head spinning. 'I heard about it.'

'That's right. He hid me and arranged for me to be rowed over to Baynard's Castle that same night.'

'But there was a price for his help.' It wasn't a question.

Philip nodded. 'I was to come to France and spy on you for him. Jack knew that we'd been friends – they know everything, these bloody spies – and of course you wouldn't suspect me.'

'But–but once you were across the Channel, you were free. He couldn't get you hanged in France for a crime committed in England. Why, in God's name, didn't you just run away?'

'What, in a foreign country, where I can't make meself understood? That's no life for a man.' A little of his normal spirit had returned.

'Then why, in the name of friendship, did you not warn me what was going on? What do you think Jeanne would have said about such a betrayal?'

Suddenly, he was shouting. 'Don't you mention Jeanne! Don't ever mention her name again! It wasn't my son she was carrying. She confessed to me just before he was born.' His eyes flicked towards John Bradshaw and he made an effort to take himself in hand. 'As for warning you,' he went on more calmly, but still in a voice that shook a little, 'Jack said that if he so much as suspected you knew the truth about him – about us – he'd slit your throat regardless, and not wait for you to show your hand about what it was you was up to.'

At any other time, in any other situation, the information about Jeanne would have rocked me back on my heels – I might even have challenged it – but something else had occurred to me. I turned to look once again at John. 'You must have killed Oliver Cook, as well,' I said slowly. 'But why?'

He said abruptly, 'We're wasting time. But if you really want to know, and as you're never going to tell anyone, yes, I killed him. He'd seen Philip, the day he took refuge in the kitchen to avoid being recognized by you. Sooner or later, Oliver would have had a good look at Philip and doubtless told the rest of you about the incident. And then it wouldn't have been long, Roger, before you started to put two and two together.' John laughed, a sound that made my blood run cold. 'Oliver was easy meat. I didn't even need to use the

358

knife on him. He was totally unsuspecting. A shove, a heave and he was overboard. Mid-Channel, in that sea, he didn't stand a chance. Unfortunately, I dropped that particular knife and couldn't find it again. Now—'

'How did you know what Mistress Gaunt told me? About the christenings?' As I spoke, my eyes were drawn inexorably to that still form on the floor and I could see the dark band of blood round the neck. The woman's head was almost severed from the body. I felt my stomach heave and the vomit rose in my throat. I started to shake, but not from fear, from anger.

'Philip followed you and was listening outside the window,' John answered with a sneer. 'You didn't bother lowering your voices and the shutters are in poor condition – lots of cracks and chinks – as you'd have seen, if you'd bothered to inspect them.' He smiled again and took a firmer grasp on his knife. 'And now, Roger, much as I regret it, it's your turn to meet with a fatal stabbing, and it will be my sad duty to carry the news home to Timothy Plummer and the duke. I daresay I'll get a bollocking for not looking after you better, but then, if you will go wandering around the backstreets of a city like Paris on your own, and you an Englishman at that, you take the consequences. No need for them ever to know that you discovered the Gaunts' whereabouts at all, or that they're dead, too. So—'

'How did you manage to kill them both without one of them putting up a fight?'

John sighed. 'Does it matter? Oh well! If you must know – and, as I've already said, who am I to thwart the wishes of a dying man? – Philip brought me here this afternoon. The woman was still alone. We said we were friends of yours and she let us in. She suspected nothing, not right up to the moment when I slit her throat. Then we just waited for Gaunt to come home.' He shrugged. 'I took him unawares. It was simple.' His expression had altered subtly. He was drooling slightly in anticipation of the kill. The scent of further bloodletting was in his nostrils, and there was a slightly manic look in his eyes. I realized with a sickening jolt that he probably was mad, but a madman who could conceal his insanity under a perfectly normal exterior. The Woodvilles must find him invaluable. He said, 'Guard the door, Lamprey!' and moved, swift and nimble as a cat, to get behind me.

The revelations of the past few minutes had held me paralyzed with shock. My brain, such of it as was still working, told me to get back against the wall, to use my own knife, to put up some sort of a fight to save my life, but my mind was reeling from the discovery of Philip's treachery and his disclosure – if it were true – about Jeanne.

John Bradshaw hissed again, 'Guard the door! Mind he doesn't make a run for it!'

Out of the corner of one eye, I saw Philip

move, but then he was shouting, 'No! I won't help you kill Roger! I can't! He's my friend. I didn't mind spying on him, searching his baggage, but this is different.' And the next moment he had lifted the latch, wrenching the door wide. 'Run, Roger!' he yelled. 'Run!'

Something in the urgency of his tone seemed at last to penetrate my benumbed senses, jerking me into life. I fairly threw myself sideways and out into the street, but my legs were shaking, weak from fear, and before I could take more than a few staggering steps, John Bradshaw was on me, trying to grab me from behind with his left arm so that he could pull me back against him and cut my throat. Fortunately, I had my own knife out by this time and managed, with a slashing blow, to wound him in the fleshy part of his right arm. I heard him curse, but a moment later, he had kneed me in the groin, causing me to double up in pain and drop my knife. I fell to the ground and rolled over, avoiding his wicked-looking blade, but only for a second or two. He was furious now, like a wounded bull, and was stabbing indiscriminately at me, intent on finishing me off and not caring any longer how he did it.

I was vaguely aware of doors opening and people coming out into the street, but no one made a move to help me. To the onlookers, it was just such another murderous brawl as they no doubt witnessed at least once a week, and at present, they knew nothing of the dead bodies in the house behind me. I managed to

361

haul myself to my feet, but without my knife, the only recourse left to me was my fists. I lashed out blindly and heard John Bradshaw laugh as he dodged my erratically flailing arms. Some men were shouting encouragement to him, women too, obviously enjoying the spectacle. I stepped back, slipped on the greasy cobbles and went down again, flat on my back.

This time, he was on me, his weight pinning me to the ground, arm raised, the blade of his knife aimed straight at my throat. I struggled, but I couldn't shift him. I closed my eyes, waiting for the blow to fall...

Nothing happened. Instead, I heard him give a strange little grunt before he toppled sideways, blood gushing from his mouth, limbs jerking like one of those jointed dolls that toymakers sell. Then, after a moment, he lay still, eyes staring sightlessly up at the dark night sky.

A hand reached down to help me to my feet.

'That was a very near thing,' Raoul d'Harcourt's voice said apologetically. 'I'm sorry I was late. I'm ashamed to admit it, but I got lost. I don't know this part of Paris as well as I thought I did.'

'Who, in God's name, are you?' I asked.

It was an hour later, and we were finally back in the Rue de la Barillerie after a journey across Paris during which my saviour had refused to answer all questions, hustling and urging me on, to get to the Île de la Cité, as though our lives depended on it, taking devious twists and turns through innumerable side streets and noisome alleys until my head spun. Now, as he forced wine down my throat, he ordered a frightened and bewildered Eloise to pack our saddlebags.

'We're leaving Paris tonight. I'll have to bribe one of the gatekeepers to let us through. As to who I really am,' he went on, turning to me, 'you've no need to know that. You can go on calling me by the name I borrowed from one of the goldsmiths' shops on the Quai des Orfèvres. Suffice it say that I work for Timothy Plummer, who's had his suspicions about John Bradshaw for some time. He sent me after you to watch your back and remove him if needs be.'

'Y–you mean ... Timothy knew I m–might be in danger?' I stuttered.

Raoul d'Harcourt – I had to go on thinking of him as that, it seemed – smiled wryly. 'I'm afraid so, but he had no proof against Bradshaw. This seemed too good an opportunity to miss.'

Once more, as at the beginning of this ill-conceived venture, I was struck dumb by my sense of outrage. I could only hope and pray that when I at last came face to face again with my lord of Gloucester's spymaster general, I would be able to find the words to describe my opinion of his conduct. But somehow, I doubted it. They simply didn't exist.

I voiced another worry. 'Why are we leaving Paris in such a rush? Why the hurry?'

'Because,' Raoul said impatiently, 'as soon as the other inhabitants of that street find the Gaunts' bodies – as they doubtless have done by this time – it will no longer be a case of a street brawl, but murder, and the chances are that you will get the blame. His neighbours must know that Gaunt – or de Ghent as you say he's called – is an Englishman by birth, however long he's lived here. And you're an Englishman. That will be good enough for them. They'll decide you have some old grudge against him.'

'Why? And how would they know I'm English?'

'Oh, in the name of all the saints, just think, man! The innkeeper, where you made your enquiries, and all his customers know you're English. We have to get out of the city as soon as possible, before you find yourself under lock and key. Do you know what's happened to the other man? The one who was with John Bradshaw?'

Philip! I had forgotten him. 'No. He must have run away. Well, we can't be bothered with him. He must look after himself.'

Eloise came back into the parlour, carrying my saddlebags. She looked rather pale, but perfectly composed. 'I'm not coming with you,' she said. 'I've decided to remain in Paris. For the time being, I'll go and stay with the Armigers, if they'll have me. I'll tell them you've deserted me for another woman.

They'll doubtless be very sympathetic, especially Master Lackpenny. I see no point in returning to England. There's nothing for me there.' Her gaze was a challenge, but I didn't respond. 'No,' she went on, 'it's as I said: there's no reason for my return. You can pass on the information I received from my cousin, Roger. In any case, everyone's going to be privy to it soon. So I'll say goodbye.' She dropped my saddlebags on the floor and walked to the parlour door, where she turned, smiling slightly. 'Incidentally, I'm not the only one of our merry band staying behind. Philip's in the kitchen. It would appear he means to marry Marthe, if she'll have him, and live with her, here, in Paris.'

There's not a lot more to say. I didn't believe Eloise about Philip to begin with, but it turned out to be true enough. Marthe would shelter him throughout any hue and cry that might arise, and, afterwards, the man who hated foreign parts would settle down and become a good Frenchman. (Well, he'd try, although I couldn't really see it happening myself.) True to his word, the mysterious Raoul d'Harcourt got me out of Paris and away that same night and on the road that eventually led to Calais. And there, on English soil, I felt safe for the first time in days.

Crossing the Channel was delayed on account of the winter weather, but a little over a week later, I found myself back in Baynard's Castle and face to face with Timothy

365

Plummer. I'm happy to say that, on this occasion, words did not fail me and I was able to give him a masterly reading of his character that satisfied even my own outraged feelings and made Raoul, who had been present at the meeting, grin behind his hand. (Later, he treated me to the best pot of ale to be had at the Bull in Fish Street.)

I did not see the duke. He had, by now, left for his estates in the North, but at a second, more private meeting, I passed on to Timothy the little I had discovered concerning the birth of King Edward. Like me, while he considered the story of the two christenings significant, he admitted that as proof positive it left much to be desired.

'His Grace will be disappointed,' he admitted, 'but if that's all there is...' He trailed off, shrugging fatalistically.

'And I'm free to go now?' I asked.

He nodded.

So I shook the dust of London off my feet the very next morning, vowing never to return.

It's unwise to tempt Fate.